GUARDIAN ANGEL
and Other Stories

T0160705

GUARDIAN ANGEL
and Other Stories

MARGERY LATIMER

Afterwords by Nancy Loughridge,
Meridel Le Sueur, and Louis Kampf

THE FEMINIST PRESS

Old Westbury,
New York

1984

Library of Congress Cataloging in Publication Data

Latimer, Margery, 1899–1932.
    Guardian angel and other stories.

    Selected from her: Guardian angel and other stories,
New York: H. Smith & R Hass, 1932; and Nellie Bloom and
other stories. New York: J. H. Sears, c1929.
    I. Title. II. Series.
PS3523.A774A6   1984   813'.52   84-14175
ISBN 0-935312-12-9
ISBN 0-935312-13-7 (pbk.)

Cover art: *Girl with a Dove*, Marie Laurencin,
National Gallery of Art, Washington, DC,
Chester Dale Collection
Cover design: Marta Ruliffson
Text design: Lea Smith
Typeset by Monotype Composition Co., Inc., Baltimore, MD
Manufactured by Banta Co., Harrisonburg, VA

CONTENTS

NELLIE BLOOM

I N Onnowac we take our summer guests to the band concert on Monday night, to the Dells at Kilbourn on the first bright day, to the glen up in the bluffs, but we always save Sunday for showing the town. We pass the old toll gate house covered with vines, rotting, its old porch ready to fall, sagging and swaying under glossy leaves and living branches. An old man used to come out and open the gate for ten cents. Sometimes he would run out at noon with his napkin tied round his neck and a pork chop in one hand. Ten cents in his brown wrinkled hand and the creaky gate would swing open. Click-click-click and the wheels would spin down the road. "Mother, I saw a red-winged blackbird. Teacher said we should tell her every bird we saw. Papa, let me drive. Please, Papa, you promised. Mother, aren't we to Nellie Bloom's yet?"

I said that when I was eleven years old, and I used to say it every time we went out to drive. My grandmother had told me about Nellie sliding down Puffer's hill in the winter. My father had added some detail about her in church. My mother had said sharply that Nellie had always had a big dejected look in her eyes from the time she was born, as if she considered herself selected for especial misfortune.

This time I had come back to Onnowac sad and desolate and when I walked down the canal road and remembered how I had once looked for birds in the marsh grass I grew sadder and wept a little for myself as I walked along. I thought of Nellie Bloom as I passed the old Bloom place there near the church with the triangle of fruit trees in back of the house and the stone wall. The sun shone on the bright bay windows and the fluted trimmings where sparrows had untidy nests. I looked up and saw queer little cornices and peaks at the top of the house. I imagined they were candles.

But suddenly Nellie Bloom was there among the blooming plants, the porch boards creaking under her light slippers, her sad face bent. There was no time between us, no space. I knew from the arch of her shoulders and her color that we were sharing the same tortured melancholy. But I was flattering myself, as young people will, when I thought that I was sharing anything with Nellie Bloom who had died forty years before. But forgive me, because the world was too much for me then. I had met only my picture of it. I was lonely and full of shrinking.

I stopped at Mrs. Alverson's window to ask her about Nellie Bloom. "What did she look like? Why did she die? What is the real story?"

Mrs. Alverson is eighty-one and she went to Nellie's christening and to her funeral and to Grandma Sweeney's. I had never heard about Grandma Sweeney before. She told me about Mr. and Mrs. Nimmons. I've always known them. Mr. Nimmons is president of the bank and Mrs. Nimmons is president of the Ladies' Aid. They seem to be quiet and kind, not at all the sort that you could imagine anything romantic or sinister about, just plain, well-dressed people who lead in prayer and whose son is in college and rides a motorcycle.

She showed me Nellie Bloom. She tried to describe how she looked as she lay in a low hammock hung between a flowering plum and an apple, how white her skin was against the sheer lavender of her gown and how black her hair as it poured down over head and ear into a dense coil held with a comb. And she described the narrow black ribbon with the locket, and the feet, one above the other at the end of the hammock, and she tried to explain what was pathetic about those crossed feet.

"We all felt sorry for Nellie when it happened and we took sides against the Nimmonses but they're good people, too, and I guess they couldn't help it. They've never missed at church and they've lived it all down."

"But what about Nellie?"

"We can't keep on being sad for someone dead forty years."

She went back with her voice and brought me Grandma Sweeney and I saw the strange old creature with her hair like a gray silk cap on her head and her forehead in three deep ridges. Her eyes stared out as if they were looking at something the mouth cannot name and yet which cannot die.

"That winter Grandma's youngest boy broke his head open coasting. And in a short time she buried her husband, too. But he was no good. I remember him sitting out near the woodshed in the sun, winter and summer, with that old pipe of his and his feet up and his hat down. Grandma was taking in washing, mind you. We felt glad when the old fellow passed on and she could put something by for herself. Then she started nursing. They called her the night Nellie fell back on parlor carpet and they took her for dead. It's my private opinion Grandma kept that girl alive for six years."

I closed my eyes and I saw Nellie Bloom coasting down Puffer's hill with one cautious foot scraping the snow, her face deep in fur, her eyes looking up and out over the rise and fall of hill to a forest beyond the river. I looked into her eyes, beyond the astonishment of her flying sled on blue snow, the cries and flashing runners, to the deep and tender distress that she held for herself. Then it was summer and I was Nellie walking home from school in a slim white dress. Dark curls warmed my shoulders and the strapped books were heavy in my warm, tired hands. For an instant I could feel the scraping of a garter and a little ache in my flesh where it rubbed the skin. You must understand that this unhappiness of mine, and it was much worse than anything that ever happened to me in the real world, made me want to be another person, made me Nellie Bloom the instant I heard she had suffered. And because I could not live my own life just then I lived hers. I became Nellie Bloom plus myself. I imagined it all and felt it and struggled through her misery and it seemed to me that she had not died and that she would never die.

And now listen to the story that Grandma Sweeney told Nellie after the sad thing happened. Can you hear her voice? Can you hear her saying, as if she were in this room: "There was a crowd of crazy men went into the desert and called themselves the self-tamers because they thought they should be something better than beasts. They called their instincts the wild beasts and they tried to tame them and make them useful to themselves. Think of those poor fellows leaving their own to go off and die like that!"

And Nellie had a long time to see herself as a self-tamer, six years, and she was lonely enough to have her instincts come out in many forms. But see her now before any of those things had happened to her, just a thin girl with a bent head and white arms bowed in her lap. See her saturated with youthful sadness, her eyes big and stark with pity for herself. Now watch Dorr Nimmons just come to town in a smart straw hat, a big handsome man, rather careless looking, with a paternal manner and darting eyes. There is the market square all crowded with people, girls in white dresses, men with canes tied with ribbons. It is Fair-time. Now—clash! bum-bum, and the band master waving his stick, one hand on his hip.

In the shadow of an elm you can see Nellie and Dorr. Groups of girls drift up and form a white circle of lifted heads while Dorr smokes and assumes that he has heard better bands in his young life. Now watch them walking home, pushing through crowds of farm boys and excited girls waving balloons, Dorr making his way deftly like a city person with Nellie's white hand holding his sleeve, her hair heavy on her neck and her pale green skirt blowing in the night wind. The wedding announcements have all been sent. The wedding gown is to be fitted for the last time next week. Nellie is to be the wife of Dorr Nimmons.

Here is Bird Brill come down from the city to be maid-of-honor. She is small and plump and her face looks even brighter and more alert because of her smart hat with quills. Slippers like Bird's have never before been seen in that town, the young girls keep bothering Mr. Hogan and Mr. Beard to death trying to find some like Bird's. But there are none like them. There is Bird running down to the corner to meet Mr. Bloom and put her arm through his and look up affectionately, dazzlingly, into his kind face.

The day the organ grinder flapped down the street like a straw man, his monkey grinning and grinding his teeth, Bird ran out and danced in the dust in front of little boys, the icemen on the dripping wagon, and Louis Rasmussen, a good-for-nothing loafer with a hunched back. Inside the house Mrs. Bloom was beside herself folding her handkerchief into a small bundle, putting her hands on her neck, whispering to herself. Finally she rushed to Nellie.

"A big girl like her. It's indecent. I won't have it. Oh, rolling over the lawn! Exposing herself and people stopping!"

Nellie ran down to her friend, afraid to disobey her mother, yet sensitive on Bird's account. She shielded the girl's legs from the street and smiled at her timidly. "Won't you come to the dressmaker's with me, Bird?"

"Oh, listen, when I get married my husband simply has to buy me a monkey and take me to Europe."

Twenty minutes late at the dressmaker's and Miss Gunther particularly uppish when city people come to look at her work, tart and cold with pins in her mouth and a pencil stuck through her hair.

"Those sleeves aren't right, Miss—Miss Gunther. Those sleeves aren't right. Oh, Nell, your dress will be ruined if your sleeves aren't right. Darling, they must be right. Oh, Miss, see there, you're missing the whole style of the thing. Put that pleat this way—not that way—like this—do you see?"

Miss Gunther unpinned the wedding gown and folded it

in an old newspaper. Then she went into the kitchen and slammed the door.

When Nellie got home she lay down on her bed without crying or speaking, like a stone, until her mother came up with some warm milk and then Bird fluttered in, the folds of her smart taffeta waist like bird wings. Nellie must go to her dressmaker. She must go tomorrow. She must have the gown refashioned so that it would have style. Bird went to the telephone and made the arrangements while Nellie lay powerless and Mrs. Bloom wiped her red, peaked nose.

Hear the tremendous rush of steam, the sound of iron wheels, the frightening speed. Watch Nellie get on. Now the train is moving, now the last moment has come and her eyes are suddenly terrified, then blank. Nellie with a big box of candy held against her and the long line of coaches pulling past Dorr and Bird.

They walk away very slowly. Dorr is so tall that Bird has to look up at him sideways and dart looks from under her quills. Now she dances on impeccable, mysterious slippers in front of a gawkish paper-boy. Now she puts her hand on Dorr's arm and whispers to it and tries to take long steps to match his. Suddenly her bright face grows pale and she buries it in his sleeve.

Can you see them that evening under vines on the Bloom porch? Can you hear Bird suggest a walk to the river and does her kiss sound cool as she stoops over Mr. and Mrs. Bloom? And now by the dark water under trees, Bird half lying against the man, gives a tiny cry. "What can I do? I love you, Dorr."

Nellie came back with her gown repaired. They tried to tell Nellie, they showed her the wistful note, but Nellie's blood turned to pain and burned those arms that had held Dorr, burned the breasts that he had kissed and the white neck where the vague little curl lay, rushed like a burning storm through the long limbs under stiff silk. Her blood burned and moved and poured through that head that had seen herself as Dorr's bride, miserable for fear she had not enough to give or would not know how, breathless for fear she might somehow prove too good for

Dorr and some of his ways, even though she felt humble now. Blood washed those images of herself in his arms, melted in love, joined to him forever, to his arms and his mouth and his legs, joined for always, always his from that instant. Blood brought the face of Bird before her and her whole body turned to fire and burned it, burned it into dust, that happy face, those hands, the little quills near her ear. And now her head tightened with iron bands and the back of her neck throbbed and she tried to speak but her nose twitched and she closed her eyes. She tried to drag up words that would express her desolation but she had no words and she sat down on the floor and put her head on her knees and those straight legs turned to wood and wood spread upward, cool and inescapable, and all those dreams that blood had washed went down beyond her reach.

They took her into the spare room and she lay like a corpse, her hair covering the pillow, her face blank and dead white. Grandma Sweeney came, setting her feet down hard. "Wake up, Nellie!"

Nellie covered her face with her hair and pressed her white hands on it. "Let me die," she said. "I'm all alone and it's dark. I've always been alone."

"Girl, he wasn't the one for you. I've had two; I know." She looked down at the floor. "God, God," She said. "Get something in your stomach, Nellie. Get your legs going or next thing you'll be the town invalid."

"I want to go where it's deep and black in the ground. I want to be planted like a flower, and never be a person any more."

I'll bet," said Grandma Sweeney.

"When I was little I was always the one to get hurt."

"Nellie, can you feel my arms? I've got hold of you as tight as I held him the night of the accident."

"No."

"Nellie, is this body all there is of you? Can you walk out as you would from the tomb? Can you step into daylight and leave that dark place, Nellie?"

Then Nellie was out every day, walking along with Grandma
Sweeney at a pace a that made the minister speak to Mr. Bloom
about it one evening after choir practice. "Really, Bloom, really,
really. . . ." But he discovered that Mr. Bloom had been
hypnotized by the old woman because he insisted with tears in
his eyes that Grandma Sweeney had brought Nellie from the
grave with her own strength. No one could shake Mr. Bloom's
faith and it began to anger people. Gussie Jorns started the story
that Nellie was hypnotized, too, and that when she was alone
she didn't walk so fast nor so far. "I knew it wasn't natural,"
they all said solemnly. "Nothing spectacular like that is lasting.
Poor little Nellie always was a sickly one." Then Grant Nimmons
died and left his place to Dorr. Dorr and Bird came home.

"What if I meet them?" cried Nellie to Grandma Sweeney.
"Where could I look?"

"Straight at them," said the old woman. "They're people,
too."

"I can't—I'll die."

You can imagine that the people in Onnowac waited for
that meeting, secretly hoping that Nellie would prove herself
no stronger than any of them, half hoping that she would fade
into death appropriately. They watched her as carefully as they
did Mrs. Bolten who was pregnant for the first time and insisted
that it was one thing to be brave when Dorr Nimmons was away
but another thing to face him with Bird. They snubbed Mrs.
Nimmons, taking sides with Nellie, and were humiliated to find
that the woman didn't need them for her parties. "I guess Dorr's
got his hands full," they would say as the Nimmons' motor went
past to meet a group of city guests, "I guess he got what was
coming to him."

At that time, usually in the morning when pigeons were
making their soft coo on the roof, Bird would think of her friend
and the shy affection that had been between them and then she
would grow sad and confused and tears would come into her
eyes but she could not imagine her life without Dorr and she
knew deep in her that Dorr had been meant all the time for her

and that it had been planned, perhaps in heaven, that Miss Gunther should make a mistake in the sleeves of Nellie's dress.

But she saw her friend's face sometimes, sometimes held it in her hands and looked down into those eyes and then she would want to rush to Nellie's house and make her understand that Dorr had been hers from the beginning and that Nellie's real love would come sometime. And Dorr rejected the church of his fathers and went to the Methodist church and said that their children would have to grow up Methodists, that it couldn't be helped. He met Mr. Bloom once and the old gentleman gravely took off his hat and said, "How do you do, my boy." He saw Mrs. Bloom hurrying out of the grocery but she lowered her sharp face and her red, peaked nose and Dorr felt less guilty that night about Nellie. But he always remembered Mr. Bloom's grave, "How do you do, my boy?" and it made him want to explain to the man because he was sure he would understand.

Imagine now a bright Palm Sunday with a clear hard sky and bells ringing. Imagine you are Nellie Bloom passing a little German church. Look up and you will see the procession, the girls in stiff white dresses with sashes and white silk gloves, white slippers; the boys in black with red cheeks and blunt-toed button shoes. The bell ringing, other bells, then the church doors closing behind the last stumbling boy, and organ music slowly rising and pouring out. And as the sounds filled Nellie's ears and the clear air rushed through her, she hurried into church and when they stood up to sing music came out of her as if she were rising from the dead and from her feet she felt herself rise and although she knew her body had not changed it seemed to her that her flesh, her hips, her shoulders, were pushing up, up, and she was all alive like something growing. And when she left the church for the first time she looked at people and spoke to them as if she had no fear of what they said or thought of her and as she passed through the drowsy, nodding groups and touched hands and brushed shoulders, she felt that they were all alive and pushing, like plants or trees, and that if they sang together the sound would carry through the whole world, through the deep earth to China, and it seemed to her that everywhere people had risen from the dead and were about to sing.

She walked down the street smiling, her face lifted, her arms swinging in strange rhythmic lightness, and all people seemed to be one great moving body, and she walked and walked up the hill to Dorr Nimmons' house and rang the bell. The maid led her into the parlor and raised one of the shades so that sun sifted in over the Brussels carpet and threw a pattern of the lace curtain on the floor. There were the souvenirs from Niagara and Saratoga and the plaques painted by Bird when she was in Miss Sydney's school. And Nellie grew smaller and smaller as she waited, felt herself shrinking down to a pygmy with big eyes and a frightened mouth, and then Bird came into the room on impeccable slippers, a burst of pleats opening at her knee like foam, her white fingers laid together. They looked at each other and they were back where they were before they met Dorr, they were two girls whispering to each other shyly, smiling, half crying, letting their eyes mix. They sank down on the horsehair sofa like feathered people, soft and strange, and then Dorr came in. He stood in the doorway, tall and grave, his cheeks flushed and his eyes frightened. Nellie's bright, lifted face smiled into his and suddenly he was on his knees with his head in her lap.

Bird's mouth still held the tender friend-smile for Nellie but her eyes were on her, hard and cold, and her fingers picked at the fluted silk in her cuffs. And Nellie's lifted, smiling face seemed like a mask when Dorr got up and walked to the window, his hands behind him. She finally said, "Wasn't it a hard winter?" and flushed, thinking they might misinterpret it, and suddenly in a tone of polite exclamation she cried, "I think your souvenirs are lovely! I wish I could go to Niagara."

And then she wanted to sink to the floor because they must not know that she had envied them or had shed tears over their elopement and they must not dream that she was forlorn again and desolate. So she told them something about the new addition her father was adding to the house so that they could see that her father was rich, too, and so that they could recall his respectable face and remember that she was his daughter. And then she said that before long she was planning to go abroad. "Not for long," she said casually, "but I think it will amuse me for a time."

She got up and shook hands, using that tender smile and uplifted face look at them both, and she urged them to come and see her but as she walked down the steps she felt her heart pound, "I hate them, I hate them, I hate them. I hope they die. I hope their house burns." And the pain from hate rose thick in her eyes as if she could never shut it out and she felt a shadowy voice in her curse them, invite horrible disasters, and she saw fire take their house and burn them until not even their bones were left, until even the ashes were gone.

And out in the clear air, in that season when all was to rise from the dead, among the early spring sounds and smells, she walked as if she were burning to death. She passed the little brown church and the memory of the morning, the bells, the singing, the clear air, hung all formed and complete above her but she could not bring it back. She could see the girls in their stiff white dresses, the button-shoed boys, and she could imagine the bell clanging and fat country people hurrying around the corner of the church but none of it meant anything to her, it was like a picture.

And then she remembered herself walking to Dorr's house and she shook with horror as if she was recalling an ugly incredible dream. The smart details of Bird's dress smote her and she decided that Bird had won him through a trick, that her clothes always made her more than she was. But no pleasure came from these thoughts and suddenly the morning seemed like a shameful dream that she must forget, and then like a miracle that could never happen again. Pity came into her throat and terror rose in her eyes and ears as she walked fast to Grandma Sweeney's house by the marsh.

Make them die. Make them die. Oh, God, burn them slowly into dust and when their child comes hang it in front of them and let it burn before their eyes as they burn and let them hear its screams and see its tiny feet curl and its hands wave in torture. Let their house burn and all that is in it and never let anyone speak to them again on this earth except to curse them. Make this happen on an Easter day when all should be rising from the dead, make them lie for three slow days and nights until even their ashes are gone. Let the fire start in their bones and burn outward and let them be conscious of all their pains, even at the end when they are in their last particles. God, destroy then that last spark that cannot be destroyed so that no trace of them can remain on this earth and they may know that they are out forever.

Nellie in Grandma Sweeney's little house by the marsh walking up and down in her new Palm Sunday clothes, walking up and down in the house that is empty now and falling gradually into the swamp where frogs sing at dusk and smoke from the railroad yard spreads and falls into the dry cat-tails and marsh grass. Grandma Sweeney, her forehead in its three deep ridges, in her eyes that which cannot be named or destroyed, has not spoken or coughed or smiled. She looks at Nellie as she stands before the little mirror looking gauntly at her strange hot cheeks, her burning eyes and the new Palm Sunday hat trimmed with bunches of wheat. She sees her stand back farther and look at the broadcloth suit made by Onnowac's best tailor, noting the careful commonplace lines, the beautiful stitching. And she sees Nellie fling away from the mirror and stand in the middle of the floor, her hands on her throat, saying softly, "I would like to tear Bird's clothes to pieces with my teeth. I'd like to get that black dress and rip it in my mouth and hear it splitting in every seam." And she walked to the wall and stood with her face against it.

God, destroy that last spark that cannot be destroyed so that they may know that from that instant their lives are out forever and that they may not even be earth that gives its life to plants and trees and can feel the soft bodies of lovers lying upon it and feel warm fruit falling in its grass and feel rain stir its substances. Put them out forever on that day when all should be rising from the dead.

And then Nellie ran to Grandma Sweeney who had not spoken and her breasts touched the old woman's knees and she reached up and put her hands on the brown cheeks and pressed them, looking into the eyes. "It's me that's going to die," she said, "not them."

She sank down then and laid her strange fiery cheek on Grandma's knee and breathed slowly. As her eyes glanced at her white hands and her stiff new Palm Sunday suit they got big with horror, but she said nothing and there were no tears on her face. She put her hand to her head as if she must cool it, comfort it in some way, and then she shaded her eyes as if she were looking off into the distance and must see the farthest object in space and she took off her new hat with the wheat and pressed her hair behind her ears as if she must listen to sounds that had been made in time by people living and dying, and then she listened to the breathing that had moved in time and she heard it like a vast painful moaning. She sank lower, she lay bent over her own knees, no tears on her face, no trembling in her body.

"They went into the desert because they thought they should be something better than wild beasts. They named their violences panther, lion, zebra, snake. They tried to tame them so that they could live together in one body. They fought there in the desert for that one thing."

Suddenly Nellie lifted her face. "He gave me something of himself and it's still in me. I know all his bones. I know his eyes and the way they look out at me. I can hear him breathing in the night. What do I do with all that? Where can I put it? Do I say to myself, 'Your real intended will come sometime,' and crochet tidies for the backs of chairs? I'm the one he loves. He was tricked away from me." She stood up. "I'm going to his house now and find out what he's going to do about it."

But Nellie walked home along that street past the scraggly orchard and the marsh where I have walked night after night, hurt and frightened, the tissues of my false world bleeding in me, my head hot and strange with visions. I have walked along the brick wall where Nellie went that day and only last week the Nimmons' heir came riding his motorcycle like mad up the cemetery road. It seems strange that he should ride past her grave on that outrageous machine of his and never know that Nellie Bloom wanted Dorr Nimmons' child, that in her were seeds waiting to be fed so that they might grow and make her heavy with life. What did I know of Nellie Bloom and that wish of hers? I was a young girl in my twenties, crazy with hundreds of head-fancies, unconscious of the vast power for happiness in the body, in the womb, in the hands that press a face, in the earth itself, where all things live and grow.

And what did I know of her sensations on Easter day, a week after she had cursed them until her blood turned black in her body, that Easter morning when she went to her window and looked out into spring coolness. Could I know the angelic brightness that came through her and out on her face or the way she lifted her arms and began to sing as she had sung that Palm Sunday morning in church? But I saw her suddenly run downstairs, I heard her sing on that Easter day as she took the armful of roses intended for her parents up the hill to the Nimmons' place. I followed her down that warm street and the brightness that was in her made her look on everyone, made those eyes look, as it were, on the pain, the secrets, the fallen dreams. I saw her standing on the porch, massed hair shining above pale cheeks, cool roses touching her skin. And now you must be Nellie Bloom in the Nimmons' parlor, holding out the flowers to Bird and Dorr. You must be Nellie as she was at that instant, washed clean of memory and all the darkness that had been done to her and that she had done.

"How perfectly beautiful!" cried Bird in her guest voice.

"It's a fine Easter day," said Dorr and creaked his new shoes.

"I like Easter in a small town," said Bird more informally, her voice a delicate peeping.

And then a quietness came upon them. It was as if the room were full of doves flying slowly, their bodies brushing. It was as if the small lost voice of each had risen higher and higher until the room was filled with voices never before heard. It rose straight, without effort, above the village bells that began to ring and the feet that scraped the walk outside.

And what did I know of Nellie Bloom and Bird and Dorr in that moment or Nellie five years from that day, Nellie five years older, her body of seeds aching, her mind big enough now to understand the terror of her body's starvation. How could I, young and scornful, holding to the roots of my unreal world, know anything of Nellie Bloom on that warm summer night, sitting with her chin on her arms in the open window by the Japanese plum, her mind on Bird Nimmons who had at last come ripe with child.

In those five years she had struggled to hold to their self-substance instead of the grim figures of her imagination. She had suffered humility and then superiority, and again she would suddenly loathe them or they would have no meaning for her, they would be like pictures on the wall. And again she would boast to them of something her parents had done or buy some smart garment, faintly hoping under her conscious thoughts that it might torture Bird with its slim smartness. But always on her face was the friend-smile and in her hands, no matter what she felt, lay the friend-substance that she wished to give them. And occasionally it pleased her to see that Bird could not keep up the strain of this companionship and that lines were coming near her little mouth and at those times a big happiness would rise in her like an actual shawled body rising from mud, smoothly dripping. And many times when Dorr was no longer beautiful to her, she could feel him straining toward her, she could hear him saying under his ribs, "You are the one I love. My life with her is hell." And it pleased her then to rise smiling and put out her cool hand in farewell.

But that night in summer, five years after the Easter day when they had met each other nakedly without the distortions of imagination and violence, that night she knew that Bird's womb was about to be fulfilled and in front of her eyes she saw that grow monstrous. And all the life that she thought was dead rose in her to curse them while she sat helpless, struggling occasionally to say, "I love them," while her mouth pulled down with scorn and loathing. And she walked up and down her room as if she had something rotten inside her that she must dig out, and she struggled with that muddy figure of happiness as if it were actual and could be met in combat. Finally she sat down on the floor and pressed her head into the bed, whispering to it, "I love them—I love them," but all through her and about her were little spirals of laughter, fine and bright as coiled wires.

The baby was over a year old before she went to see it. She went up to the porch and then stopped to see if pain would rise so strongly that she could not go in, but no pain came, only shyness, and when she saw Bird she kissed her on the cheek and for a second she saw the three of them as they had been on that Easter day when they had risen from the dead. The same smile was on her face but inside her it was different, inside her was the darkness and stupor of death and the gestures of death that go through movements without meaning. She forgot about the baby and kissed Bird again. She inquired about Dorr and his business and the new bird bath in the garden.

When Bird excused herself, she looked at the new carpet and the smart hangings at the windows. She recalled the subtle arrangement of tucks in Bird's frock and then began wondering about the new cement walk that was being put in on Main Street past the library. She heard Bird come into the room and she was conscious that something lay soft and heavy in her lap, but she was also aware of not noting these things or commenting on them. She told Bird it would be a good thing if they would put in cement walks all over town.

"Father is on the committee and he's very anxious to put the thing through. He used to be mayor, you know, and they all respect him. He has a lot of influence but I doubt if the city will go into debt even for such important improvements."

"I know," said Bird, her eyes twinkling. "Aren't people stupid about things?"

"Yes, they are. Father says he was up against all the vices of mankind during his term as mayor. He was simply helpless."

"Don't be so hard on them," said Bird softly.

Nellie looked around the room strangely and then down at the child in her lap. "Oh, God," she said faintly and stood up, but Bird had her baby in her arms before it fell.

That evening when Grandma Sweeney got home from old lady Anderson's, she found Nellie sitting with her back against the wall staring at the sea-shell doorstop. It is said that her face was stiff and terrible and that when she struggled to speak it was as if her throat was frozen. She looked up at Grandma Sweeney, but she did not try to talk, and no tears came into her eyes, but she put her hands often between her breasts as if there was something there she wanted to tear out and throw on the floor. And after a time she got up and walked back and forth, her hands on those strange, fiery cheeks, and she kept clearing her throat as if she was trying for the last time to force herself to say that she loved them, but her throat must have been frozen because her eyes stood out from her head as if she were dumb.

And once she sat down on the floor and looked at her body in horror, at her legs and arms in such a strange lonely fashion that Grandma Sweeney suddenly crowded her into her lap and they sat there without speaking as it grew darker and darker and the lights of Onnowac went out one by one. The night train came through with its monstrous churring and screaming, but Nellie did not sigh or speak, but lay there against the old woman. When it grew colder and the darkness was thick like felt around them, Nellie pressed her cheek against Grandma Sweeney's and put her arm around her neck. But she made no other sound or movement all through the night.

MR. AND MRS. ARNOLD

N O one knew what Mrs. Arnold believed; she never said much. Mr. Arnold played extravagantly with words but no one knew what he believed. They thought they loved and hated one another but they could never be sure.

"Darling," said Mr. Arnold. "Oh, nothing, nothing at all," he shouted suddenly at her mild face. "I wish you wouldn't wear that confounded cap, please. Oh, wear it if you want to."

From Mrs. Arnold radiated silence.

"What do I care! If women want to wear caps let them." He waved his arms. "Shall I order some of that sweet cider when I go past the store?"

Mrs. Arnold nodded. She removed her cap, smiled up at him, and suddenly replaced it. "Cider is always good this time of year," she remarked.

"I've never had a good glass of cider in my life. When I was a boy, yes, once I did, I take that back. No, I don't take it back. No one knows how to make cider properly. Oh, the cutthroats that try to do things nowadays. The bloody highwaymen, the grocers, the butchers, the garage men. . . ."

Mrs. Arnold turned her tatting.

"Infernal cowards, all of them," he boomed, "can't face life."

"Can you?" asked Mrs. Arnold, rocking, tatting.

"What's that? Were you speaking to me?" He went to her,

kissed her, patted her busy hands. "That's all right now, don't worry about the cider. I'll order it."

"Thank you, dear." She smiled and removed her cap.

"Good Lord, if a woman can't comb her hair, she'd better keep it covered."

"You'll find your umbrella in the hall, dear."

"Umbrella?" His mouth fell open and he stared out at the bright maple leaves on the lawn. "Are you crazy?"

"I am always sane," she said and added in the same voice, "never sane."

"Well, if you want me to take it I'll take it, I'll do anything to please you. . . ."

"Don't take it just because I want you to, take it because it's going to rain. No, I won't let you take it just to please me, dear."

"But I want to take it. Where do you keep the umbrellas? Can't a man ever find anything when he has to go down town?"

"Here, dear," she said and handed it to him. "You're sensible to take it. I know it will rain."

Mr. Arnold flung the umbrella and pitched out of the house. With respectful precision Mrs. Arnold raised the umbrella to its feet, brushed its coat, and led it to the rack. Then she laughed.

The telephone rang. "Hello, hello, hello!" said Mr. Arnold. "I ordered the cider. Want anything else?"

"No, dear."

"What's that?"

"I don't want anything else."

"Don't want anything after I've gone to the bother of calling you up? Can't even think up something to repay me for the trouble, can you?" He banged the receiver.

Mrs. Arnold took the breakfast dishes into the kitchen and filled the dishpan. She made suds with flakes of soap and watched the water make the glasses clean. Then she wiped the dishes and noted reflections on their surfaces; she wiped the dishpan and hung it up. For luncheon they would have some soup, some celery, hot muffins. . . . Her smile pricked the stiffness of her face. She took up her tatting, rocked until she saw the postman, then put the kettle on.

From the dining-room window she saw Mr. Arnold flying to his food. She covered a plate with a white napkin bordered with hollyhocks, for the muffins. The door banged, a man groaned. She knew her husband was ready for his meal.

"Come into the dining room, dear," she called.

"Don't I always, dear?" he answered.

His skin was sulphur-colored, his face solid, his body big and broad, but his eyes proved him perishable.

Mrs. Arnold tasted her soup. "Will you say it's good?" she asked.

"All soup is good."

Her laughter was neither bitter nor amused. It was a plain flat sound.

"Well, do I have to say that everything you cook is splendid, wonderful, excellent, incomparable? Can't you let me forget that I am eating? Where are you going this afternoon?"

"The club, probably."

"You be careful at the crossings. Now, listen to me. Dear," he cried, rising, bending over the table, "you're going to be run over one of these days."

"I suppose so."

"You can't ever watch where you're going. You expect people to get out of your way and the bandits nowadays won't get out of anyone's way. You ought to know it, dear!"

"Will you have some tea?"

"Certainly I won't! Have I ever been a man to indulge my stomach?"

"I had on my yellow crêpe when I bought this tea." She put her chin on her hand and looked out.

"If I'd known thirty years ago what I know now, I'd have set the world on fire."

The woman tasted her tea and heard him call from the porch, "Goody-by!" She examined a dark spot on a silver spoon;

shuddered. "Don't forget your umbrella," she called.

He charged back to the doorway. "And make an ass of myself coming home in the snow, I suppose. Yes, you want to make me ridiculous in every way, don't you?"

"It sometimes snows in October." Again she withdrew, into unlimited space, he judged, from her look. "A rather nice little bowl."

"Who cares where we bought it? No wonder I'm a madman living in the same house with you. Not a day can pass that you don't make your remark about that bowl."

"You are looking for cake again?" she asked half sweetly. He rushed from the house.

She lingered at the table and watched the suppressed look of the heavy silver imprisoned there on the white cloth. She moved a spoon close to the sugar bowl and fenced a delicate cup with forks. Then she carried the dishes into the kitchen and filled the dishpan with water. She would not go to the club that afternoon. It was raining. The grocery boy threw open the back door and set down a jug of cider. She laughed.

It was almost dark when she opened the door to two men supporting her husband. She brushed a bit of mud from his sleeve and placed a pillow in his chair.

"I don't want that there!" he cried, enraged and trembling.

She turned to the men, fastening up a strand of pale hair. "It was very good of you."

"Yes, wasn't it?" gasped Mr. Arnold.

"Knocked the wind out of him all right. Too much careless driving, I tell my wife. Ought to be punished. But he'll be around, this is nothing."

"Oh, nothing at all," sneered Mr. Arnold. "Those high-waymen can do as they please. What if they do knock a decent man down?"

The woman opened the door to the men. She came back to her husband and suddenly kissed him. She took his hands and they looked at each other.

"I tell you I could set the whole world right if they'd only listen." His mouth looked surprised, half-frightened, as though he had formed his last sentence.

His wife moved softly and slowly away. "There's something quite good for supper," she said without intonation.

THE FAMILY

1

THE instant Mr. Beale entered the house Mrs. Beale drew
up her right shoulder and blinked three or four times. Then
she poured boiling water on the tea and told him dinner
was almost ready. The little Beale ran into the garden, her sad
startled eyes on the rhubarb, the radishes and onions, the straight
rows of flowers. She walked with her hands clasped behind her,
looking from right to left stiffly as if she thought she was being
watched and must show how honestly she was inspecting every
leaf and how great was her appreciation of the garden.

"Come right along in and eat your dinner!"

The little girl swung round, her fingers on her shoulders
and marched slowly and gravely up the stone walk to the house.
She slid into her chair and tied her napkin round her neck all
by herself, looking up at her father and mother between her
fallen hair.

Mr. Beale looked straight ahead of him, as if his eyes were
seeing something far, far off, as far away as the Baltic Sea or
the Indian Ocean, and he held up his knife and fork dripping
with gravy. "I try to make everyone happy," he said gruffly, "I
try to do good to everyone. I try to think right and talk right
and do right. Who ever does anything for me?"

"Please, you're dripping," said Mrs. Beale gently.

"I haven't got a friend anywhere." He couldn't help but remember his mother and the way she held him on her lap once after his brothers had chased him through the timber tract trying to get his watch away from him.

The little Beale stopped eating. She took hold of the red string tie on her sailor suit and stared at the buffet with the rows of tumblers on top and the watermelon picture just above. She seemed to fold up and grow smaller, her lips, her cheeks, shoulders, arms, all but her eyes and they grew fixed and big. She seemed to have stopped breathing and then when her mother bent to serve the pudding she let her finger move up toward her neck, over her cheek to her eye and then her mouth jerked down and she let her head sink to her chest.

Mr. Beale half rose, one hand jammed on his napkin, the other pointing toward his only child. "Now, what are we going to do with you? You're a coward, you haven't got any digestion, and I don't know what's to become of you." He sank down again and took a piece of bread. "I suppose we'll have to let you grow up into an invalid like Irma Hoar, always hanging to your mother, weak livered and not worth anything at all to humanity."

He pulled out a large white silk handkerchief and began pushing it into his ear. His eyes were far off again and suddenly he said, "We live so our children can do something more than we have, so that they can do better, think better, and be better men and women than we've been, and so they can leave the world better." He turned his sad eyes toward the window, swinging his chair around and shoving his dishes away with his elbow. Over the neat grass plots children were leaping and screaming, tumbling over dogs, tearing at each other's hair ribbons and thrusting out tongues. They began throwing sticks for the dogs to run after and they set up a great screaming when one little girl rolled backwards into a bed of zinnias. Old lady Peppen ran out then with her umbrella and children and dogs galloped off down the cement,

"Those are *children*," he said. "They know enough to get out and play and have a good time while there's a chance."

"There's been a flood in Ohio," said Mrs. Beale.

"There's been a *what* in Rio?"

"A *flood*," she brought out with great effort, all her pleasure gone.

"Well, I can't do anything about it. I'm sorry for all the unfortunate people in the world, but I can't stop the rain or the snow or any of the things that cause human suffering. If I could I'd do it, but I can't . . ."

"Stop, stop, *stop!*" cried Mrs. Beale with both hands pressed over her face. Her hair was arranged in a small vace on top of her head and drawn low on her forehead. Now she was leaning forward against the table, her arms folded in her lap, and her young eyes on the brown glazed teapot. When her husband stopped talking she let her shoulder sink down so that the ruffles on her collar brushed the white lobe of her ear. Her forehead and face grew placid and sweet as if she were thinking of soft white hens in hay or waterfalls of silk displayed on a shining counter. She poured herself another cup of tea, holding the cover with her forefinger. "Gizzie," she called, looking toward the door into the kitchen, "more hot water, please."

Gizzie burst in, setting an old straw hat with a buckle in front on her head. She always wore this hat in serving and kept it on a hook just inside the pantry door where she could jerk it in a hurry.

"Yes, Mrs. Beale," she said and rolled her dark glossy eyes at Mr. Beale who had turned away from them and was sitting with his head in his hands, his legs far apart. The room seemed full of his breathing. He seemed to be breathing out something that settled and congealed on them until they were small and still under the coating.

"I want you to fill the teapot, Gizzie," said Mrs. Beale faintly.

"Awh, Mr. Beale," said Gizzie and then ran into the kitchen snuffling. "He's the best hearted man in town," she told her friends. "Always bringing a present home, raincoat or something expensive. Mis' Beale is nice, too, but she's too educated or something to make over him and he's gotta be made over. But I stand up for the both of them. It's that little kid that gets me going. They'd be larks if it wasn't for her."

Mrs. Beale drew a long breath as if air were hard to get and she had to draw against a great dark substance or mass that was pressing on her. The little Beale sat with bent head, staring out at her father through her hair, tears glittering on her long fair lashes.

"Did you like the pudding?" asked Mrs. Beale.

"Do I like what?"

"The pudding."

"No," he said, "I don't like anything."

Mrs. Beale jumped up and burst into the kitchen where Gizzie was standing over the kettle, the teapot in one hand. "Give it to me, Gizzie," she cried as if she were smothering. "Give me the teapot. Oh, I know you think I'm crazy," she said staring into the girl's face, "but I can't help telling someone. I want to roll my eyes round and round and then seize my nose and wind up my face, just as if it's a clock," she cried in horror, shaking so that the teapot lid clattered. "I want my face to strike my death." Then she laughed. "Pour on lots of water," she ordered. But Gizzie couldn't get over it. "You watch Mis' Beale," she told her friends. "There's something out of the ordinary there."

Mrs. Beale took her place again. Mr. Beale put his spoon into his pudding. "It's all right," he said and ate slowly, his head down. Mrs. Beale knew that in a moment he would go to the pantry and pull out an old cook book of his mother's and begin reading over the receipts. "One cup butter, one cup figs, one half ounce raisin juice, seventeen eggs . . ." But he shoved his plate away. "Nothing tastes rich," he said. They moved into the sitting room. The little Beale sat down under the dictionary stand, fearing her father would suggest a game of ball when he saw how sad and frightened she was.

But Mr. Beale couldn't even play a game of ball with her because when he threw she would cover her face with her arm and stand there a martyred figure, nine years old in Buster Brown oxfords and a white sailor suit with a red string tie. No matter how often he told her she was a coward she would always automatically throw her arms over her face when he threw and when the absurd game was over she would dart to her mother with little whines of fright in her throat, her hair falling over her cheeks. But their joint suffering came when she was called upon to speak a piece at the church for the Christmas exercises. She would go about like a dead girl for days in advance and on the night of the celebration she would have no voice left in her. When it came her turn she would have only strength to get up in front of everyone, under the glittering tree with paper angels and stars, and stand gazing idiotically, water coming out on her forehead and sparkling in the tender fuzz around her lips.

"Her baby work is driving me crazy," cried Mr. Beale. "Where is she? Dorrit, come here!"

She came out from under the stand, bumping her head something frightful, and looking at them with her lips trembling and her sad eyes opened full upon them in terror and helplessness. Sometimes she was led down the street and pushed into a crowd of children and ordered to play. Other times unexpectedly, she would be tested as to how much she knew in arithmetic or how well she was doing with her piano lessons or lectured on her bad handwriting.

Mr. Beale pounded into the hall and came back with a large mysterious box. Mrs. Beale trembled as he raised the lid because she knew it was another present and when he brought presents there was "no living with him," as she put it. It was a net dress for their only child, trimmed with silk rosebuds and ribbon edged ruffles. He shoved the box at his wife, ordering her to dress Dorrit, "and don't be all day doing it, either. When I get home I like to see something of my family and not have them leave the room and stay away a couple of hours." Then he put his head in his hands, his legs far apart. "Awh, Mr. Beale," called Gizzie from the dining room, "don't you want some of my cucumber pickle?" but he didn't look up or answer.

He wondered why he couldn't make his family like him better than they liked themselves. When the little girl came back he did not move.

"Say, Mis' Beale," called Gizzie cheerfully, "Mis' Beale."

"What is it, Gizzie?"

"I guess we're going to have a rain. The walk's all covered with toads in back."

Mr. Beale rared up. "Of all the freaks," he cried, scowling darkly at his wife, his voice husky, his hands shaking and spread open.

"Shame. Control yourself."

"Always got to fill this house up with freaks. Confound it, anyway."

He saw his only child then standing squarely in front of him, her fair hair tied on top with a monstrous bow and hanging in soft light curls on her shoulders. She looked beautiful, her white baby skin, her bare dimpled arms, the firm legs and shining eyes. He took out his glasses. Something rushed hot behind his face and fell thick in his throat. He stared at her, one large hand held over his cheek.

"Stand back so I can see!"

She moved back timidly but with more spirit than they had ever seen in her, and when she was ordered to turn she even gave a shy hop on one leg.

"Stand still like a Christian." Then he blurted out without wanting to, as if the words were saying themselves, something about "she would be crying before night, anyway."

"Awh, can I see Mis' Beale?" asked Gizzie, her head hanging in the door. "Awh, say you wouldn't know her." She knelt on her stiff knees by the child, her great squeaking button boots stuck out behind her, one side of her dark hair rolled up in electric curlers. "Run and kiss Papa," she whispered to the child. "Throw your arms round his neck." She fell back on her heels and threw out her arms to show the child. "This way," she said and smiled largely. "Oh, if I had a nice Papa like that I'd thank him and let him know. I'd show him I was grateful and that he was the best Papa in the whole world."

The child's nose twitched and her eyes got big and frightened. She clutched her dress with both hands and stood as if she could never move, her eyes watching her father, following him as he paced up and down. Once or twice he snorted so that if his child finally did rush to him impulsively, throw her arms around his neck, and at last act like this only child, it would not be because of the present but because of him, of his love that he could not talk or act or let out, of the foolishness in him for both these people, his wife and child, that could only come if they would first do their part.

"My, my," said Gizzie, "my, what a bad little girl. Run along to Papa and thank him."

"You leave this room," broke in Mr. Beale. "And let me tell you right now," he cried, glaring into her face, "I never expect anyone to make a fuss over me and I don't care what she does or what her mother does. I give and I don't expect any return. I work my head off and I don't expect any thanks, and I'd have you know that you ought to be locked up for your infernal meddling in other people's affairs." He began shaking his finger at her, his eyes by now wild and hurt. "I don't want her to thank me, can you get that through your crazy head?"

The little girl darted out of the room, they heard her stumbling quickly up the stairs, her slippers clattering on the bare steps, and finally when she had reached the top they heard a sharp scream, as if she had been holding her breath for a long time and now the cry came down on them, cutting through the room, desperate and lonely. Mrs. Beale ran and Mr. Beale knew that now he was farther away from them than before, he knew that now his wife would fold the little girl tight to her breast and rock and rock, her face pressed gently against the soft long hair, and perhaps all her own loneliness would go as the child's arms went tight around her neck and clung to her for help and love.

"I know you don't mean half you say," said Gizzie, shrinking back from him as if she expected a blow. "My uncle Harry

Needles was just like you only he was a musician, he played the flute. It was solid gold and I used to clean it for him with vinegar and ashes."

He pushed her aside impatiently and went back through the house to the kitchen and then out to the garden where the corn was. He pulled ear after ear from the drying stalks, looking up mutely at the roof of his house. Then he leaned over and pulled up a turnip and began eating it, the sand grinding against his teeth as he chewed. He thought of the additions he could make to his home, the dazzling sun parlor where birds would fly in and out and flowers would grow all winter. That would make it the best house in town. He felt proud of the way the roof sloped down to the clean boards and the roses and vines over the screened windows made it all look inexpressibly quiet and peaceful. The grapes were already formed on the arbor at the side and in the fall the heavy blue clusters would hang rich and full almost to his head. He looked back at the roof and saw an imaginary observatory rise and glitter on the very top. He saw himself inside looking out at dark spaces and whirling planets that revolved in the deep endless dark, gold stars and comets and meteors, all close to his head.

"It's good to be alive on such a day," he called to Mrs. Hoar who came out to water her flowers, holding her starched dress away from the leaky watering can. He walked nearer and nearer, his head slightly bent in respect. "Those asters of yours are the best I've seen this year."

"It's too much responsibility" she replied shortly. "I sometimes think we'll have to give up the garden. There's so much to do in the house and cellar."

"Nonsense," he cried. "You don't know a thing about it. Nothing's better than fine flowers." He stepped over into her garden plot and began walking up and down between the rows of plants, telling her how she could change everything around and improve it vastly, knocking the head of flowers that he did not like or thought were in the wrong places. "Now then, thow out all those vegetables and simply fill this in with flowers."

It seemed to him that she answered tartly. She turned her back and pulled up a weed, the wind swinging her skirts round her legs tightly. Then she walked up to the house, her weight going over on her right side, the crazy blue dust cap flapping its ends in her neck. He felt disgust run through his gums and out on his mouth. He stepped back into his own yard, certain now that his wife had done something to offend her, and then he thought of his mother who was friends with everyone in the town, who went where the sick were, who sent large loaves of bread to the poor and always gave largely when a family was burned out or had sickness. He stared at the sickly bushes in the side yard and he remembered vividly his daughter scuttling behind one of them when she saw him coming, then crouching, her eyes closed, a small beaver hat set on top of her fair hair. That one time he had been overcome by her abject, mute cowardice and had passed by, but other times when she considered herself hidden from him he would force her out to stand before her maker.

The wind raised up his hat and he reflected that the winds and storms of God could lay waste to the land and the fury of waters could wash everything away, all traces of homes and gardens and miserable lives. He felt as if he had been struck over the head with a mallet and as if the shock went down to his toes. Now a deep murmur of thankfulness went all through him and he heard himself thanking God for his child, his wife, for his home that he loved and the safety and warmth inside. He rushed in. "The fact of the matter is, with all our faults the United States is the greatest nation the world has ever seen. We stand above them all. We stand for democracy, right thinking, for right living, decent living, and we live for the next generation, that's our religion, that's our whole life, the next generation that is to make humanity better, leave it with higher ideals and hopes, a bigger conception of life than we have ever known. . . ."

"I know it," said Gizzie, holding up a knife covered with snowy lard, "I know right thinking is everything. Now, Mr.

Wilgrub got cured of seizures, he had them every time Mrs.
went to Milwaukee and he was cured with Christian Science
and Theosophy."

"I've practiced all those religions all my life. There's good
in all religion. But the important thing is to live up to the
constitution of the United States."

"That's just what Uncle Harry Needles was always saying,
every time it'd come night he'd begin and if I'm educated at all
I owe it to my Uncle Harry because he was the smartest in
books of any in our town, they all said so and he had things in
the paper and . . ."

Mrs. Beale moved into the kitchen, her face stiff and
remote as if she were far away.

"Got toothache?" he asked.

She shook her head and then shuffled away in her soft
slippers. He remembered her bright face above the set of furs he
had given her, the eyes as he had handed over all his money to
her. She could have anything he had, he would save her in a
fire or a wreck, he would always take care of her and he had
already given his life to her, first to his mother and sisters and
then to his wife, he had sacrificed himself from the time he
could remember to a pack of ungrateful women who were always
at his heels. He took the whetstone out and spit on it. Then
he began sharpening his knife blade.

"Now it's on," said Gizzie, but he did not look up. "Better
eat while it's hot," she said but he paid no attention. Finally
he went into the dining room but his wife was not there in her
place. He started to shout for her wildly and then went to the
window instead and jerked up the window shade, letting it roll
to the top with a bang and then flop over the roller, winding
the pull tightly. He turned around and faced the table under
the large bright shade that made the cloth dazzling white and
the plates with their gold bands shine and gleam. He saw the
pickles in a fluted glass dish with sprays of flowers and he leaned
over and took one, hiding it when Gizzie came in.

"Ain't you down yet?" she asked. "Where's Mrs. at?" She

went off through the house on her squeaking shoes.

He paced heavily so that his wife in the room above would know that he wasn't eating, that he couldn't eat if she wasn't there to hand him things and talk. He wondered about his child. "She'll have to be a teacher," he thought, "no one will want to marry her." But a teacher would know how to change the next generation, make it better, nobler. He felt the sweat stand out on him as he thought of his girl leaving a spiritual mark on everyone.

"Do you want gravy, Mr?"

He turned to Gizzie. "When I take a day off from the store I expect to be entertained, I expect to have a little consideration shown me and look at this!" He waved his hands over the loaded table and the empty chairs. His heart felt so sore and open that he could not speak. Then he heard Gizzie snuffle and her squeaking boots trod back to the kitchen. He remembered the day his father took him to see Dick Bacon's sick bull. He could see the mud, the flies stuck in it and circling above, singing like hornets. Home in the wagon, buckwheat cakes for supper, a lamp in the center of the table. He bent his head lower. "Pass the bread, if you please." Plates piled with bread white as snow, platter heaped with hot sausages, his father saying the blessing, freckles on his mother's hand seen through eyelashes in the lamplight, in the peace, amen.

(Interval)

In the night Mrs. Beale got up and went to the open window. She leaned out and smelled the cool dark air, she felt as if she were wandering under the trees down there in the dark garden with face lifted and head empty, heart empty, all young and happy. Tears started to her eyes and she said to herself sternly, "I am not unhappy. I am a wife and mother. I am respected in town wherever I go."

But she saw the Mrs. Beale who had stood by the open window thinking of her baby that was not born yet, she saw that Mrs. Beale as clear as day. She had on a wrapper with pansies in it and her hair was in a bang just above her brows and done in a knot at the back. Below that pale brown hair was the face which looked as if it was all open with wonder and large, inarticulate understanding and anticipation. She saw it all, the sun on everything, the dog licking her puppies all over, and she saw the warmth and understanding that had streamed out of her to the dog, the garden, as if it had been something tangible. She could see it streaming from her eyes, her arms, her whole body. It went into the small fruit trees just coming into bloom, it seemed to blaze down on the ground and fertilize it and make it thick and sharp with green sprouts, and it seemed to be making the blossoms on the trees open out.

That day she had thought of all the dogs and cats and lambs just born into the spring world, all the colts and calves and chickens and pigs, all the blossoms being born from buds and the buds from stems and seeds. She seemed to strain up out of her pansy robe, out of herself toward everything growing and expanding, as if this was a moment she would never forget and she had closed her eyes as if it should be even more important, more sharp, since she was never going to forget any of it all her life. It had seemed easy to her that day to go into the warm garden, or to drop down on the earth in the sun, and while those buds were opening and the dog was licking her puppies to let her child be born. She remembered the way she had sank back in her chair at the thought, trying to experience it, head back, feet stretched out, toes stretched. She had smiled mysteriously, her eyes very large and glittering, and her hands had fallen open on her lap.

"Where's the hammer," Mr. Beale had cried from the cellar, and she had called back gently, "I think it's in the kitchen drawer, dear." And then he had appeared, "Where did you hide that confounded hammer anyway? I wish you'd get some system and order about you." She could see the long gray cobweb hanging off the end of his glasses. His lips had trembled, his breath coming through clenched teeth.

Plate of meat. Dish of sauce. Dish of potatoes. Plate of bread. Tablecloth clean on Sunday. Napkins clean on Wednesday and Sunday. Bed of petunias. Jack Miller passing in new car. Mrs. Peppen watering grass. Two sisters from the Sacred Heart passing in black robes.

"Women like that should be shot."

Would God punish a woman who married someone she didn't really love? Would He wait until she got along in years and then deal some dreadful blow? Oh, that day in her pansy dressing gown with her hands fallen open on her knees, her baby in her, *in her,* she had thought of the cemetery in winter, she had seen her mother with a velvet band around her neck and a coffee cup in her hand. If a woman did the best she knew how, if she was brave in childbirth and endured all of it, would that be paying God back for the wickedness she had done? If she endured it all without a shriek or a moan would God overlook her not loving her husband?

"They are a menace to all right thinking men and women. Such women should be beaten in the streets. What good are we as human beings if we can't raise children and leave the world better than when we came into it. All through the history of mankind these women have been a menace to the home, to biology, to sociology and to the real purpose in living. It's a serious question and one that is beginning to stir the minds of men all over the globe."

She had put her face in her hands and looked out, her eyes wide and bright. She had made a soft sound in her throat as a man went by leading a little child. She saw her own child and thought of the miracle of having it out in the world, of placing it in a chair, running toward it with arms out, catching it up while its gold curls shook over its happy pink face, watching it stoop uncertainly to pick up a speckled hen's feather from the path.

"Aaaaah, there he goes, the dirty thief to charge me twelve dollars for that job of cleaning. I'll let every tooth in my head rot and fall out before I go to him again to be robbed. . . . Oh, well, be a thief in this world and you'll be rewarded, you'll get the good things of life, everyone will smile at you if you're only thief enough. . . ."

She had struggled up out of her chair, her nose twisting idiotically, her hand on her throat. She had looked startled and anguished, as if she felt she were swaying dangerously and would eventually hit the floor. "Well, anyway, I feel happy to-day."

"You're always happy when you don't have to see much of me."

"That's not true, that's a lie. I love you. It's a lie. I love you. That's a lie, that's a lie." Her voice was low and hard. "Lie," she said with a heavy thick tongue.

She started upstairs, taking them slowly, Mr. Beale following, begging to do something, asking if he should call the doctor, Gizzie, Mrs. Hoar, asking if she didn't want some ice cream or if he couldn't get a rig and take her riding out to the point where she had such a good time that Sunday after they were married. He had shaken the sleeve of her dressing gown, twisted it in his fingers, pulled it, demanding that she tell him what was the matter, what he should get, swearing he would do anything in the world for her if she would only tell him what to do, what she wanted, what had made her so sick.

She had sat down in the same chair by the window, her lips shut tight, fear and nausea all through her. Then she had looked into his face, he was so frightened, his hands on her, his mouth twisted, and he had put on his glasses so that he could see her better.

"I'm nothing but a toad!" she cried. "I'm a snake. Oh, I want to come out, I want to drop off my skin, Oh, you, too, your snake skin, Oh, God in heaven, don't forget me. . . ." Then she had unbuttoned her slipper and rubbed her swollen ankle.

Mr. Beale shot toward the door. He did not turn as he spoke but kept his hurt face away from her. "It's a shame I don't gamble and drink and use bad language. That's the way to make a woman love you—that's the way to succeed in this world, be a thief and a devil and disobey every one of our Lord's commandments."

She had made herself lie back, saying that no one in the world was completely happy and that it was better to have a man who was steady, didn't smoke or drink or carry on, than to be dragging around after someone you would love insanely for a year, say, and then cease to love. Wouldn't it be better to live quietly, wouldn't God at least respect a woman more who took a man who was good and honest and had a fair business than to live wildly in the flesh? And yet she felt guilty. Her ears roared as if tides of blood were rising and she managed to get out of her room and down the stairs, calling wildly to her husband who came running, his glasses glittering on his vest, his gold chain glittering.

She closed her eyes and threw herself against him as if he were a wall, and cried, "I love you—I love you—I love you." The she began to moan as if all those dreams that had settled in her since childhood had come back, the face and body of the ideal man who was to love her, the one made for her in heaven, the one they had ordered her to wait for, wait, wait. "Oh, help me," she cried and turned her eyes to him in panic and dark remorse. "Oh, tell me anything that's true." He had to get the doctor.

The dark still air blew onto Mrs. Beale and she stared into it as if it held all her life that had gone, as if the Mrs. Beale in a pansy robe was somewhere in the dark, imperishable but unknown, unrelated to her now, and as if that child in the womb, so perfect, so loved, was also unknown, unrelated to the little girl she loved and who had cried herself to sleep in the other room.

In all the dark houses all over the world, she thought, are people who once were happy, who knew a day that was above all days, and now they can't remember how they felt or what it meant or what it was for. I am Mrs. Beale, a wife and mother, respected by the doctor, the dentist, our butcher, in the electric office, in the gas, general coal, trusted by the egg man, the vegetable man and in the fruit market. I can charge wherever I please. Our credit is good. No one needs to know what I think or feel about anything. That is my own. I can nod, no matter what is said, whether I believe or not, and know in myself what I really believe and I don't care what anyone in the world believes just so I can have peace and quiet and no one drips on the clean cloth. I will ask Mrs. Grouse to-morrow how her hip is and if they have to operate.

But by the time she got back into bed all her emotion had slipped out of her, she felt vacant and strange but not unhappy. There was nothing in the world to be tragic about, she thought. People were as pleasant as they knew how to be, and yet she had a queer image in front of her eyes that would not go. It was a dog rooting in autumn leaves, smelling with his moist warm nose over dry, imperishable leaves, each different, each vivid and crisp, and it was so sharp in her mind that tears came to her eyes but she felt no sadness, only a little shudder in her arms because she understood so little and didn't begin to know the why of anything on earth.

2

Everyone in town thought it was remarkable that the little Beale girl should pass in school each year because from reports she never answered a question that was asked her, never worked her problems at the board, and when the examination papers were passed she always sat staring idiotically at the teacher who was writing the problems in big clear figures in front of them all. The little girl simply sat with her hands clasped in front of her on her desk and looked helpless, as if she knew she couldn't even work them wrong. She would have been sent to an institution some said if it weren't that her parents were of good family and well read, they took all the magazines and had beautiful flowers. The Hoars told everyone that the little Beale was passed from year to year because of the gorgeous bouquets she took to her teachers.

In any event Mrs. Beale was always overcome with pity and anger whenever she paid a visit to the school. Once she was humiliated by watching a spelling down and witnessing her daughter being left until the last when they were choosing sides and the teacher hurriedly pushing her over to the group where she belonged, the indignant leader being unwilling to call her name. The child stared at them all as if she had no notion of where she was and when she was called on for a word she simply opened her mouth but no sounds came out and her eyes got bigger and bigger. Another time Mrs. Beale saw her snowballed in the schoolyard, pelted with snow, and yet unwilling to run, afraid to run perhaps, and walking sedately along, pretending to be oblivious, her large eyes straight ahead, her mouth twitching.

"She's not like any of my family," said Mr. Beale.

"Honest," Gizzie Needles told her friends, "that little kid gets my goat. They give her the world and all and she just stares at them stupid. Can't even tell time and her Papa bought her a watch and all for having the measles."

Year by year she rose in school, through the grades, into the high school finally, and each year she seemed more death-like, her eyes strained far open and her mouth drawn small and firm. They sent her off to college, "far away" was all she could reply when they asked her where she wanted to go so they made it five hundred miles from home. "Don't it beat all what they'll take in now," Gizzie Needles said, "and she's begging to come home. I always read her letters early in the morning before they're down. She's begging."

Now Dorrit thanked her father for all the gifts he had ever given her, for the net dress, the little watch, everything, she thanked him with words that seemed to pitch out of her and burn and crack. She thanked her mother, she thanked her for bringing her into the world, she begged them both to let her come home. In every sentence was love, love, something about the fires and pains of love as if she had been torn out of their bodies and lay dying.

"If she comes back she'll be an invalid," said Mr. Beale. "No, I set my foot down. She has to stay. No more baby work."

But they wrote back to her with strange fire, meeting her love, her loneliness, her despair, but telling her she must stay and then after a time she began sending them pictures in her letters, great colored flowers that would never rot, flowers that were full of life that never changed. Mrs. Beale pinned them up in her clothes closet, she didn't want Gizzie to see. Mr. Beale looked at them privately and shook his head, he knew that if he said they were good he would be partial and dishonest.

They didn't let her come home for Christmas, it would be too far and business was bad, but she could come for the summer. They met her at the station. She got off the train gravely, her eyes filling with tears as she looked around her. She had on a small hat with a white rose over the ear, a soft rose that pressed her fair hair, and she wore a strange dress of no particular period, all folds and much too long, to the ankles, and everyone in town had hers short.

"Good heavens, girl," cried Mr. Beale, his hands nervous and his face screwed up.

"What?" she asked.

"Why, nothing," he said, laughing, "nothing but that confounded dress of yours."

"Oh," she said.

Mrs. Beale began twisting up her nose and mouth and rolling her eyes around, even sighing in little gasps. She took hold of her daughter and kissed her many times. Then her head suddenly began to shake as if she couldn't help it and the cords of her mouth and neck stretched tight and her eyes went shut. She had a crisp new handkerchief in her gloved hands with a B done in blue.

"Why, Mama," said Mr. Beale reproachfully because the station platform was crowded.

But his daughter was facing her mother as if her hands

were tied, saying over and over, "Mama! Mama! Mama!" and yet not touching her mother or seeming to see her. The next day Gizzie Needles told over town that Dorrit was still a freak but she answered now when she was spoken to and was improved in small ways. "But she's got the funniest dresses you ever see. I looked over everything last night. They went to the show."

The first morning at home Dorrit went up to her father with mysterious pride and dignity. "I have something to show you." The tightwaisted dress with the full skirt made her look frail and she had a bunch of field daisies pinned on her. Her hands were very white and she held them out from her, open. Her head was back and her large eyes were looking deeply into his.

He got up laughing. "Well, let's have it over with," he said good-naturedly.

She led him to her room and then stood in the middle of it, her face flushed and proud, the mysterious smile on her lips, her lids almost closed.

Mr. Beale looked around nervously. "Well, what is it?" he asked, his voice cracking. "What have you got to show me? I'm busy this morning."

"Can't you see?" She was laughing now, little gay laughs that darted out of her and she kept moving her hands toward the walls.

He put on his glasses and looked around. "I can't see a thing except these walls that need going over."

"How do you like the pictures?" She dropped down on the bed as if her legs had given out, her hands clasped between her knees and her whole body rigid.

He went up to them and took off his glasses. "Why, they seem to be all right. I never could get much excited over painting, though. Where did you get them?"

"I made them."

He looked at her with his mouth fallen open.

"I painted them."

The walls were covered with pictures of happy families,

the father, the mother, and the child, painted in bright sun among flowers and birds, painted with love in their faces and hands, love in their hands and arms that touched each other, and all three in some strange way were entirely separate and yet interchangeable, as if they understand each other's parts, as if they understood so well that they need not speak. And here there was no love withheld, it was all over them, it was part of the bright light that came from their flesh and their deep happy eyes. Each was a picture of a family, but a family that had never appeared upon the earth.

He sat down heavily beside her. She did not look up at him, but stared at her shoe, moisture coming out on her forehead. He straightened his shoulders and set his tie right. "Well, I'm no judge," he said in a high voice, "but I do know one thing. A good painter has to know the laws governing every move. He has to learn them and stick to them. He has to know anatomy. He has to know how to paint his object so that it looks like the real thing and if the real thing was put beside it the painting would look more real. This is done through a knowledge of law. Just as the universe is run and governed by law, created through law, so is painting and everything else. Look at the laws of the United States. What is there to compare with them in the whole history of mankind? Nothing. Absolutely nothing. We are unique. We stand to-day a unique and powerful people. We have banished liquor and brought the home up to where it now stands. The fact of the matter is there is no nation that has ever attained the dignity, the power, and the glory of the United States of America. Your ancestors made this country what it is and remember that as long as you live. Your blood is in these institutions, the blood of your ancestors is there. When this was a vast wilderness . . ."

Mrs. Beale came in nervously. "Aren't they lovely?"

"When this was a vast wilderness your ancestors came here and with their brains and their bodies they created a world that was absolutely new in every feature and law, they startled the rest of mankind, they . . ."

"Excuse me," said Mrs. Beale, "aren't they good?"

"Well, if she's going to paint she has to know the laws." He began pacing. "The thing to do is to get a safe profession and then go into this when you're sure of taking care of yourself some other way. Now, this is fair enough. You teach for five years and make a success of it and we'll let you take up painting and give it a try. Of course, if you were a genius that would be different, but as it is you'd better make a success in some other field first."

Mrs. Beale pushed the moist hair back from the girl's forehead. "I think Papa's being fair enough, don't you?" she asked gently.

"Now if you could ever get to where you could make pictures for magazines or advertisements," he began.

"I wouldn't do that."

"Well, listen to me, young lady, if your painting is any good you ought to get money for it and let people see it."

She sat with her face lowered in that habit of childhood, the hair falling over her eyes and her hands clasped tightly. All of a sudden they heard Irma Hoar call her mother into the house.

"Aaaah, those two are enough to turn a man's stomach. No, you learn how to support yourself before you do any funny stuff like this. Well, I said they were all right but I don't know a thing about it. What do your teachers in college think?"

"They don't like them." She raised her head and stared straight into his eyes.

He stopped short. "I suppose you think they don't know anything. Well, let me tell you a thing or two. They've learned the ropes, they know the laws, and don't you suppose they can tell the difference between a painting that shows promise and one that doesn't?"

"No," she said shortly, her cheeks red as fire and water standing out around her mouth.

"Well, what are we sending you to school for? What do

you think you're there for if it isn't to study and learn from them?"

"Let's stop right now," said Mrs. Beale. "Let's forget all about it and if you'll tell me what you want for dinner, Dorrit, I'll have Gizzie tend to it. She likes to know ahead."

"I intend to know why you think we're sending you to college?" He stood squarely in front of her but she did not look at him or answer. "You listen to me for once in your life, young lady. I want you to learn how to support yourself and I want you to make a better job of it than I've been able to do. It's time you braced up and faced the world the way the Lord intended us all to do, with courage and backbone. At this rate you're going to be just like Irma. . . . Oh, Good Lord, what's the use of talking? What's the use of anything?" He leaned toward one of her paintings. "Is that a dog or a bush?"

She stood up on the bed backed against the wall, her arms, her skirt covering the picture. Her white hands were opened above her head and she looked up at the ceiling, her mouth drawn small, her eyes large again, strained far open.

"You always liked apple dumplings and we've got lots of cream to-day," said Mrs. Beale, swallowing and choking. "Let's make up our minds we're going to be happy even if everything isn't just as we want it," she said very low.

Mr. Beale closed his eyes as if they hurt him. "You think there's a lot of people in this world that don't know anything and that you're too good to tell them anything. You're on the wrong track. People aren't the fools that you think. And, Good Lord, if you can't paint a dog so that it looks like a dog and not like a bush, I'd say you weren't much of a painter and never would be. You've got a lot to learn, my young lady, and some day when your father is dead you may think things over and learn to respect him and decide that you could have learned something from him after all."

Dorrit began to shake her head. She shook it steadily, her lips pressed in a white line and the wet strings of hair beating her cheeks. Then she put her hands over her face and stood

motionless in front of them, one side of her skirt hem loose and
dipping down, a small run in her stocking. Mr. Beale drew the
wind up through his nostrils in a tremendous snort and left the
room.

"Come, sit down, relax. Why, Dorrit, nothing is as bad as
you think," said Mrs. Beale. "You know what good dumplings
Gizzie makes and if you can't think of anything you'd rather
have I'll go down and tell her it's to be dumplings. Why, Dorrit,
why, my little girl," she said as she saw her daughter sag and
fall down on the bed, her arms out limp, her hair tumbling
down in her neck.

"I thought he'd understand," she said, pressing her white
hands on her cheeks. "They mean something. I thought he'd
see. Oh, I painted them for both of you. I thought—Oh, I
thought——"

"Everything's different from what we think," said Mrs.
Beale and stroked her daughter's hair. "Nothing is like what's
in our heads."

"Nothing," she choked out.

"I know Papa's unreasonable but he knows the world better
than you do and he's lived longer than you have. I think you
ought to show him some consideration and make him feel that
you respect his opinions even if they are different. Why should
you be right? Nobody's right, maybe, and it doesn't matter
anyway." Her head was thick with memories but they turned
about in her so fast that she couldn't examine them. "Listen,
dear, we must tell Gizzie what we want for dinner because if
dinner is late then the dishes will be late and that will spoil the
whole day."

"But what are they for?" cried Dorrit. "Why did I paint
them and what do they mean and what difference does it make
what they mean and who cares anyway—you're right—who
cares. Well, I'll tell you one thing," she said very low, sitting
up and wiping her eyes. "I care—do you hear me—I care and I
don't care if I'm the only one in the world that does—I care!"
she shouted.

"All right," said Mrs. Beale gently, "but don't wake the neighbors. You'll have them all wondering what kind of home this is and what sort of people we are." She clasped her brooch that had come loose. "I think you're getting to be a great deal like your father," she said reproachfully and went out.

3

On the following Sunday Mr. Beale walked with his wife and daughter over to the cove across the river. They went slowly, cars passing and leaving dust on their shoes and faces, they followed the small paths through the woods where birds whipped out of low bushes and flew to the branches above. Mr. Beale protected them from a large snake that hissed under some leaves. He raised his stick to strike and then in good humor let it slide away.

"You thought best not to kill it?" timidly suggested Mrs. Beale, not wanting to criticize but thinking how she would fear those dry leaves on the path and the small sounds from the deep grass all around.

"If we mind our own business we won't get hurt." He went on ahead, his hat off, bending to go under the branches and then holding them back for his women.

"Finest place in the world for a nice house," he finally said. "How's this for a garden?" He pointed to masses of pink flowers in the swamp ahead.

"Oh!" they cried and plunged forward not noticing that their heels were enormous with mud and grass and bits of dried dung.

Birds sang unexpectedly and made soft sounds among the leaves as they flew out and rose, descended sharply, lighting to preen, swinging themselves on a tender branch. The Beales wandered over to the edge of the water and sat down in silence, lifting their heads. Mr. Beale threw his hat down with force and took in long noisy breaths of the cool shady air. Mrs. Beale was

smiling and vacant, her face all light gold and her soft eyes on
the moving water. She broke little twigs in her fingers and made
houses with the pieces. She hummed as she built and once she
gave her daughter a little pinch on the ankle.

Dorrit looked at a young leaf that was spread on her knee.
"I'm going to wade," she announced.

Mr. Beale flushed. He saw both his women in the stream
holding their dresses above white indecent thighs, laughing
foolishly, exposed and ridiculous. "Don't be a fool. Sit down
like a decent girl with your parents."

Mrs. Beale leaned toward Dorrit and put her arm over her
shoulder, her wedding ring flashing, and whispered something.
Then the two hung together in sun, their faces set sadly on
something far off, beyond him, out of his reach. Their feet lay
crossed girlishly in the grass. The girl, her head on her mother's
shoulder, seemed to fit into the curves, the softness of her side.

He walked away into the woods, cutting a young green
twig and chewing it, stepping high over violets and young grass.
It seemed incredible that he had ever been worried, irritated or
angry with any one. He made plans for his observatory. He
would buy his wife something nice and then be satisfied when
she didn't make a big fuss over him. He would buy his daughter
something. He'd like to get a fur coat. He could see her in grey
squirrel with a velvet cap and a little soft thing on top. He
would never be angry with them any more for not being impulsive
with him and warm and glowing, even though his way was right.

No, all people had their rights, all people were free and
no one should put out a hand to hold them. He would give
Mrs. Hoar something nice, after all she was a mother. One
night, in the farm house, in the darkness, in his bed—Oh, the
pure winter air that had poured over him then, the pure sheets,
white and cold, the light soft blankets above, his brothers
snickering over Minnie Predd. "God intended all of us to be
happy like this all the time. It's our own fault when we let our
ugly dispositions get the better of us."

He hurried back to where they sat. He tried to join them,

touch them in some way, enter their lives. "This is what I call having a good time," he began in a loud voice. "It's the only decent, right minded way of doing it. Some men have to smoke or drink or run wild with women to have a good time but this is what I call simply ideal in every feature. And isn't it a lot better than ripping through the country in a car, running people down, making a big noise?" But he did not stop for them to reply. "Isn't this doing the world a whole lot more good? Now take tobacco. Tobacco has done more harm in the world than anything else except liquor and wrong thinking. Liquor is the curse of humankind. It turns men into dirty beasts with no respect for women, no respect for civilization, and no respect for the conscience that has been put into us by God and kept in us through generations of honest, decent, Anglo-Saxon people. The time was when we were all as savages, and some of us are still in that state or not far from it, but today we stand in the most glorious period of mankind, the most fruitful period the world has ever known. Just the conception of the League of Nations shows that. America today is the most important nation in the world. She won the war, she has the money, the ideas, the ideals, and the courage to spread them far and wide, all over the planet to the dirty foreigners, even, with their false ideas about women and the home and government, on to the stars." He leaned back against a tree, his eyes damp and fixed. "The fact of the matter is, we are a great people, the greatest the world has ever known. No influence equal to ours has ever come upon this globe in the history of the race. No country . . ."

Dorrit jumped up, her head thrust forward, and started away into the woods.

"Where are you going?"

"Away!" she cried.

He went after her. "Come back here!"

"I won't!"

"I said to come back!" He plunged through the bushes until he came up with her. He caught her arm and jerked her around, facing him. Her eyes were large and wild, she was stiff

with resistance, she bared her teeth in his face and pressed her
head closer to him, straining up from her shoulders, then
panting, unable to form words with those frozen lips.

"Have you gone crazy?"

"You've ruined my mother's life."

He shook her slender wrists and his eyes half closed. He
could see the crumpled organdy dress with ruffles and a dragging
soiled sash. Hair in strings. Breasts rising and falling as she
gasped and knocked herself against a tree. He heard his wife
coming through the grass. The silence, the sun in broad streams,
a bird singing. Outside his rage he saw the slender girl, her teeth
chattering now like an idiot, her hair falling in the old fashion
over wrists and face. The bushes parted.

"Oh, can't we have peace?"

"No!" cried Dorrit. Her feet bruised the ferns as she ground
her heels in to hold herself up.

"What are you quarreling about anyway?"

"Our quarrels are over for good!"

"What do you mean?"

The girl backed off, not looking at either of them, her face
turned toward the trees in sun, the dazzling patch of yellow
flowers in the distance. "I'm never coming home any more. I'm
never going to see you again." She held her chin grimly.

"Damn your foolish talk anyway. Don't you owe anything
to your parents? Isn't it about time you repaid them for their
worries with a little kindness and consideration? Isn't it up to
you to live for them instead of for yourself?"

"Who do *you* live for?"

"My family—society—the next generation."

"Well, you're a fool to do it."

"Stop!" cried Mrs. Beale. "I won't go into that line of
thought. It doesn't do anyone any good. Stop now, when I say
so."

"I'll say it a million times. Anybody's a fool to live for a
society as rotten as this and for homes that are rottener. What
business have you to live with my mother? You're not her

husband or my father, you've never loved her as she deserves, you've never spent a real hour together in your whole lives and you never will. Don't I know the quarrels that went on before I was born, and they're going to go on until I take her away from you. Yes, I'm going to take her far away and love her as she deserves so that she can be happy for once. Oh, the nights I spent, the dreams, the . . ."

"Some time your father will be dead," said Mr. Beale.

"Good! Die—*now!*"

"I'll be—dead." He turned to his wife who was holding her skirts above her high laced boots that were flecked with damp. She evaded his startled hurt look and kicked up a bit of sod with her toe.

"Don't expect me to enter this," she said coldly. "I've tried to please every one and keep peace. I've tried all my life to have it quiet and smooth and I can't do a thing with either of you, there's no handling you. . . ."

"Yes," said Dorrit, "he'll always be a tyrant and you might as well admit it."

Mr. Beale looked quickly at his wife as if he expected her voice to suddenly rise in his defense, to shame his daughter, to remind her of the things he had done, the way he had sacrificed, the way he had toiled for them all his life and only once ordered a tailored suit for fifty-five dollars. Those eyes of his wife's should look at him now in trust and respect, they should be lost in him, her whole being lost, his prisoner forever. But she kept pushing her toe under the bit of sod and her head was shaking as if she were trying hard to hold back something. He could not speak. He waited for those words that would justify his life. He waited for his wife to prove that she was loyal, as if now she would be proving it to the whole world.

"Well," Mrs. Beale finally said looking sadly around her and dropping her skirts on the wet weeds, "now that we're all thoroughly miserable we might as well go home. All of our happy times end this way."

He went on ahead, seeing nothing, his legs guiding him

without his mind around the soft mud slides and ooze pockets. He heard their damp feet squeak in their shoes. Then Dorrit spoke in a strained desperate voice. "Why do you always have to play safe, Mama? Can't you choose between us? Oh, my God, how can I make you see the evil you're doing in staying with him."

4

At home, when his daughter came down with her suitcase, Mr. Beale got back his voice. The sight of her there defying him gave him new strength and courage. He ordered her to stop. She dropped the suitcase and looked at him from a stony face, her arms stiff at her sides, the air of a stranger about her high heels and street suit, her creased gloves. Even her scarf looked new and different and he had bought it for her, bought her everything, shoes, suit, hat, and all that was under. This angered him all the more.

"*Now* what are you trying to do?"

Her expression did not change from the dark impersonal stare. Her mother sat near the table mending a long run in a white silk stocking. She did not look up and she sat as if her ears were plugged shut and she was listening to other sounds, she looked as if she were seeing other things—then the room, the lamp, the books on the shelves, the blue crockery stand for umbrellas in the hall.

"All right," said Mr. Beale, "how far do you think you can get? You're still afraid of the dark. Twenty years old and afraid to cross the locks, always get dizzy in the middle when you look down at the water. You'll be a nice one out in life, you will. You'd better see which side your bread is buttered on and try to please your parents just a little." He opened his evening paper and adjusted his glasses, looking over them gravely at his wife. "Charlie Utter's got the grippe. Well, can't you be neighborly and telephone and see how he is? I don't see why you never want to do what's right."

The girl stood there, still dark and defiant, her eyes wandering over the room she had always known as if she knew it would never leave her mind, as if the row of books would always be there, the lamp, the picture of a squirrel with his paws up. Then she looked in shame at the floor, frightened perhaps at the memory of the locks and the time she had trembled there in the middle, clinging to the iron rail, and her scotch cap had blown away into the dark ugly water.

"Have you no respect for your mother?" he cried.

"Stop!" said Mrs. Beale. "Stop right now." She did not look up but stayed bent over her stocking, taking small even stitches, her needle gleaming as she pushed it through the fine silk.

"I want you to look at your poor mother," screamed Mr. Beale. He jumped up suddenly and threw the paper over his head so that it opened and rattled down to the floor. "For the first time in your life think of some one besides yourself. Think of your mother who has sacrificed her life for you."

The girl put her hands over her stomach as if she were being drawn down by a heavy sudden pain, a strained, piercing look in her mouth and eyes. "If I could only forget you both," she brought out. She bent forward, closing her eyes. "You're in me. I've suffered more over your lives than you have. I've thought of you more. Oh, I want to lose you, I want to get rid of this rotten world, too, where people do everything by chance. They marry. . . ."

"What do you know about marriage?"

"Too much. Too damn much. They all marry by chance and children come by chance and it's all run that way—I've seen it."

"Hah, a lot you've seen. You're awfully wise, aren't you, telling your parents about life. Get some sense in your head if that's possible and learn to think for yourself instead of copying all the crack charlatan thinkers of the day."

"I'll show you—you'll see—you'll find out what I really am some day."

"So you're going to show us what a big gun you are, well, that's very nice of you, I'm sure."

"God," called Mrs. Beale in a strange voice as if she were speaking for help. She put her head on her arm. In her hand was the white stocking, the needle sticking through it.

Dorrit seemed to stretch out toward her mother, she put out her arms and all of her body curved toward her. "Please come with me."

"I've done the best I knew how all my life," said Mrs. Beale. "I couldn't have done it any different. I don't know any other way."

"But, Mama, I'm going to take you away with me, we're going together and you'll see how happy I'll make you. We'll be together all the time, just the two of us, all alone, and we'll be so happy. You'll never need to worry or cry or anything. It's going to be wonderful if you'll only come."

Mrs. Beale covered her face and began rocking in her chair, making the animal sound that had come from her when her daughter was born, only not making it so deep. These sounds were more like frightened animals in the cold. Dorrit ran to her, knelt in front of her trying to pull the hands away from the eyes, pleading with her, kissing the hands, the little curl in her neck, begging her to come, to go far away with her forever. She tried to pull the covered face against her, tears coming down her cheeks, and she tried to fold the woman in her weak protecting arms against her breast.

"Yes, you women. Well, stick together, both of you. Oh, get out of my *sight!*" He plunged out of the room.

Mrs. Beale gave a shriek and went after him, slipping on the little rug between the two rooms and striking her head against the sharp corner of the door moulding. But she ran after her husband, a trickle of blood on her temple, and when he suddenly turned around, his shoulders heaving, she dashed at him and clung, her eyes closed with blood, running over them, and her mouth saying over and over, "Husband, husband, husband."

5

Gizzie Needles told every one about Dorrit's leaving home. Those she couldn't see in person she telephoned and when she got new information she added that eagerly. "Awh, Mr. Beale," she would say to herself when she thought of him, "always did good to everybody, you did, and now look where you're at." She told about his business that was failing because he would rather win an argument than make a sale and she described Mrs. Beale and Dorrit. "That girl, say she's absolutely crazy. Something not quite plumb there. You should seen her dragging those pictures after her. She'd leave her good grips and lug them pictures instead. And they're all of what I'd say were the insane. Nobody ever saw anything like them in this world and in her grip she had one of people without a stitch on. Oh, she'll come to a bad end. You can't go on that way and have all the good things fall your way all the time. No, she'll go crazy herself before she's through."

But Mr. Beale looked more wild and hurt than ever before and when he took off his hat he had a noble aloof gleam about him that made Gizzie catch her breath. Now that she had lived longer she saw that she was the only one to have made him happy, she was the only one who knew just how to make over him and get things going nice. She was the one, not Mrs. Beale—too cold, too educated—she told herself, pressing her hand hard against her chest and wrinkling up her face. She thought once of suicide but she couldn't bear to go without telling him, without rushing up to him and showing him once and for all her feeling, then knowing when she went into the dark cold water that she would live forever in his mind, in his strange cruel head. "I'll be insane," she often thought.

When Mr. Beale heard that Dorrit was living at Mrs.

Utter's rooming house on the corner of Mac and Franklin Streets, he went to his wife.

"Mama, we've got to do something."

Mrs. Beale raised her head and looked out of the window. He began pleading in a demanding, helpless tone, half whispering finally, but she would make him no answer. She stared at the men who were lined up across the street watching in dumb fascination dirt being thrown up by the shovelful out of a pit. Then Mr. Beale walked up and down, that stark look of grief and anxiety all over him. "Mama," he said, "you've got to get her back. Put on your hat and coat and go after her. You can't stand this."

Mrs. Beale wet the corner of her handkerchief and rubbed one of her finger nails. "You know you won't sleep a wink tonight if you don't go. Better go now. Oh, I've never seen a woman like you. Never want to do what's right, never on time, never ready to be generous."

"I don't want her to come back here," said Mrs. Beale pulling a small shawl over her shoulders.

He fell back on his heels staring at her, a white silk handkerchief fluttering from his fingers. "Haven't you got any instincts that are human?" he said hoarsely. "Aren't you a mother in any sense of the word?"

"I suppose not."

"You don't want your own child in her home."

"This is my home," said Mrs. Beale. "From now on I'm going to have peace in this house. There's not going to be jangling and turmoil every half hour and I'm not going to put up with nagging and the rest of it. I'm going to have peace."

"Shame on you," he cried. "You'd turn your daughter into the streets. . . ."

"I haven't turned her out. She can keep on in college. I'm willing to keep on giving up so that she can be there but if she ever does come back both of you must do as I say. I won't have any more shameful arguing and quarreling at my time of life. . . ."

Gizzie Needles came in looking rather sheepish and took

the salt cellars off the table. Mr. Beale did not look at her but
sat with his elbow on the window edge looking out at the smooth
rolling lawns and the bushes at the side of the house. The little
girl had hidden from him there, her beaver hat set high on top
of her long fair curls.

"I've got a pain under my right shoulder blade," said Gizzie.

"Pain under what?" said Mr. Beale.

"My right shoulder blade," she repeated.

"Well, I guess there's one thing I'm not to blame for," he
cried. He jumped up and waved his arms over his head. "I've
always had a pack of ungrateful women at my heels and all I
can say is go to a doctor and send me the bill."

"Awh, I ain't that bad off, Mr. Beale. Say, if I was that
bad off I'd not a peep outen me. I wouldn't upset you for
anything in the world."

"I suppose not," he said, "and don't leave the furnace door
open again."

"Well, we've been burning the garbage," said Mrs. Beale
indignantly. "I told her to leave it open to cool off."

"I'd like to know what the city collects garbage for, I'd like
to know why you can't be like other people for once and do as
others do. Is there any law prohibiting you from setting it out
in the garbage can like a Christian or do you always have to be
doing something special? Are there any ropes on either of you
that are keeping you from acting like rational women?"

"We have reasons for burning the garbage and you wouldn't
understand if I told you," said Mrs. Beale quietly.

"Oh, you fiend!" he cried and left the house.

He rang the bell at Mrs. Utter's and finally Dorrit came
into the little parlor. They breathed in the red plush that was
everywhere, the red satin paper on the wall, the red door of the
stove. Everything was red and thick and close to them, pressing
them together, and every time they looked up eyes disappeared
behind the folding doors.

"Dorrit, I'm real awfully sorry." He stared straight ahead
of him, his gaze set far off, far away beyond them both. "Your

mother sent me to tell you to come back," he brought out uncomfortably, not meeting her eyes. "She's about out of her mind. I left her in a bad state."

He saw that she wasn't going to speak, and that she was probably going to sit and stare at him with her large eyes, her hands folded on that crazy, no fashion dress, the fair hair low in her neck. As he looked over her head at the thick red paper he thought he saw all the daughters in the world and it seemed to him that they all loved and respected their fathers, that he was the only one who had an ungrateful, disobedient child. But she sat there in front of him, her hands folded, nothing in her face to show that she was his child, no fires of love anywhere in her or her mother.

"Your mother's in bad shape. I'm worried about her."

But the girl did not move. He pulled a chair close to her and tried to look into her face for a while, thinking that something might come to him that he could say that would change everything all of a sudden. But he couldn't. He got up and grasped the back of the chair, pitching his voice to the tone he used in lecturing people, but as he spoke his face twisted horribly.

"We're in a wonderful world, a *wonderful* world. We have everything, every opportunity to do good, every chance to help humanity. Everything in life is *right*. We're given chances, great opportunities, even living is a privilege. If we don't naturally like living we must make ourselves. We must conquer weakness. We must strive to know God's purpose for us and live up to it. This is a happy world but happiness is not foremost, truth is foremost, and honor, and decency and the constitution of the United States. There's vast opportunity for all of us but at the time we don't see it and when we do see it's too late, we can't go back. I don't know about others but I regret every damn thing I've done in life from the beginning. I've done it all wrong but I can't help it. Do you hear me—*I can't help it!*"

Dorrit looked at her father but she did not move, she made no gesture or sound of understanding him, she merely stared with large eyes at his nose. She did not suddenly jump up and put her arms around his head as he sank down on the red plush and she didn't even reach out her hand to touch his.

"Get your hat and we'll go," he said firmly.

"No." She stood up very straight, her hands at her sides. "You tell Mama goodbye for me."

"Listen," he said very low, bringing out the words through his strained lips, "it's going to be different now, everything's going to be different at home."

"It can't ever be different," she said.

"Now, now," he said, his teeth clenching together, his lips drawn apart. "You be a good girl and keep on with school and you'll come out all right."

"Of course I'm going back," she said briefly. "I'm going to stay with the Lorski's until I finish."

He looked as if he had been cracked open by lightning and now he drew his mouth together terribly and his eyes turned toward the floor as if he could not, dared not think of her leaving them now, going into the world—away, away from them forever, never to see her again, his little girl, the child he had loved all his life and lived for and brought presents to and tried to bring up right.

"Are they good people?" he said shortly.

"I suppose you wouldn't think so."

"You know good people as well as I do," he bawled out. "Anybody knows a good honest person when he sees him. There's no question about that, but if you're planning to live with a lot of common low down foreigners and thieves I tell you right now that. . . ."

She drew herself up as if she expected a blow from somewhere. "I'm going to be a painter," she said.

"Well," he answered with infinite pleading, "can't you be that at home where it's safe? Gizzie's a freak but she's good help and you won't need to do anything. Mama's going to be sick in bed if you don't come. And you can keep to yourself as much as you want. I don't know how Mama's going to pull through this."

"I understand Mama now."

She seemed more distant than ever from him and when he watched her folding into herself and withdrawing more and more he suddenly shouted, "Go to the devil then and I don't give a damn. I've tried to do good to everyone, I've tried to think right and talk right and be right, and you can all go to hell from now on." He went blindly to the door and ran hard against Mrs. Utter who was standing in a dark corner near the folding doors.

6

Now when Mr. Beale was mentioned everyone had a good laugh. He hadn't talked the arm off any one since his daughter left home and all he would say no matter what was said, was simply, "Well, I'm sorry but I can't help it." Mrs. Beale appeared more often at the clubs and now she wore younger clothes. Gizzie Needles told her friends that it had been Dorrit who selected her mother's costumes. "Yes sir, and just like her, too, to trig her out like a widow and all. Mis' Beale looks ten years younger now and she doesn't buy a stitch without my looking at it first. Sends everything home."

Mr. Beale was often seen inspecting the locks or the bridge and after supper at night he was always bounding up out of his chair. "Someone at the door."

"There's no one at the door."

"Someone at the door," he would mumble and go into the front of the house, throwing the door wide open. Then he would stare out into the blackness, take off his glasses and peer into the bushes and frozen vines. He would begin mumbling to himself, his head sunk down between his shoulders.

"We can't afford to heat the outdoors," Mrs. Beale would cry. "Do come in!"

"Someone stepped on the porch."

"Well, then let them ring the bell."

He would finally be closed out in the darkness, feeling around the frozen shoots and frosty branches, stumbling over wire netting and fallen trellises. One night after feeling around in the dark, trying to make out that figure, listening for the voice, he stopped still, his white forehead gleaming in the dark, and he didn't put out his hands to feel any more and his eyes were no longer squinted in desperate searching but came wide open. He looked ahead of him, his face set, as if he knew something and had always known it but could never make it come true. Gizzie Needles came to the door.

"Awh, Mr. Beale," she cried, "come in. You'll catch your death out there."

"Good Lord," he thought to himself "don't a man's intentions count for anything?"

"Mr. Beale, Missus is having a fit."

"Well, I didn't tell her to, did I?" he said.

He went further into the cold yard, surprised that he wasn't stumbling, walking where the ground was frozen and uncertain but keeping his balance as if all were smooth. He walked over the frozen flower beds at the side of the house and the dead bushes scratched his hands as he passed. He felt a roar inside him, as if all his nature were loose and tumbling and rolling inside him, he felt dizzy as if all of him now were loose to pitch and boil in giant waves and whirls that brought his eyes shut and made him reach out for support.

"I was marked," he gasped, "no one wanted me in the world and when I got here I couldn't make any one want me." And then in the center of the tumult he felt a fine spiral gnawing, as if sharp teeth were in his flesh and bone, as if his nature that had always had its own way was now destroying him, slowly gnawing him to pieces while he could only wait in horror. "And damn it," he said aloud as if he were justifying himself in front of a roomful of people, "I knew the right way,

I knew all the time what was right, but something wouldn't let me do it."

He stared up mutely at his house. There were giant shadows over it, dead vines rapped the windows, the roof spread down and made eaves where bits of hay stuck out, but there in the dark and the cold the whole thing looked alive and warm, like something he had built that could never die. Just as it was, without the observatory on top, without the sun porch with birds and flowers, without any of the additions he had made in his head for it, without anything but just what he saw in front of him—this was his house, his home, and there were warm lights in the windows as if it had life inside and as if when the storms of God had carried it away something of it would remain, something would always be there.

Inside Mrs. Beale was holding her glasses to the light and breathing on them, then rubbing them. She kept shaking her head as if she didn't know she was doing it but her face was placid and sweet. "Gizzie," she called, "bring my other glasses. They're in the top drawer of the sideboard."

Gizzie was in the pantry, her head against her straw serving hat, her cheek near the large tarnished buckle in front. "I'd tell a lot about this buckle if I'd a mind to," she often said mysteriously. "It's been in the Needles family for generations. Sir Henry Needles gave it to his bride in Wild Rose Castle, Needles, England."

She went into the living room. "Yes, Mis' Beale," she said. Then she waited, all her weight on one large black button boot. "But I do think I'd ought to call Mister."

"No," said Mrs. Beale quickly. "He's happier where he is."

7

Dorrit Beale never came home for another vacation and when people, just for fun, asked Mr. Beale how she was he would stare over their heads and say, "Very well but busy."

They would repeat it at home when shades were drawn and snow was piled high at the windows. "Very well but busy." "And why didn't you say 'What keeps her so busy?' " someone would ask and then they would throw back their heads, their hands on their sides, and all laugh heartily. The little children would laugh because their mother was laughing and everyone would eat more.

But a big surprise came when Alma Utter came home from Chicago one evening and called in all her friends. She had gone to the Art Institute that morning "because I never could get enough of art and anyway I'm always interested in the different lines of thought people have." In one room were paintings by Dorrit Beale. "The backgrounds of them were fine," she told her friends, "and the 'tetnic' was perfect, only the Dutch to compare to, there's no question about that."

"But what were they *of?*" Mrs. Boots asked emphatically.

"Oh," said Alma, looking at her husband for help, "you say, Will."

Mr. Utter burst out laughing. His face went pink all over. "Don't ask me to describe them because I couldn't look at them. Made me feel funny."

"Well," said Alma, "I think the world and all of Mr. and Mrs. Beale. We've traded there all our lives and we think highly of them but I don't know what I'd say about those pictures. Of course hanging up on the wall like that with other masterpieces and all, you don't feel in a position to criticize exactly, but what they are supposed to be of and what story they're telling. . . . Oh, go on away," she said to her husband and when he went into the woodshed she explained that the pictures were of naked people and "you couldn't tell which was which hardly." She flushed and looked confused and offended. "I don't see the point in that. Well, anyway, they were all active," she explained, "but I was simply wild about the backgrounds. The figures didn't mean one thing to me. Honest, I can't see the sense when we have such nice clothes now in not painting them on people. How would we all look going that way and if none of us does why does she paint that way. Why, I was upset over it. Of course, there are statues and all that and proper in their place but to have her from our town, I don't know. But the backgrounds were just fine. If I could have one with just the background I'd even hang it up somewheres."

"When they's such pretty scenes to paint all around, houses and the marsh and the country, cows, flowers, my I don't see," said Mrs. Niman.

"Why, yes, something that's good to look at that we all know and that's *real*."

"Well," said Alma sadly, "those weren't like nothing we've ever seen or would want to see or think about even. Some folks there were making over them but I just couldn't even though she is from our town. And don't tell, I don't want it spread around, but Will was taken sick to his stomach. He had to leave even if we did pay."

The one reproduction Mrs. Beale saw in a city paper made her shake with grief and fright. It made her think of their position in town, of the butcher and the postman and the clerks everywhere. When she bought anything or paid a bill there was always the glowing respect that a good name brings and the low voice, "Anything else, Mrs. Beale?" "Nothing else, thank you, Mr. Butzlaff."

Mrs. Beale met Mrs. Utter on the street and tried to evade her but Mrs. Utter began urging her to come into the house and have a chat. "Now, that's a shame, Mrs. Beale. I don't see anything of you any more. How's Mr. Beale?"

Mrs. Beale had a soft startled look on her face. "He's having some bridge work put in."

"Well, I said to Mr. Utter yesterday, I said, 'The Beales are as happy a couple as we have in this whole town,' I said."

"I guess we are," said Mrs. Beale.

She started walking home very rapidly, holding her head higher than usual. Her face was rigid with the expression of placid joy she had made for it and had held on all afternoon in front of her friends. She pulled her scarf close around her neck and bowed pleasantly to old Mr. Grouse who was wheeling his lawn mower back from the repair shop. She kept imagining herself in her bedroom, taking off the gay face that was over her real one, taking it off as she would her hat and putting it away in the darkest corner of her closet until she should have to go outside again. She would not dare look in the glass at her real face, at the dark horrible lines of disappointment, the cheeks sunken with shocks of all kinds, the head dented and dark with worries. She gave a little shocked cry of self pity and wiped her nose. Oh, to lie down deep, to rest, to die, to be buried in the peace of the quiet earth.

"How do you do, Mrs. Evans, lovely day. Yes, quite well, thank you. He's having some bridge work put in. No, I must hurry home and keep him company. He's restless without me."

She found Mr. Beale pacing the floor. "I'm going to Chicago," he said.

Mrs. Beale sank down. "Well, I hope you aren't planning to send Dorrit any money because I can hardly get along as it is. Your charity always comes out of me in the end."

"Well, say," broke in Gizzie, the pearl buttons on her calico gleaming, "I heard that one of those pictures of hers sold for, I think it was two thousand or something like that."

Mrs. Beale's mouth dropped open but Mr. Beale made no sign that he had heard. He stared at the sparrows on the lawn.

"But I said to them, 'Say, did you see the check?' and they said, 'No, but it's straight all right,' and I said, 'Well, you wait until you see the check and have it in your hand, then's time to believe.' "

"Please bring me a glass of water, Gizzie," said Mrs. Beale.

"Say, and if I was you, Mr. Beale, I'd pull every last one of them pictures down from the walls and have done with the foolishness. You've a right. You're her father."

"Who taught you that a father has rights?"

She began to giggle and went off for the water.

"Maybe I can get them taken down," said Mr. Beale as he left for the station. "I'll do what I can."

When he reached the city he went straight to the gallery and when he got inside and saw his daughter's name printed on a booklet he held it up as if the name was a new one to him. Then he walked through the room where her pictures were hung, trying not to see them, his hat in his hands, horror and guilt on his face. He went back slowly, forcing himself, his head sunk down between his shoulders and his stomach out.

He drew up in front of the first, a naked woman in sand. Bright sky and water. Two enormous gulls with opened wings. A huge happy baby seated squarely on the woman's stomach and the woman's head pushed deep in the sand, chin up, a look of such definite animal delight in her face that he shivered. He went on until the room seemed to fill up with the happy naked figures of men and women and children, until the sun was there behind him and his shoulders were hot with intense gold light. Sea gulls were in the room, you heard their enormous wings, the ocean was there, and everywhere he looked he met one of the supreme bright looks of radiant bliss. He wanted to sink down, he wanted to sneak out in shame, and he felt guilty, as if the people in the room knew that this was his daughter, the child who was to make humanity better, his only child who was to make the world grander, fulfill God's purpose on earth, leave a spiritual mark on all. The sweat came out on him as he imagined himself saying aloud. "My daughter painted these freaks that have never been seen on earth. I brought her up right but my wife spoiled her."

But the dramatic touch came from Irma Hoar who went around the world with her mother the following year. A friend, Mr. Coburn, promised to show them Paris and one night at dinner Irma asked to be taken to the Latin Quarter. Mrs. Hoar was happy that it was Irma who asked because she was eighty-two and didn't want to appear eager. So when Mr. Coburn turned to her she pretended to be giving in and indulging Irma.

"But, Mother, *you* say," said Irma, her eyes glittering.

"Well," said Mrs. Hoar, putting one hand over the other, "it doesn't matter to me just so I'm on the go."

"Now, isn't that wonderful?" cried Irma. "Oh, Mr. Coburn, she is interested in everything, more interested than the young people we see over here."

"As I said before," Mrs. Hoar broke in, "I have no preferences. I did want to see Shakespeare's birthplace on account of the club at home but I've seen that and now I don't care what I see." When Mr. Coburn left that evening Mrs. Hoar said to Irma, "I never thought Jim Coburn amounted to much when he was around at home, but I guess he's real well to do."

The next night, seated in a restaurant in the Latin Quarter, Irma could hardly see from her excitement and the tumult of associations she imagined for all the people. One man she was certain took dope, he had the look of Edgar Allen Poe in his face, and there were women there that she knew had no moral sense. She tried to imagine what that meant and what it would be like. It even seemed all right to speculate about such things now that she was in Paris. It startled her strangely to find that here one could do anything and at home one couldn't even imagine doing anything. She wondered what part she might have played in the wild life of the underworld and then had to take herself in hand as barriers in her gave way.

Mrs. Hoar's eyes were wide open, darting here and there, gathering details for the clubs at home. She saw a long haired man who reminded her of Jeff Boots in Rio and while she was staring at him Mr. Coburn tapped her arm. "You're missing something," he said and indicated a table toward the center of the room.

"Why, they're all drunk," whispered Irma, staring sharply.

"And a woman with them" said Mrs. Hoar.

The five men were ragged, indolent and foreign looking. They pounded the table from time to time and then threw themselves back in their chairs howling with laughter. Irma eyed the girl more closely. She felt a jolt go down her as she recognized the hair and eyes, the startled mute look. She pressed her mother's hand so tightly that the woman chided her and licked the place with her tongue, staring at it through her glasses. Irma watched the girl's movements and occasionally when her voice rose she caught a sentence.

"The fact of the matter is, America is the greatest nation the world has ever seen," and, "in the history of mankind there has never been an influence as far reaching, as profound, as religious, as that of the United States of America."

The girl clasped her hands behind her back and puffed out her cheeks, letting her voice sink down in her throat. "Indeed America is teaching the world how to live, she is showing the dirty foreigners how to respect womanhood, how to make homes, how to live always for the glorious next generation and how to turn it into honest, God fearing men and women. . . ."

She paused and the men at her table pounded with their feet and their fists until she started again, pursing her lips and scowling as if at a formidable audience. And then she suddenly stopped short, stared at them all, her mouth twitching, and laid her head down on the table, her arms still clasped behind her back.

"See," said Irma, feeling a deep exultation, "she isn't happy."

"How can *any* of these people be happy?" asked Mrs. Hoar.

Irma felt chills go up and down her as she stared at the head lying on the table and thought of how dramatic it was, her mother not knowing it was Dorrit Beale and no one in New Bedford knowing that she was seeing all this and watching the girl who had been brought up among them.

"How *can* such people be happy?" asked Mrs. Beale again, more severely.

"I was just wondering," said Irma.

TWO IN LOVE

W E decided after much argument and debate that we were really in love in spite of our physical attachment. Since then he has telegraphed me every two weeks asking permission to come and see me, and has followed my invitation with: "But do you really want me?" and that, an hour later, with the time of his arrival. It is very nice.

"Hello," he always says at the station. "How are you?"

And I always answer: "Very well, thank you," in spite of my painful stomach disorder.

"You got my telegrams?"

"Yes, Ronald, thank you."

Then he laughs and lights a cigarette and I am glad that my uncle isn't there to see him because he calls every cigarette smoker a dirty dog and I wouldn't want Ronald insulted by anyone but me.

"Dear," he said suddenly as though he had practiced it. "I haven't had my trousers pressed since the last time I was here."

Then I look at his knees and they look so funny that if it were anywhere but Ashland I would feel proud.

"They were bulged in the beginning in the interests of love so you don't mind, do you?"

When we reach home my heart falls through to stone and lies there helpless. I realize that I must discover him all over again. I realize that we are not as wonderful as our letters led us to believe. It is a sad affair.

Then Ronald goes to the big chair where my mother sits and shakes hands with her and acts as though he knows her better than he does me. But he doesn't. And she doesn't like him very well because she's deaf on one side and he speaks low. Suddenly the air falls apart and I want to fall into it and never see any one connected with love again. It is a frightful moment and one that I hope I can never forget. So I always start laughing because it doesn't do to let a moment see that it can make you miserable. Oh, I know. I've knelt to those horrid moments and had them simply beat in my head with their sleeves. So I just laugh as loud as I can.

And my mother says quietly: "The china closet, dear."

That's where my medicine is, but it doesn't do me one bit of good and I may die soon. I don't care though.

"Mother, Ronald brought you a box of candy, but he's too bashful to give it." Then I pretend that I am Ronald giving it and I stumble around the way he does only I can't look as silly. Now that I think of it he is silly looking and I don't like him very well even though we are in love.

Well, that's the kind of terrible time we usually have and he's perfectly unknown to me. I know every one better than I do him and it isn't that exciting kind of unknown-ness but that other. The kind that makes your eyes feel wide open and as though you've been deluding yourself for a good long time. That's the terrible kind of unknown-ness that I've had to contend with. We know then that we're complete strangers so we have to act as though we aren't. Then when my mother isn't around he comes near my chair and acts like one of those furry cats that he knows I like and I pet him but we don't get worked up or anything. Then my mother comes rushing in and sits down between us. I pass the candy.

"Ronald, this is good candy," says my mother, looking at the hair I've upset. If she only knew that it wasn't one bit of fun doing it, I always think. After that she doesn't leave us alone for one minute and we live through a dreadful afternoon. Ronald grows more and more silent until I have to play the piano to keep from bursting into tears. I look at him sometimes with his lips stuck out an odd way and his feet just crazy and I always know what he is thinking. He is saying it over and over. "All of our troubles come from sex." If that means anything I haven't found out yet.

Then we have to eat dinner and that's just awful because I am a vegetarian, due to my painful stomach disorder, and Ronald eats almost nothing but meat. To have to watch him chew the flesh of animals and swallow it, is more than I can endure, so I don't watch. But I see it just the same. I'm that way. And then we move into the living room. We *move* in. No one walks in our house, or runs, or does anything active. We move as if we have trains and my mother sits down in her chair, on guard for the evening.

In those hours after dinner I always miss my father. He died. Sometimes I wish my mother would, too, because she keeps me from kissing Ronald when I want to and now that I think of it I'm sure that she is to blame for all our trouble. Ronald and I would probably be in love all the time if it weren't for her. Well, she ought to die. But I might not say that to-morrow. And I think she is fond of me.

The doorbell rings. In walk the Gaulsen girls and behind them the Briggs girls. In Ashland any unmarried woman of good family is called a girl until death. Annie Gaulsen keeps widening her eyes at Ronald all the time and it reminds me of the way city men go at me when I look at them too long. But Annie is a protected woman and doesn't know about such. Then Nellie tries to pretend she thinks that Ronald is just as good as any of us.

"Well, Mr. Manchester, what do you think of our little village?"

"To tell you the truth," says Ronald, "I never see it."

Nellie turns to my mother. "Annie made the most delicious pudding for dinner today. It was perfectly delicious."

"Annie is always doing something interesting," says my mother.

"Isn't she though!" This from the Briggs girls. "That hat she made your mother is too charming for words."

"And now," says Nellie, "she's making one for me."

"How ingenious of her," cry the Briggs girls. Then they start talking about Europe. They went when they graduated from high school thirty years ago, and they always tell about it in a delicious abandoned way as if no one else had ever been. Ronald loved it.

"Stick around Paris much?" he asked.

"Tell me, dear," said Laura Briggs to my mother, "tell me where you got that perfectly darling little rug over there. I've seen such rugs in the House Beautiful—yes, we've taken it for years—and it is exciting to actually see one."

While they are examining it I grab Ronald and drag him into the library. We light the candles and sit down in the same chair. It begins to be nice.

"Ronald, I've been awfully angry with you."

"Not really angry. You couldn't be angry with me *now*, could you *now*?"

"No, no!" And I kissed him but I felt like meat.

"We aren't ever really angry any more."

"But I don't know you," I said.

"Let's take that for granted."

He seemed much older than a college boy and not at all like one. I ought to say that I would be in college, too, if it weren't for my painful stomach disorder.

"It's nice," he said suddenly, "that you kiss me even though you are bored."

"But I'm not!" Again I felt like meat. It must be that I always do when I lie.

"But you love me, anyway, I'm sure of that."

I didn't want to think and all of a sudden I felt as though I was him. It wasn't necessary to tell him so and we just sat that way for a long time. I had just time enough to get in another chair when my mother appeared.

"It's a shame," I told her, "to leave two young people alone like this—unchaperoned. I shall never be the same again."

She sat with us the rest of the evening and it made me furious because I knew that if I were in love with a minister or a lawyer she would let us be alone most of the time. So I went to bed early and dreamed about trees and flowers and it was hardly light when I woke up, but the sky was beginning to be lovely, and the roofs looked as close as the branches. I put on my slippers and my negligee and walked right into Ronald's room.

"Hello, Ronald!" I said.

He reared up and then remembered where he was. "How do I look in bed?" he asked, offhand, but I knew he was surprised.

"Better than I thought."

"Well, well," he said, and put out his hand. "Kiss it!"

I did.

"You're cold. You're shivering. Why don't you get in bed with me?"

"Oh, no," I said and did at once.

For a moment we were lifted into something strange and timeless but that's all I know about it. I said: "I like being in bed with you." Then I went. And all the time I was drawing my bath I wanted to tell some one about it. I couldn't think of anything else and I knew if I told my mother she wouldn't be able to either, so I didn't have any one to tell. Wasn't that pitiful? But that moment has hung above me like sound and color and scent.

Breakfast was different. It was a pleasant meal and I felt handsome and Ronald looked it. It was as though we were existing in a delicious space just inside the one my mother was in, a space she knew nothing about. I felt rather sorry for her. Then I reached under the table for Ronald's hand and there seemed no doubt about our love.

"Isn't there something awfully amusing in this room?" I

asked my mother, but she looked very cross and shook her head. "Ronald and I are going walking," I said. "We can't stand this laughter here. Something is laughing at us."

How terrible that I didn't know then that I was the one who was laughing. I—but we went on walking and came to a fallen tree as soon as they do in the movies.

"Darling," said Ronald, "I'm yours. I've said it before but this time I mean it."

"I shall always love you," I said and then I was kneeling to him and I could feel a crown on my head and wonderful jewels on my neck and yards and yards of velvet and fur falling around me. I laid everything before him. But he tried to kneel to me and to do that he had to fall flat on the ground, so we had to laugh.

"Come on," he cried, "we're going to elope."

I felt sharp and definite all of a sudden.

"We're going to Paris to-night."

"Wouldn't we have to go to New York first?" I asked. "And what about our clothes?"

"You really sound human," he said. "God, I'm glad to know that you are."

Such terrible sadness ran through me that I could hardly speak—and laughter. I thought: "We're only pretending. Love isn't like this. It's something else." I said aloud: "I can't believe that we're really in love. Love is different."

He moved away from me as if I were poison. "You're afraid. You're going to fail in this too."

"I never fail in anything," I cried. But that laughter was running up and downstairs in me.

He was quiet for a long time. "I love you," he said finally.

"You don't know what love is."

He began to laugh. "I understand you," he said.

"No, you don't. I don't myself."

Then he fell into an unseemly rage. "You're a coward that's afraid to step out of her own dooryard. You're afraid of reality. I've tested you. The tiniest things can set you way off. I know perfectly well that if I had come here with my trousers pressed everything would have been different. But I don't mind that so much," he said, "only I thought when you were sure that you loved me it would be different."

"You're taking what I say under emotional excitement as being true. You can't do that."

"Oh, rot!"

"I can say that I love you for eternity and know that I do but all the time something can tell me there is no eternity."

"If you're really in love time doesn't matter."

"I know. Oh, kill me! Kill me!"

"Nothing doing," he said brutally. "You'd enjoy it too much."

"I thought life was a holiday," I said wistfully, knowing that I was being deliberately child-like.

"How will you ever know what it is?"

There seemed to be no tissue between us, no blood in common, nothing. The agony of that sudden separation was like death. But I laughed. "This is real," I thought. "We ought to stand alone like this."

"If I fit into your picture of me, you love me. If I don't you have no use for me."

"Ronald," I cried, "I never do that!" But I saw the blood of that lie drip into the grass.

"I love you in spite of it," he said. "But try to see *me* sometimes. Will you?"

"Oh, I will," I said and kissed his knees.

"This is no time for that," said he and the day was one of misery.

He took the early train the next morning and on the way to the station he told me his dream. "I was in the gutter weeping, with my head on a dog. Some theatrical people passed and a woman with a large hat and a patent leather belt gave me a ticket for the show. I went and sat in the first row balcony and I felt better. Then suddenly, for no reason, I began weeping again and every one looked."

"Oh, Ronald!" I began to cry. But I didn't mean it. And I waved to him as the train went out. On the way home I decided to clear away all the images I had of him and find out directly what he was like. I cleared for days and spent my nights nursing the clearings. I knew that pity must not remain, that kissing was only a palliative, that love to endure must strangle sentiment. I knew all that and I used that knowledge as a whip.

He came again and he had as much existence as vapor. I knew that something in me was making him unreal. I think it was the laughter, but I was helpless.

"What has happened?" he asked.

"I think my mind or something has killed our love."

"Don't say that!" he begged. "Minds make it better."

"Mine didn't."

"Damn it all, pretend anything you want to about me just so you love me—pretend anything—I don't care."

"I can't."

"But you can! We don't have anything to say about this."

"Why do you ask me to try then?"

He tried to kiss me and then he moved away. "You look like Miss Muffet," he said and stared at his hands for a long time.

"Oh, it's untrue, I love you, I love you!" I felt as though I were talking in my sleep with that laughter self a shadow. I wondered suddenly what it would be like to really love. It hurt me to wonder that. "I love you," I said again. Then I waited for something to happen, for that delicious space to open and let us inside, for us to be changed back again with the tissue between us firm and our blood the same. But nothing happened. He stood there as empty and vacant as the moment itself.

"I wish you would stop bothering me," I cried, and laughed when he looked hurt. "I mean that!"

And now I am alone.

GUARDIAN ANGEL

For Meridel Le Sueur

W E were passing out of church, nodding and smiling largely
from our false, too-kind Sunday faces. We were being
moved along the aisle toward the back, our feet pushing
in little steps forward with the crowd. We glanced down to see
if we were about to scrape some one's heel and the aisle carpet—
why, even as we looked at it, the very instant we stared, we
couldn't recall the color. We were leaning forward from our
shoulders so that our necks felt soft and full of sweet low
murmuring—"How do you do? How is your mother?" And
suddenly we smiled at the ceiling, over the heads of solid citizens
in glazed white collars, their hands out shaking other hands,
their fixed benevolent smiles the same for all. We had to push
in our hips to get around the end pew and to turn into the long
narrow aisle at the back. She jerked my arm. I felt her cold
breath on my cheek as I turned. I looked suddenly into her face
and I could feel her heart beating. "Aunt Grace, *that's* the
room," she said.

The long wooden drop that shut off the Sunday-school
parlors from the rest of the church had been raised and I peeked
into the room. We had gone to that room as children but I
never remembered seeing it as part of the church before. It
looked so different. She simply hurled me toward it and I turned
and apologized to Mrs. Gunsaulus, whom I had almost upset.
"Do forgive me. . . ." She grasped my arm hard and then she

let go and went into the center of the lonely place. A ragged
song-book, the edges softened into a kind of gray fluff, was lying
on a frail varnished table. A small organ, with red velvet behind
the ornate openwork design in the front, stood at the right near
a flock of ugly, clattering, hard chairs. I had seen those things
most of my life, but now, as part of the church, they all looked
different from ever before, more exposed, more bleak and worn.
The carpet was like that other carpet. I looked and all the time
I was seeing it I couldn't recall the color. My niece put her
hand on her forehead slowly and then dropped it, gazing straight
ahead. She looked slender and childlike in her flowered silk
with the hair hat pressed back in front and her startled, tender
face all exposed and gleaming. She was like a little child who
has lost her voice and swallows and swallows to regain it, twisting
her handkerchief around her thumb.

"I thought this room was enormous," she brought out
finally.

I felt her shocked breathing go through me. I always feel
it when she is scared or disappointed or about to cry. "Oh, you
couldn't have thought that, Vanessa," I said.

"But there must have been hundreds and hundreds here
that night of the bazaar. I was only four but I remember the
crowd. I was so frightened of everybody that I just wrapped
Mamma's skirt around me any time any one looked at me. All
I can remember are huge moving black skirts, like tents, and
the most I could see was a silver belt-buckle and sometimes I
felt a hand come down on my head for a second. Then that
door over there came open and the room seemed to be even
larger and like a ballroom. The floor looked bright and slippery.
I remember that," she said firmly.

We both glanced down at the carpet. "How extraordinary,"
I muttered.

"Yes, it was, Aunt Grace. She came in that door over
there." She looked up at me. "Fleta did," she said softly and
looked away.

If you had seen us there I couldn't have made you believe

that this twenty-year-old girl and myself had ever sat under the grape arbor at my house laughing in the sunshine with our heads back on our shoulders and our hands lying free, palms up to the light. You couldn't have believed that this child could open those awed lips and send out a strange peal of laughter that made me join and started off old Mr. Bates in the vegetables and weeds to laughing, too, and waving at us through the corn. You couldn't believe that her sober face was ever shining with the most delicious open laughter that united every one in a second and made us all want to protect her and keep her happy. Oh, she would go rocking off down the garden path sometimes, her golden head among the flowers, and lean against the apple boughs just to laugh, her face turned toward the sky, her hands and body limp against the tree, open to sun and light. Sometimes at a picnic, with yellow leaves shaking down all around us, she would go into a perfect delirium of joy so that her brooding, self-absorbed face was transfigured and we would one by one join her with delicious laughter, laughing at nothing, absolutely nothing, as the yellow leaves fell. But she is an only child and subject to rages and resentments as well.

"You aren't listening to me, Aunt Grace," she said, twitching my sleeve. "Fleta came in that door. She had on a cream net dress over rose-colored satin and it had a long train. Little children were riding in the train . . ."

"Now, Vanessa," I said, "they couldn't . . ."

She looked resentful and insisted that they did. "They were swinging from the ruffles on her sleeves and hanging from her belt and shoulders. She moved slowly—like this—and she was looking straight ahead at some one and walking toward him, smiling and holding out her hand. I had always been frightened before. I had never made a move to leave Mamma at any sort of party . . ."

"But you always laughed when you got home," I said.

"Oh, sure I did, but this time I was good and scared of every one and I broke away from Mamma and walked across the room to her without any fear at all. Those little children were hanging to her like sleepy fat bees, but I pushed right through and took her hand. She looked down at me and I looked up." She stood very still, a look of serene awe around her head, her face lifted angelically as if again she were looking up, up, with rolled-back melting eyes. "Oh, that door opened all of a sudden and my life was changed."

She forgot about me. She stared at the door as if she were acting the scene and re-acting it, over and over, her hands even making little ghost gestures of surprise and then homage. And there in her neck and eyes was shining the weakness of her, the inability to make up her mind or grasp a situation, and in her parted lips I saw the dark struggling part of her, the solemn, never-resentful self-absorption.

"Why, even when I used to come here six years ago to Christian Endeavor it wasn't like this. I can't understand why it's changed so, got so much smaller. Why, it even looks mean."

"I think it's having it all thrown open. I brought the children one day in spring to a little recital and it looked much better than it does to-day."

"Oh, I'm so glad. Then it isn't just me, is it? You know I'd hate to think I just imagined things different from what they are. You know one does hate to think that."

"Yes, of course," I murmured.

She gave her pealing, unexpected laugh, as if she had seen through all her illusions and for a second was shining out above herself and her blindness, transformed into that golden all-laughing being, warm with sun and life. But I knew she was merely laughing because we were stepping out of the empty church door into the Sunday noontime of our village. That was always her greeting for the outdoors—her enchanting intimate laughter.

Across the street at the engine-house four men sat pressed into armchairs, arms folded on chests, feet crossed, pipes going. We could see the new fire-engine through the large open door and I remembered the days when four great black horses would plunge into the street, men hanging from the ladders on the side of the rattling engine, little boys running down the road behind. The minister's boy stepped along with his enlightened chin held high, his bland pink cheeks shining with cleanness and health. I am sure Vanessa did not see him when she answered his cordial, rather effeminate "Hallo." I am sure she saw only a vague face and suit passing outside her.

I know, for example, that at four years of age at the Presbyterian bazaar she hadn't seen Fleta Bain, whom all of us have known for years. I saw Fleta, too, that evening. I was about eighteen at the time. I remember her perfectly. Her dress did not have a train. Four meager children with sleek thin hair walked beside her. Fleta herself was distraught and grief-stricken, her large eyes full of misery and pity for the race, because, I have since decided, she saw in each person her suffering self. I heard somewhere that she was wretched that night because of unrequited love and she had come home from the city to our village for peace and a quiet, painless life, leaving in the past all the chaos and violence of the other, the dark hurt of thwarted purposes and desires. She was heart-broken that night, almost too miserable to know where she was, and behind her walked her abominable old aunt, Clackie Weir, wearing one of her atrocious bonnets that she created out of plush and ribbons from candy boxes. Some said that Fleta had martyred herself for her old aunt, that she had no other relatives, and she felt the most remarkable and unselfish love for the creature. Others said they pitied Aunt Clackie because she had a lot to put up with from Fleta, who tried out all her lessons in spirituality and the higher life on her aunt.

"You know, Aunt Grace, I think I have to stop and tell Fleta about—just now," she said very low, looking ahead with that intent eager look.

"But it's so near lunch-time."

"Oh, Fleta doesn't think of *food!*"

"No?"

"Of course not. You know I met her February 20th, 1904, and then I got to know her awfully well on March 10th, 1927."

"Must we stop, dear?" I said. "You know I ought to get home to Wendall and the children. You go, and let me run along home."

"No," she said shyly. "No, I'll only stay a moment. I want her to understand how my life changed that night in 1904. You know, Aunt Grace, she is so . . ."

"Yes, I know," I said hastily.

Fleta always makes me feel as if she pitied me because I am a married woman and the mother of twins. She always reminds me of my struggles in Chicago when I went there to become a great singer. When I sit down in her house I am aware that I have failed. I see myself suddenly as I once dreamed I would be—singing with my head back, my voice entering all the people and rousing them so that they too would feel a singing in themselves, a mysterious response to my voice. Oh, perhaps I hate Fleta Bain. And perhaps I am deeply indifferent to her.

The door was standing open. Vanessa had rung. I prayed that old aunt was either in the cellar or the attic. She was so stingy she wouldn't accept an invitation out for a meal if she had food that might spoil. She would stay at home and eat it.

"Oh, Fleta!" cried Vanessa.

The big screen door opened and Fleta stood in the dark doorway. She was smiling her mysterious little smile. She wore an ordinary dress and it hung longer in back and was bunched and gathered around the waist abominably. I was sure that aunt of hers made her wear it for economy or perhaps she wore it as discipline in some of her spiritual studies. Vanessa had forgotten me. She was standing in the hall, one hand on her chest, the other clinched out in front of her.

"What darlings you are to come and see me!"

I peeked and Aunt Clackie was absent. "We can stay just a moment. Vanessa has something she wants to tell you."

Fleta turned to her with shining eyes, her lovely thin mouth opened, her long fingers with their bird-beaked nails working mysteriously as if she had some concealed tatting. She

spoke gently, her voice low and deliberate, but there was
something enchanting in the secret special thing she made out
of Vanessa's merely wanting to tell her something. She made it
all into something strange and lovely. Suddenly our being there
together, waiting to hear words—just words—waiting to speak
from our throats and hearts something inexpressible, made me
see Fleta for an instant as Vanessa must always see her. She
glanced at Vanessa and then as she looked at the girl's rapt,
almost trancelike face and body, such a look of sadness and pity
came on her face, such patience and deep, deep sorrow and
understanding, that I had to like her.

"What is it, Vanessa?"

The girl took hold of the curtain and fitted the edge over
her finger. She didn't know at that moment that Fleta was her
whole life, that she needed and loved and wanted no one but
that women's face and soul there before her, that infinite
understanding and tenderness making all the world so strange
and splendid, and her whole being vital and angelic. She
swallowed and smiled helplessly.

"How are your little children, Mrs. De Vries?"

Now the moment changed. The mention of children, the
recalling of my married state, gave me that darting suspicion of
Fleta. Something cold and hard entered the room. Her face was
the same but I felt a coldness, like the cold that seeps out and
slowly paralyzes. Above her head was a large framed painting of
a madonna with a very fat bare child in her arms. Perhaps the
aunt had hung it there. Below the picture, below the glorious
mother-curves and breast and generosity sat Fleta, her sorrowing
face and hurt eyes pointed straight at me.

"They are always well."

"Oh, how unusual. I thought children were always having
things."

"Just little sicknesses," I said.

"Oh, don't let's talk about *children!*" cried Vanessa.

"No? Are we to talk about you darling, instead?" She

laughed enchantingly. "All right, let's talk about Vanessa. She is beautiful. She has something to tell us."

"I can't in front of Aunt Grace."

I really could have slapped her for that. Fleta made it seem not at all rude by taking us both to the window and showing us a bird's nest in the crotch of the big tree near the window. Again I felt some unutterable sorrow in her. I must have shown it in my eyes, my voice, the way I put out my hand to protect her and show her that I understood, because she was cold again. I saw that she pitied *me*.

"Good heavens, when women say they are perfectly satisfied in giving up their careers I always wonder if they are being really honest. What about you, Mrs. De Vries?"

"I feel as if my singing helped to make my children. They wouldn't be as lovely—"

"Now, Aunt Grace, you know they are perfect wretches. Why, that little Byron actually tottered over to me carrying the encyclopedia and crowned me with it yesterday. If you put out your hands to pet them they grab your finger and bite you. My word, lovely, if that's what you call lovely, if that kind of atrocious animalism is—"

Fleta laughed heartily. "I'm sure I could never wipe a child's nose," she said.

I was furious. I looked at the door. I closed my lips and counted to twenty. Before I could suggest going, Fleta had again pressed my arm with a sudden change of feeling. I saw a kind of deep regret on her face again and all her spirit seemed to warm me gently, as if in her heart she longed only to make people glow and be rich in their qualities. Now she looked much younger than her age. Fleta was fifty-one. But when the coldness comes she looked ageless—ninety, one hundred and fifty, even. She said to Vanessa, "Dear, come and tell us now. We must know *now*."

All of Vanessa's smartness had gone. She couldn't speak of her experience in the church in an ordinary tone of voice. She couldn't say anything about it in front of me. I was outside.

I didn't understand. I wiped the noses of children and the chins of children all smothered in cream of wheat. "Vanessa," I said, "I'm running along now."

"Oh, just a moment, Aunt Grace."

I went to the doorway. "No, I've stayed too long. No, really, Fleta."

"Wait outside," Vanessa whispered. "Please."

I waited outside the screen. I looked at the bridal-wreath that made a snowy bank all around the cottage. I remembered Aunt Clackie in her monstrous sunbonnet with the long gingham cape in back and the starched strings poking in the nasturtiums around the elm. I remembered her sharp voice that was always out of patience. "My soul and body!" or "Good *lands!*"—always said with more disgust than I could ever summon. She was thin and old but she had always taken supreme care of herself, never eating anything that might shorten her life, doing anything that would endanger her health, or putting any sort of strain on herself. No one in Lodi had ever liked her. All of us, with the exception of a very few, pited poor Fleta, and some said it was a great mercy Fleta could take up New Thought and Yogi breathing when she had to live with Clackie Weir.

I thought, when I saw the pansies in a tiny decaying box, of Fleta's career, of her bowls of flowers on magazine covers, her graceful little garden scenes in color, always faint and yet real enough to pass. I wondered if you had to choose between those flat pointless little pots of daisies and sprays of fern and large beautiful flesh children that grow in you and break out of you into the world to sing and be wonderful. I knew that Vanessa would always be a Bodley in her strong body, that she was physically the child of Belle and Edwin, but in that other part, the part that shines through the body, she was Fleta's child. I wondered then if a time would ever come when she would break out of Fleta to come to life in the world of flesh and blood and truth.

"Like blueberries," said Fleta at the door. "That delicious taste. There's nothing quite like it, is there?"

Vanessa stood awkwardly. She moistened her lip as if some forgotten taste of blueberries might still be there, hidden in the skin. "Oh, I don't know what you mean. I don't remember."

"You've eaten blueberries and you don't remember? Good heavens, Vanessa! They are like nothing else on earth."

All the blood rushed into the girl's face as if she had been struck on the cheek or across her startled eyes. "Oh, you aren't angry with me, are you?" she cried. "Don't hate me!"

"But, my darling child, why should I hate any one? I don't get mad. I don't know what that is."

"Then you don't hate me for not knowing blueberries?" she said softly.

"Well, for land's sake quit lettin' in all the flies in the country!"

It was Aunt Clackie Weir. I said good-by in a hurry. Vanessa stood there stubbornly while Fleta closed the screen door. I saw that Fleta's face was white and trembling. She moistened her lip, stiffened, and then relaxed and said with pitiful gayety, "I haven't let in *quite* all the flies, Auntie."

Vanessa mumbled in a wretched awkward way. "Let's talk about time and space again. I read that book you gave me. I think he's wonderful but I don't understand that about immortality very well. I wish I could—"

I heard a crackle and whistling of silk. I saw an old white face full of fury and disgust shove Fleta away from the door and turn on Vanessa. "It's time decent folks was seeing about their victuals," she shouted and slammed the inner door so that we heard the key fall out of the lock. As Vanessa staggered away she saw Fleta behind the living-room curtain, waving her hand and trying to smile gayly.

"Oh, that wretched, ugly woman. Oh, sometimes I think I could actually—yes, I mean it, actually kill her." She was trembling so that she could hardly speak. She pulled off her hat and let the wind blow her bright hair, shoving it back and back from her smooth forehead and her ears. "How did she dare mention food when we were talking about immortality?"

"She's an old lady," I reminded her.

"Well, then she ought to know better."

"We ought to know better than to call at lunch-time."

"Nonsense! Fleta doesn't care about food. She would rather find out about immortality first. She would be satisfied to fast for weeks and communicate with the masters on the other side—"

"But, dear, that's Miss Weir's house, remember."

"Well, she needn't think *she's* going to be immortal. I should say not. Only the most sensitized, the most highly spirtualized will be saved and kept from the wheel of experience, from Karma."

"How do you do, Mr. Bope?" I said.

He lifted his hat. He had soft white hair and he always wore good clothes. He was the president of the Coöperative Gas Works and a widower with two daughters, Julia and Jane. His name was Pliny Bope and he was our richest citizen. They always said he had the first dollar he earned but he kept up his house very well and the lawn was always lovely, the best in town. Grass was about the only thing that grew on his place, the flowers usually died. There was too much shade. Vanessa's father, my brother, Edwin, was one of the stockholders in the company. Edwin usually made bad investments, but when he made this one and put in everything, we patted him on the back because anything Pliny Bope was connected with made money and made a lot of it. Any firm that he was with wasn't going to lose, no matter what the conditions were, because money was a matter of life and death to him, and he would give his leg or his lungs before he lost even a part of his fortune.

Vanessa said finally, "Fleta is investigating Mr. Bope. She says he's responsible for a lot of the suffering here in town on account of the low wages he pays. She's checking up on Mr. Bope," she said threateningly. "Mr. Bope in particular and I'm going to speak to Papa. Perhaps he could do something toward helping humanity. Say, where could I get some blueberries? I had them once but I can't remember how they tasted." She flushed when she admitted that. "As I remember them—well, I just *see* them, that's all."

"That's all there is to them," I said.

"Perhaps for *you*," she replied gravely.

"Don't be an idiot," I said.

"Now, Aunt Grace, I don't think it's very nice of you," she began. But I saw she was far away from me. I could have called her anything. She was unaware of me. She had withdrawn into her personal mist, into her real world, where she stood alone with Fleta, being slowly transformed into something as nearly like the woman as possible. It wasn't merely an intellectual domination. Vanessa drank the woman in through her pores when she was near her, she drank in her being on those days when she rushed to her house, her arms filled with Persian lilacs, her face uplifted, worshiping, like an angel adoring, and then pressed the cool moist flower clusters into Fleta's brown exquisite arms.

"Fleta's birthday is on Thursday. She's invited me to come over. There's going to be a children's party. When I told her about that night in the church she said right off, 'Let's *ask* some children on my birthday and we'll have a beautiful time with them.'"

I told Vanessa that would be awfully nice and instantly she said: "But we aren't going to have Byron and Myrna. They're too young and I don't know what Fleta would do if they acted natural and started biting people's hands."

"My dear," I said, "my children don't bite, and if they did bite I think it would be very disloyal of you to tell about it, and I consider these stories you tell not disloyalties but downright lies to pamper Fleta's defeated maternalism." But she hadn't heard me apparently. I heard her murmer something about blueberries and the next day I found her at the table, all alone, a bowl of blueberries and cream in front of her. She ate slowly, tasting the mild vapid fruit to the full, one hand supporting her bright cheek.

"Well?"

"Well yourself."

"How do you like them?"

"What?" she asked.

"Blueberries."

"I—I haven't decided yet. I—I think—I wonder if these are the way they are meant to be—"

"I'm sure they are." She looked so perplexed and sad and startled over it. I ought not to have gone on but I did. I couldn't hold back. I said: "That vapid washed-out fruit always makes me think of all the meager frightened things on earth, those precious, rare, tasteless, pointless, flat, *tasteless*—"

"I'm going to take her a box for her birthday. I think she would like that."

"Yes, that would be called a pretty attention," I said.

"I'm making her a birthday cake, too, but don't you dare tell any one. It's the first I've ever made of this kind—Tropicana cake. One layer chocolate, the next orange, and the top lemon."

"Good heavens!" I cried. "Whose recipe?"

"I found it in a magazine called *The Pathway*. I'm going to make white frosting. Had I better cook it?"

"You'd better let me help you with the whole thing," I said.

"No. This is Fleta's cake. Everything I make for her is my own. Everything I do for her is all from me, earned by me, and I shall always be that way forever." She took another listless spoonful of fruit, the milk dribbling down, and chewed. "I kind of like these, Aunt Grace," she said. "They grow on one. I really didn't like them at first. They didn't taste like anything. But now I understand about them. I can't name how they taste but I like it. They are something one must learn to like, though, like beets."

II

The next day Vanessa came early. She had the box of blueberries all wrapped in fancy paper napkins and in her other arm she was carrying a large platter edged with fresh rambler roses. In the center was her birthday cake, the one she made for Fleta, her Tropicana cake or whatever she called it. The icing was soft and oozing, it bulged in places and looked too thick and sweet. But the effect was lovely if you didn't contemplate eating the mess, the pink rambler roses with the soft shiny leaves and then the mound of soft pure white in the center.

"Vanessa, dear, it is awfully pretty," I said. "The whole effect is lovely."

She was flushed and haughty. "I think it looks terrible." She had even cried over the cake. I could tell. She saw how miserably unappetizing it looked. "I burned my hand and I almost begged you to come and make me another but this is Fleta's and she will understand," she said proudly. I saw that she was waiting to be purged and overjoyed by Fleta's inspired vision of the platter, that she was contemplating a triumph. I knew that when Fleta's sad eyes looked at it, when she spoke in her tender special way about it, that Vanessa would be uplifted. I knew that Vanessa was waiting for that now. She was telling herself too that her ideal of a cake for Fleta was so perfect that of course anything she made would look mussy and sad.

"Come on, Myrna," she said patiently. "You can carry the berries if you'll be careful. Here." She laid them in Myrna's outstretched eager hands. "Now walk gently, Myrna! Those are for Fleta."

The children each had a gift for Fleta. Byron had made her a picture of a tiger in a cage. It was colored with his crayons, and really he has talent. The tiger simply roars out of the picture at you and his stripes are the most like real tiger stripes I have ever seen. Myrna made a princess on a large white paper. The lady wafts along in her white robes, and her feet look as if they are artificial, but her face is as cool and remote as the face of a princess. I am carrying a large armful of summer flowers and I have on my green voile with the hand embroidery.

"Now you and Byron are going to behave, aren't you?" asked Vanessa sternly.

"Oh, *yes!*" they cried at once.

Byron simply jerked at my hand to be up in front with Myrna and Vanessa but he was too small to walk alone. At the door Vanessa said to me, "How can I see Fleta alone?"

"We'll arrange that," I promised. I prayed that she had disposed of that hideous old aunt.

Fleta threw open the door. She was in lilac muslin. Her hair was done in intricate waves and little loose waterfalls, all shining under a net. Her face had that special light in it and two little children were reaching up at her from the side, waving colored beads and boxes.

"Look what I gave her!" said Joan Davis. She pushed a red box with a picture of a mouse on it under my hand. "Look!" she insisted. "Come on and see the other presents, Mrs. De Vries." She clutched my hand, dragging her whole body back on it, her weight on her heels.

Fleta laughed. "I'm so happy to-day," she said. "Oh, *Vanessa!*" But Byron pushed up between them and thrust his picture of a tiger into her hand. "Here," he said gruffly, and showed his teeth and gums, twitching up his nose and making a horrible deep noise in his throat.

"That means tiger," I said.

Fleta clapped her hands over the picture, her face soft with delight and surprise. "No, this *is* the tiger."

Byron simply jumped up and down.

"What did *you* bring her?" said Joan Davis to Myrna. "Let's see it."

Myrna shyly unrolled her princess.

"I brought you a store present, didn't I, Miss Fleta?" said Joan. "Yes, I did. It cost ten cents. I bought it all myself. My present is the best here. See that mousie?" She bent down on the floor to show Myrna. They both bent over the box, their loose dresses falling softly as they pouched there like birds.

I herded them and drove them before me into the living-room. They ran at once to the open window and pointed out the robin on her nest.

"Sssssssh," I said. "She's keeping her eggs warm so the babies can come out."

They stood with parted lips, hands closed and half raised before them, little shy smiles on their faces. Sally Maggs put her lips against the screen and made a warm cooing sound in her throat.

"I wish we could get the babies out."

"Could you be borned from a boy-bird, Mrs. De Vries?"

"Our goat's going to. It's going to come right out of him."

"How nice," I said, "and may we all come and see it?"

"To-morrow? To-morrow?" cried Byron. "Mamma, to-morrow? Can we go to-morrow?"

"Some time," I said.

"We was all little tiny babies too once."

"Mrs. De Vries was a little tiny baby too."

They put their elbows on my knees, leaning forward, straining to get their faces closer to my face. I just sat there making those warm indistinct sounds in my throat at them. I loved them so much that I couldn't bear it.

"My Daddy was a little tiny baby once. He said so."

"When's the party going to be?" some one cried.

They all slipped out of their mysterious sleepiness and one rushed to the door. "Miss Fleta, when's the party going to be?"

"Ssssssh," I said. "Come here and tell me a big story."

Fleta came slowly, her little face cold and set, one bird-beaked hand on her cheek. She turned to Vanessa and said, "This is something important. I want you to promise."

"But why?" murmured Vanessa. She too looked cold and different. Her orange frock was brilliant in the dark room. Suddenly she turned to me as if we were alone and said, "Aunt Grace, Fleta wants me to promise never to make another cake."

"It can't be that bad, Fleta," I said. "Let's taste it."

Fleta smiled politely.

"Fleta," I repeated, "let's taste it. Let's start the party."

"Yes, yes, Miss Fleta," cried the children, stretching up their arms.

She looked distraught and bleak, cold gray like stone. Her lip was raised and she gave little laughs and yet she seemed to see none of us. Finally she said, "There are plenty of people in the world who can make cakes. But there are very few who can do what Vanessa was born to do."

"Can you be borned from a boy-bird, Miss Fleta? Can you? Can you?"

She put her hand down absent-mindedly and stroked his head.

"I want to do what others do and what I can do, too," said Vanessa.

Fleta just smiled and turned her back to Vanessa. She went to the window. "Did you see the nest, children?" she asked.

I saw the sad cake on the hall table. Its sides had bulged out from the heavy frosting and there was a great oozing rent at the bottom. The rambler roses on one side were just beginning to turn ghastly, as the white slowly gained on them, covering their color and freshness. "After this, Vanessa," I said, "don't expect to find good recipes in magazines called *The Pathway*." Just then Tom Chettle opened the screen.

"Hello!" He said it like an explosion, his cheeks fiery and full of wind. He gasped and smoothed his hair down before he went to Fleta and held out a package that once was white.

"Oh, thank you, Tom. How sweet of you to remember."

He had to turn away as she untied the string. It was candy in a red box with a gorgeous lady looking out of a rose. I am sure he selected it because she looked like Fleta to him. Vanessa moved away in scorn and stood so that her back looked rigid. I knew she was protesting and that she knew just how her back looked to all of us, turned coldly and squarely against our foolishness.

"Come," said Fleta to the children, "the party is going to start."

III

The wood is charming when you get to it. You first have to climb over an old stile, and then follow a levee which has a tarn on one side and a cow pasture on the other. I always call the dark side toward the river, with those bleak strange trees and the pools of scummy green, a tarn. You can see the highway and the Caledonia hills if you look across the smooth pasture with the deep green places where the cow hoofs have sunk. We got over the stile very well, Fleta leading as if she were exploring a new land, her enchanted eyes moving from the tarn to the silent green pasture and the blue hills in the far distance. I was at the very end, half carrying my little Byron because he isn't used to walking in the country. Suddenly I heard Fleta call back in her clear even voice, "What are we to do to-day, children?"

Sally Maggs simply screamed, curls shaking, "We're to protect the trees!"

"Yes, but what else?"

"We're to clear the path for those who are to come," said Tom Chettle gruffly. He jerked down his blue sweater and dropped his head. Then he jumped high in the air and laughed idiotically, showing all his teeth at one of the little girls just behind. He began walking crazily to cover his embarrassment but the little children gravely started to pick up all the branches and leaves and twigs on the path. Ahead Fleta had stooped with her lovely secret grace, to airily pick one twig as an example. Then she walked on, her face toward the blue of the distant hills, and behind her the children came, picking furiously, trying now to outpick each other, panting, damp, and just ahead of me Vanessa, picking not only twigs but roots, stones, bits of glass, tinfoil, apple cores wilted and brown, and tossing them all gently into the deep soft meadow grass at the side of the path.

We sat down in the farther end of the pasture with the large tree behind us, making it shady and silent, a mound of yellow sand just ahead with a shallow pool left from the high water. I shall always remember those bodies of little children fluttering around her. They put up their warm arms to her, their bright faces swept hers as they peered into her splendid eyes, they thrust up their faces now and then with quick laughter. We sat around Fleta in a semicircle, her honey-colored hat, all lacy and twisted like a nest or a hive, on the grass beside her.

"Please sing something, Mrs. De Vries," said Fleta sadly. She sat turned away from Vanessa and I thought she was deliberately avoiding any reference to her.

"When's the party going to be?" said Byron gravely.

"Why, darling," said Fleta, "I had forgotten. The party's going to be *now*," she announced.

"Could I do something?" asked Vanessa, coming around and looking humbly at Fleta.

"Nothing at all, thank you," said Fleta. She did not look up. "Tom, let me have that basket, please."

He handed it to her simply shaking with delight and embarrassment. "Can I get water, Miss Fleta?" he asked. "Or—"

"No, we aren't going to have coffee or lemonade," she replied.

She leaned over the basket and drew out little packages wrapped in gay paper napkins. These she handed to the children.

"No, no, don't peek," I said.

Then she gave each child an apple and an orange and sat up suddenly coy and smiling. We unrolled our packages and saw in the center of each paper a dented, rather sodden sandwich filled with hard cheese. The soft bread had been torn in the cutting and great clots of butter stood out on top. "How lovely," I said quickly. "Look, Byron, see the big bite I'm going to take!"

"I don't want mine," he said.

Now Fleta broke off a tiny morsel and as she chewed held her fingers over her mouth. She looked around her, her eyes softened and vague as if she were eating something indescribably delicious, the other hand spread open beside her on the grass. Vanessa with great hungry lips and eyes watched every movement but she did not imitate Fleta. She sat as she always sits in the country, breathing in the sun and air with her body. Tom Chettle bit off pieces of his sandwich sharply with his head lowered. Suddenly he jumped up and fired his paper napkin, rolled into a moist wad, across into the trees.

"We aren't supposed to do that, are we, Miss Fleta? Are we? You said we shouldn't ever throw paper at the trees."

Fleta was holding up a little empty cracker box, the decorated kind that animal crackers come in. It was empty but she had saved it because of the animals painted on it and the whole thing was a circus cage. She held it up and said, "Shall we play with this?"

They looked embarrassed and ashamed, as if their lady was a bit foolish but they didn't want to let her know they knew. Some of them turned their heads away. I saw Vanessa spring up and cry at them, "Don't you even know how to *play?*"

"Well, Byron can draw better than that," said Myrna in a shrill voice. "He drawed a tiger that's better than that." The children turned to her and looked, their mouths very cross and impudent. "Byron can draw anything but his are all different. He can't make two of anything. But I can make as many as you want." She began pulling grass and heaping it in front of her.

"Yes, Byron *can* make a real tiger."

"Not really real," said Sally Maggs suddenly.

"Yes, Sally."

"No, our Lord Jesus makes the real tigers."

At the mention of God the children sat shyly with mouths slightly open, damp curls falling in their eyes, their fingers stuffed in their mouths. Lockets gleamed on dotted swiss and there were grass stains on white socks. Tom Chettle had bent his head again, his cheeks fiery, his knuckles white on his raised knees. Vanessa watched Fleta, her whole face very sad and humble, but the woman never once raised her eyes to the girl.

"Yes, God makes the real tigers, Sally," said Fleta. "Let's try to do something nice for God every day. Each one of us— every day."

Sally pitched over backward in embarrassment, covering her whole face with her little hands. She lay there on her fat side, peeking out at Fleta. The older ones were flushed and uneasy. They stared ahead or turned to giggle self-consciously behind their hands as Fleta looked above, gentle fixity in her raised head and sad, disappointed eyes.

The meadow cows, the young calves, and the baby bull stopped grazing and came closer, came slowly over the grass with their soft eyes fixed on Fleta, their hoofs heedlessly raised over the heads of daisies and mist flowers, a foam like egg white stained with green dropping from their grinding jaws. They came gradually and when Fleta lifted her eyes again, saying softly, "God lives in everything. He is in all," she saw out of the corner of her eye the cows slowly advancing, steadily, without noise, almost without motion. She knocked her bird-beaked fingers against her chest nervously. Her lip raised over her small grayed teeth. Her body jerked back and she stared at them for a second as if fire were coming from their nostrils, as if their sad, melting eyes were rolling and insane. She saw them with derelict teeth dripping black foam and iron hoofs that could tear off a scalp in an instant.

She jumped up and put both bird-beaked thumbs into her mouth, one eye following the friendly startled cows, the other calculating the distance to Barden's farmhouse. "That place over there is nicer," she brought out coldly. "Come, children, let's play we're pilgrims crossing the valley of terrors unaided."

She led the way rapidly, the children plunging after as if it were a game, the disappointed cows standing motionless. Tom Chettle pushed the little girls aside to catch up with Fleta, he even pushed Vanessa to reach her. They all cried out in resentment as he passed them, his elbows out. He ran on to Fleta, who was far ahead, a bright gold star for good attendance in Sunday-school shining on his blue sweater. I saw him slip it on while Fleta was talking about God. Mud was hanging in fangs from her high heels, her eyes were small with terror. Tom drew up beside her. He stretched up, filling his loose clothes like a man, shielding her from even a bird's-eye view of the meadow cows. Then he took long hops, his arms held out as a screen, his boots squeaking deep in the grassy mud.

Suddenly I saw her look full at him, her small mouth drawn down in iron resentment and her eyes glossy with scorn. He mumbled, "I'll take care of you—" and she replied, "Indeed, you needn't," and helped herself over the stile. He fell back, gulping down a great blubber in his throat. Then he passed us on the path where he had hopped so fantastically, head down, hands deep in pockets.

"Good *for* you," one of the little girls was brave enough to cry and some others repeated it. One child advanced and gave him a push with both hands, but he only jerked his cap down over his eyes and disappeared in the gloom of trees and bracken.

"Now, we're going to play a guessing game," said Fleta, her arms opened to us, her head turned toward the spot of soft green under forest trees.

"I guess you was afraid of those cows, Miss Fleta," said Sally Maggs.

"Come, come," said Fleta gayly. "find your places. Each one has a guess."

"You was afraid, wasn't you, Miss Fleta?" she repeated, in a high excited voice.

"Here's your place, Sally. We're ready to begin." Fleta suddenly waved her arms as if little bells were ringing on them. She hummed and even danced under the spreading tree. "Guess— guess—"

Sally stood by herself, her lips drawn down, and began to cry with uncovered face. When Fleta finally came toward her she turned away forlornly, covering her face with her hands, and when the woman knelt and put her arms around her she suddenly turned with a long deep cry and threw herself against Fleta, clung with her white hands and warm arms, crying, her back rising with sharp sobs—"You was afraid of the cows—" She screamed wildly now, her whole body wrenched and moving. "You was—you was—"

Fleta picked at the hands clasped on her neck. She tried to lift the arms, the head. Then she said sharply, "Come, Sally, we're waiting for you."

"You was too, Miss Fleta!"

"Children," said Fleta and they all turned to her. I turned, too. "Listen, children, I want to explain something." They shivered at her tone. The river lay behind us, glassy, cold, moving toward another larger river showing the brown sand under the amber ripples near the edge. The children looked down restlessly and then they glared at little Sally who pulled away and stood in guilt beside her lady, dirt streams running down her swollen face, her hands as her sides, her head bent.

"Aaaaaaaaah, shame, shame," said some one.

"Aaaaaaaaaaaaah."

"I am not afraid of cows," said Fleta. "If you must know why I came here," she added sadly, her eyes tinged with lovely soft reproach, "it was because this is cool and right for our game. Isn't it?"

"Yes! Yes!" they all cried.

One little girl jumped up and faced the shamed Sally who was sniffing and gasping with drooped head. "I'm, going to slap—yes, sir, I am, you're a naughty nasty girl."

"Hush," said Fleta. She got down in the grass before them and knelt, holding their hands in hers, bending toward their quiet startled faces. "Let's forgive her. Let's kiss our Sally. Come, children, let's kiss our Sally. She's sorry and so are we. We're sorrier because she thought so badly of us—we're sorry for *her*. But it's all over now."

The children stood where they were. No one made a move forward. It was very still. Fleta rose. She closed her eyes and the light poured down through the green leaves.

"Let's promise to always be honest," she said. "Let's all of us make ourselves be sincere and honest and brave. That's the way we pay for the privilege of living—by being honest and open in return." She dropped her hands to her sides, looking ahead through the dark trees that grew down to the river. Then she said, "There is so little we can do on earth, there is such a very, very little possible for us to do—people will let us give them so little, they will take so little, that the one big thing left for us is honesty. Money honesty. Justice. Truth—even in the smallest things." She put one hand over her mouth for a second and then she looked at Vanessa. "If we want the new world to come in place of this dishonest, vulgar, cheap one then we must work and be honest in everything—that is the first requirement, the foundation of *everything*.

Oh, as she spoke I wanted to sing. I felt the way I used to feel about audiences. Only now I was the audience and Fleta was doing to me what I always longed to do to them. She was making me want to throw out my arms and look at every face and pour out a tremendous song. And even the little ones felt something because they took long frightened breaths, moistening their lips soberly, and then looked down and kicked the sod. Vanessa simply sprang toward Fleta. She closed her lips tightly and yet we heard a groan that seemed to come from the soles of her feet and rise in torment through her whole body. She threw herself down on the ground before the woman and put her face against the bottom of Fleta's skirt.

IV

She walked in as if there was no feeling anywhere in her body.

"Vanessa!" I said.

She looked at the carpet.

"Vanessa!"

Her eyes were dull, her whole body looked as if it had been cast out of some warm permanent place onto rocks. Her face had the vague set look of some one paralyzed by a fall. She stiffened her arms in front of her and pushed them hard between her knees. Then she lowered her head.

"Is your father all right"

She nodded. I felt relieved. I am always expecting something to happen to Edwin. And I thought how just like life it was for me to have been sitting there thinking up something new to eat and to suddenly hear that my brother had broken his leg or lost the little money he had left. And before Vanessa came in I was imagining an entirely different existence for myself—I even saw myself husbandless and childless and me climbing a cocoanut tree in a palmleaf skirt. When you think things like that something always happens to make you grateful for just the plain daily reality.

"How's your mother, Vanessa?"

She nodded.

"Did you stay and talk with Fleta?"

She stood up and began walking up and down in front of me, pushing her hair up from her forehead and setting her teeth down on her lip.

"Just tell me what you think of this, Aunt Grace. I signed up—concert—one night at the dormitory and then we decided to go walking instead—Robert and me. And four times I answered present in gym class so Margot wouldn't need to appear and I told Miss Evans at the hall that Minnie Huggett had gone to see a doctor but really she went to the Orph matinée. Do you think that's so terrible?"

"Let me think," I said.

"Oh, what's there to think over? Every one does it. It's nothing. We don't give it a thought."

"Well, I don't think it's awfully honest," I said.

"Do you think it shows that I'm vile? Oh, Fleta said—" She clapped her hand over her mouth and turned away for a second. Then she swallowed and pressed her lips together, gazing at her shoe. "She said that for a person of my development not to realize that I was lying was worse than for some one else to lie and know it. Oh, she said that her life would mean nothing— nothing—Oh, does it all mean that I have something rotten in me? Am I really dead like those other people on this planet that lie and steal and don't have anything in them to say what is right and what is wrong? Will I go on and on and not be able to stop and does it mean that—Oh, she thought I had a divine voice in me that would speak—"

"Now, Vanessa," I said, "I think it all means that you're getting awfully careless but if you feel sad about it—"

"But I don't!" she cried suddenly. "I don't. Get that into your head now. I don't and I never, never shall. I don't see anything wrong in it. I think I was being generous to do it for them and no one can make me feel that I'm vile for having done it."

"But it was certainly not honest, Vanessa," I protested. "It wasn't horrible but it wasn't honest."

"And I don't care. I want to be dishonest. I want to lie and steal and kill and do everything bad because I am bad and I don't care, I'm glad I am, I'm glad of it and I'll never speak to Fleta again. I will never look at her again in my whole life. If she telephones me I won't go to the phone. If she sends me flowers and begs my pardon I won't acknowledge it. She is— dead—dead—" she repeated and threw herself down in the chair, her hands gripped over her eyes.

"Don't do that, darling," I said. "Every one tells lies but just don't tell any more. Be reasonable about it. Fleta didn't mean to hurt you."

"She did."

"I know she didn't. She's alive. I felt it this afternoon. She wants to put something good into the world that will make us grow and worship more and be happy and know what we're doing and getting. I really loved Fleta to-day when she spoke."

"*You* don't know her!" she cried, sitting up.

"What do you mean?"

"Every one talks about knowing Fleta. No one does. Oh, that's why it's so terrible—I know her—I understand—and no one else can—they *can't*—"

"Perhaps."

"Oh, she said that I was hardened in a way she would never have suspected. She said I could commit a crime and

have nothing in me to speak the truth and make me know—
what I had done. She said her life meant nothing—nothing—
Oh, does it all mean I'm not fit to help her make humanity—
better," she cried and covered her face. "Oh, Aunt Grace, what
shall I *do?*"

"Just don't tell any more lies," I said.

"Oh, I don't mean *that.*"

"What do you mean?"

"Oh, Fleta, Fleta," she murmured. "No one—no one is
good enough to know her. Everything she does is a gift to the
world but they can't see. No one can accept what she has to
give because no one can see. And now perhaps it was all a test
and I'm—vile—dishonest—I lie and I don't know I am lying or
really care—and I don't know now what I have actually done
or how enormous it really is—and it is a test and I'm not good
enough, I haven't measured up and she has tried to teach me
how to be in life."

"What do you mean?"

She got up impatiently, as if she couldn't speak, shaking
her head back and forth and drawing up long breaths and then
sighing horribly. Finally she sank down on the couch. "How
can you be so casual about it, Aunt Grace?"

"But it isn't horribly important. Every one has done
something like that."

"Well, if you want to know it, I'm not going to be loose
and dishonest like every one. If you can overlook anything as
dishonorable as that, then I can't respect you, Aunt Grace."
She turned her face away, her chin high.

"Darling," I said, "I'd rather tell lies than be snouty and
feel that I was better than other people. Really."

She walked over to the fireplace suddenly and held her
body rigid, drawing her face together in agony. "What do
you mean by that?" she asked. "No, don't tell me! Don't tell
me! I don't want to know the satanic things you have in your
brain—"

I was startled. I picked up my hemstitching, feeling rather

strange. I tried to remember what I was going to say. It seemed as if I had swallowed my words. All through my head was the odd vacant sensation you have when you try to remember some one's name, for example, or a telephone number or street address. Then something just rushed into my head and filled it. I hadn't thought of it from the day I concealed it from myself in deep shame. I was in the first grade and some one had found a cheap fancy brooch in the playground. It was very ornate with a bulge in the center and a woman's face painted on it. The hair was floating and very long with some flowers caught up in the side. When the teacher held it up and asked if it belonged to any of us I stood up immediately. I said aloud, "That belongs to my Aunt Ella. She works in Bloom's store and that's a picture of her when she was a girl."

I stood there solidly and the teacher questioned me. The pupils stared with open mouths, leaning forward on their elbows, their moist lips following my words. One boy was making pictures on the varnished desk top with his eraser. I remember the long soft gray marks. I knew I had told a lie and yet I believed what I had said. I knew it was false and yet I couldn't stop acting as if it were true or stop believing in some strange way that it was true all the time I knew it wasn't. I had all kinds of defenses ready in case any one should question me but the teacher put the pin in her desk and asked us to open our readers to page fourteen. It seems to me now that I have always felt odd when that number fourteen comes in. It seems as if I have tried to remember something that lies in the back of my mind. When I read directions for knitting—"cast fourteen stitches"—I have felt odd. I remembered that now. Suddenly I seemed to understand something about my whole life and other people. I felt more life inside me.

"Let's be happy, Vanessa!" I cried impulsively. "Let's compose a song. I want to sing magnificently."

"It's seeing truth in a big way instead of the small usual way," she said. "I have been living in the small usual way like other people. Fleta is above all that. She is uncompromising.

She sees all our little motives and actions." She jumped up. "How she must suffer, knowing what we are!" And then, as if she couldn't endure another instant of self-denunciation and remorse, she said, "Could a person come out of something like that—stronger, Aunt Grace? Could a person be a bigger person for having suffered it?"

"Oh, you darling child," I said.

"To thine own self be true!" she said in a deep ringing voice. She looked at me as if I were old and had forgotten something important. But I couldn't believe it was so very important. She stood over me and half shouted, "Aunt Grace, what road are you on? Where are you going? Are your innocent children going to stand with the builders or the wreckers!" Then she went out of the house.

V

Belle called me on the telephone. "Come over this evening and cheer us up," she said. "Edwin is worried about the talk he had with Mr. Bope. He's so upset I wish you'd come if you possibly can and bring Wendall along."

We went. I put my hand on Edwin's shoulder for a moment and then sat down where I could see his face. He was staring at the toe of his shoe, his arms crossed, and his mouth set in that stiff stubborn line that makes his chin solid, even stony. I felt a sharp pang for him because he has always thought of his family in terms of the things he might do for them, the solid costly way he might care for them, and his eyes are always turned toward that vision of the future that he must have, where he will be able to stop and enjoy his wife and daughter and his material possessions, as the reward for having toiled so whole-heartedly.

"Things look bad," he said drearily.

"Oh, don't let's talk about it now," said Belle. "You know nothing has happened yet."

"But it will," he said fatally. "It always does."

"But, Edwin," I said. "I'm sure Bope wouldn't permit the works to fail on account of what he would lose."

"Of course he won't fail," said Wendall. "Bope's a good business man, he's sound as far as money is concerned—sound. Don't worry about it, Edwin."

"That's true. And we've known Pliny for years and he isn't ever going to lose money. We know that."

"I'll grant you that," said Edwin. "But perhaps if he lets it fail he can gain. Had you thought of that?"

Belle turned up her face to him with all the lines showing and the worn sweet look around her mouth, one hand raised, her lips parted in a kind of protest against Edwin's violence toward an acquaintance. "Don't let's think of it, dear," she said. "I used to worry," she added, turning to me, "but somehow I can't any more."

As I looked at them I remembered those two a long time ago; Belle in her going-away clothes, her face positively dewy, an astrachan cap on her head and bands of the fur on her wine-colored gown. Edwin was nervous that day, smiling and shaking hands a great deal, but worried between the eyes, tense. Jack Morris was there, too, being very polite to them both even though Belle had refused him twice before she became engaged to Edwin. And the last thing Edwin said to me as he kissed me good-by was, "Grace, we're going to be happy. In two years I'll have more money than Morris ever dreamed of having . . ."

Here were the same lamps they had been given for wedding presents, the rug, the set of Shakespeare and Dickens on the bookshelves. There were the cheap chairs they had bought cheerfully with visions of the finer, softer ones in their minds making them content. There was the same old table loaded with books, one of the legs in need of glue. And Edwin's manner was so different in his home that I realized again why Vanessa never laughed anywhere except out-of-doors. His eyes were always so disappointed, so persecuted, and he sat brooding, in hurt silence, or else he talked in a booming voice that silenced the women.

"How about some bridge?" suggested Wendall.

"I'm expecting to be bankrupt in about four weeks, Wendall," said Edwin, looking up and unfolding his arms. "Well, I've always lost, I've always got the worst of it, and I've done nothing but worry all my life. If I lose the last of it now it'll be almost a relief to me," he said, whitening, bringing his fist down on the arm of the chair. "It'll be a relief."

Belle looked down weakly at her rings. "Perhaps we need the lesson," she murmured and began rubbing the back of her hand.

"Edwin, is it really so bad?" I said.

"Yes."

But I couldn't be sure. Edwin has always seen things in terms of calamity and I never can decide whether he is giving the facts or merely punishing himself and his family by anticipating the worst. The only hopeful statement I can ever remember him uttering was that one after his wedding, "In two years I'll have more money than Morris ever dreamed of having. . . ." Why did this scene suddenly come before me? My father, Edwin and myself sitting waiting to go to church, waiting for my mother, who finally came down looking beautiful in her feather hat and boa, saying, "Dear, may I have a dime for the plate?" Father replied without changing expression, "Dear, I don't think I have a dime." She went to her purse that lay on the desk. "Then I shall have to put in a quarter," she said serenely. Instantly he shoved his hand into his pocket and said with great dignity, "Dear, I believe I have a dime. Yes, dear, here it is." At the table he would notice that the baby liked something and he would say, "Mamma, give Irving yours. He likes it." My mother always smiled gently and gave it to Irving, giving my father a quick indulgent look.

I used to turn away, suffering horribly, and each time I vowed I would find something in life more important than money. But Edwin felt humiliated in a different way. He made money his goal so that he could be generous with it, giving his wife all that his mother had missed, giving his daughter the things his sister used to long for, and above all being generous with people, with our village, giving public buildings, donating huge sums with his name heading the lists, being the supreme benefactor of all, the wealthy, indulgent father of the town. I am sure he wanted to feel that every one's material happiness was dependent upon him and he wanted to show the whole world how a man with money ought to act.

"Well, what about some bridge?" asked Wendall again. "How about you, Belle?"

"The table's over there, Wendall," said Belle, wiping her lips with her handkerchief. "One leg is loose but shove that side toward me."

"Good," I said. "Come, Edwin!"

"Papa," said Belle gently, "please play with us."

"Well, if you want me to play, I'll play," said Edwin as if he were conferring a favor. "Personally I don't think much of bridge or any other card game."

"Yes, I know," said Belle. "How pretty that dress is, Grace. I like it very much."

Just then Vanessa flew in. "I've got the grandest news," she cried. She saw her father and adjusted herself to him, sobering, as if she must always respect his grief and disappointment by a cold grayness. "You'll never guess."

"Then you didn't fail that trigonometry the way I said you would?" asked Edwin.

"Oh, *Papa!*" she cried.

He laughed. "Well, what is it?"

"You all have to guess."

"We are," said Belle. "But the suspense is too great."

"It certainly is," said Wendall. "Are you and Robert eloping or something?"

"Well, you might better do that than hang around Fleta Bain," said Edwin angrily. "That woman makes me mad all over."

Vanessa stiffened. "Clackie Weir has a beau," she said, all her excitement gone.

"Good Lord!" cried Wendall. "Since when? Who is it?"

"Guess."

"That's altogether too hard."

"I thought something was up the other night when I went over there and saw her singeing the hair off her arms out in the kitchen over the gas. Honestly she was. Now, Mother, could I make up a thing like that? Could I? She was. And her cheeks looked that odd purple, just like a turkey when you first unwrap it and get it ready to pick and draw. Honestly. But I tell you, I saw her . . ."

"No, no, dear," said Belle.

"Well, who's the lucky man?"

"You'll never guess."

"Oh, out with it!" cried Edwin impatiently.

"Pliny Bope!"

Edwin threw his cards down on the table. "Lord, that robber had it coming to him!" He began shaking his head over the table, laughing in a strange shocked way. "He's going to have a sweet life from now on."

"I noticed Miss Weir had a new hat," said Belle. "It was remarkable-looking."

"But they always are." I offered.

Belle put her hands up and began describing it with gestures. "This front part right up straight and trimmed with pieces of ribbon from candy boxes and tufts of cotton and actually those cherries you put on Christmas trees. She looked so private and sedate coming out of church that I didn't approach her."

"But one doesn't anyway," said Wendall. "Does one?"

"Oh, sometimes I ask her about her health."

"Really? How extraordinary." I said.

"Dear," said Belle, turning to Vanessa, "will you make us some coffee?"

"Sure."

Suddenly Vanessa came running back. "Oh, and Mr. Bope

is wearing white wash vests with pearl buttons, and Jane and Julia told every one that if he does marry Miss Weir he has to buy them each a car. But they know how to get around him, they said, and they can get the cars even if he doesn't marry her."

"Oh, what's the use anyway," said Edwin.

"But Fleta's going to see about Mr. Bope."

"And what does she think she can do?" asked Edwin, facing his daughter.

"Fleta won't let him do it," she said, giving her head little positive shakes, her face looking stern and exalted. "He can't keep on the same path if she explains it to him and shows him that he is working for death instead of life. She'll force him to see. Why, she said yesterday it was our duty to save him from doing it for his own sake, not for the sake of the money but for the sake of saving him from spiritual wreckage. We really are our brother's keeper," she said softly.

"I see. And what's Mr. Bope going to be saying to all this?" asked Edwin.

"Fleta can *make* him see."

"Well, she's a remarkable woman then."

Vanessa whitened and caught her lip with her tooth. She looked at her mother for aid and Belle finally said weakly, "We all know that Fleta means well."

"Oh, it's more than that!" cried Vanessa. "Why, what good is it to live and be wonderful the way she is if no one is capable of seeing and understanding? Oh, I don't see . . ."

"That's true," said Belle, "we don't appreciate any one enough."

"But Fleta says that Mr. Bope is beginning to agree with her about spiritual things. He's been at her house almost every evening and she has been showing him things he has never seen before."

Edwin got up and went out on the porch. I followed him. He had his hands in his pockets and he was staring straight ahead. He looked so honest and shocked that something clouded over my whole life, everything I had ever enjoyed or earned or loved, and the future seemed almost too dark to contemplate. Somehow, I couldn't face Edwin's life, so I said lightly, "I'm sure you're just being pessimistic."

"He went over the whole thing. He has all the figures down plain. It almost convinced me. He's going to put the screws on us—a hundred per cent assessment—I could mortgage the house but that wouldn't be fair to Belle and Vanessa. He has us framed."

Everything around us was soft and dark and I felt suddenly that there was something hopeless about living. I always believed it was our fault if things turned out wrong and that we had the privilege of being noble and rising above misfortune, but now, standing in the dark with my brother, I was sickened down to my toes. Then suddenly in the center of me I realized that I believed in a God who dealt things out to us, who gave us some compensation for everything. If he took away money, he gave something in return; if he let us suffer for a long time, then suddenly he brought us something to pay for our misery. As I stood there I saw that I could never give up this childish, weak belief, as if there was a spiritual bookkeeper in the clouds who kept the accounts. I discovered with a strange feeling deep in me that the belief was part of me and that it was as real as my arm or throat or breast, just as Bope's money was an extension of his physical body, something he lived through and expressed himself with.

I put my hands in the dark moving leaves near the porch. "I am sure, Edwin," I began.

"Yes, so am I. I've got about a month."

"But, Edwin . . ." I was ready to tell him that he wouldn't be happy if he did have a lot of money, more than Mr. Bope or Jack Morris. I was all ready to give him one of my lectures on human values versus money values. I cannot describe what happened to me. Suddenly I saw my brother. I saw, I felt, I understood my brother as he understands himself. I understood human purposes and I turned my face away from him. Everything inside me was utterly still. I felt a quietness over us both, like death, like the clear strangeness of death. I saw my mother lying in her coffin, her white face, her white hands, that puff of tulle around her neck. I remembered telling myself that she was dead, but I couldn't believe it and I suddenly ran up to her bedroom to ask her how my hair looked in back and if I should order more potatoes. Then in the cemetery, under those bare trees with drops hanging in the cold, in that instant when they lowered the coffin, I heard a shriek. It was a deep unearthly sound, like an animal and a woman in labor, and when I realized that it had come from my mouth and that my jaws were standing open and my eyes bursting out of the sockets, I ran down the hill and through the trees and graves to a muddy field.

"Oh, it is so still to-night," I said, closing my eyes.

"Yes, Grace," he answered.

"Do you remember what mother used to tell us?" I began and then I rushed back to Wendall and Belle and Vanessa. "We must go. Yes, really. Good night. . . ."

When we got outside I put my arm through Wendall's and tried to warm me on the inside where I felt so cold, so empty. I got closer and closer as we walked. Then under the dark trees I said, "I want to see my mother to-night," and all of me was shattered and aching. We went on in silence and I remembered my mother's face in adversity, the magnificent smile, the eyes, the way she sat by the window looking over the snow piled about us with forlorn sparrows huddling in gray flocks on the white under the frozen bridal-wreath.

"Oh, Wendall," I said.

He did not speak but I felt his arm and then he said "Grace!" in that sharp direct way. His voice went straight through to me. Something new and fresh sprang to life in me, rising slowly above all the deadness in me and in the world, flying full into my breast and opening, warming me until I suddenly said his name again and kissed the back of his hand, bending to it, holding it against my cheek in gratitude. Then I lifted my face. The courtyard park was empty and silent. I saw the church ahead and the post-office and the street-lamp at the corner. The new part of me suddenly blazed out of my pores and it made me stop for a moment and look at the enormous sky and then I longed to drop down there in the mud of the gutter, my chin against his knees, and say, "Thank you—thank you—"

                                        ♦

VI

The Matt Beviers gave a dinner-party the other night and Mr. Bope was there. It was one of those parties that ends with singing around the piano and it was extraordinary to see Mr. Bope singing. Matt Bevier and I were sitting on the couch watching the others and suddenly Mr. Bope sprang across the room to the piano. His white hair blew out behind him—it is very fine and thick—and he threw back his head, stood on his heels, and opened his mouth into an enormous round O. He held it while they turned over pages and pages of music, and from time to time he would close his jaws, moisten his mouth, and then throw back his head and make that tremendous round O again. We didn't hear one sound from him but he must have been holding the same note with all his feeble strength.

Every one spoke of his spryness. When a lady dropped her handkerchief or bag he simply leapt across the room, knelt on an agile knee, and presented it to her with a bow before the other men had decided to move. He was flushed and eager, very kind and talkative and polite, but he got to discussing stocks with his host, and Mrs. Bevier had to go to them and tap them on the shoulder when Julian was ready to play some Beethoven for us.

"I—I—I—I—he was stopping at the same hotel—a millionaire—fine fellow—just as human and natural as you or I—gave me a tip on the market—" He looked into Mr. Bevier's face and rose.

"Julian is going to play," she whispered.

He began to clap vigorously, clearing his throat and bending back on his polished heels. "Very talented, very talented," he said in a whisper that we all heard.

I was fascinated, thinking of him with Miss Weir. He has made Edwin suffer so much that I was glad in my vicious heart that he was going to marry her. It would balance things up a little. Fleta was always saying she was going to investigate his wages and she had tried to do something, one way or another. Once she came to Edwin. But every time I thought of him at the piano, sending out those tremendous notes that he held with his whole strength for such a long time, his whole face goose-like and the loose flesh in his neck purple, I had to think of something sad to keep from bursting out laughing.

"Will you look at Bope," whispered Wendall to me. "He jumps around as if he's had something to drink."

"Don't, Wendall," I whispered, "I shall die, I mean it."

Mr. Bope was coming toward me rapidly. He sat down, leaning forward, and said, "Mrs. De Vries, how are those fine children of yours?"

I felt possessed. I wanted to shout, jumping up and down, "There's going to be a third, there's going to be a third." But I looked him in the eye and said, "Quite well, thank you, Mr. Bope. How are your girls?"

"Excellent. Excellent. Yes, indeed. And Edwin?"

"Not so well," I said. "He's worried."

"I see—I see—Will you excuse me, Mrs. De Vries?" He bowed. "There is something I must see our host about. It's been delightful." He sprang over to Matt. "I'm convinced we can't make a cent out of it, Bevier," I heard him say. He took out his pencil and an envelope and made some figures. "Of course that sort of thing is very nice but we'd never make a profit. Let's see. Two thousand times seventy-eight—"

"Wendell, we're going," I whispered. "Do you mind?" Then I went over to Edith. "Good night, Edith, it's been lovely."

"Yes, Edith," said Wendall, "we've had a grand time."

I walked toward the door with Edith and she said, "I've been hearing gossip. Is she really engaged? Is it true?"

"Vanessa?" I said. "Isn't it awful, Edith? Here I'm her aunt and I don't know."

"We'll have to ask Fleta," said Edith and laughed.

Wendall came then held my cape for me. When we got outside he said, "You know I'd like to be able to say something definite, seeing I'm her uncle."

"Well, I'd like to be able to at least pretend that I knew and was keeping a secret."

"What does Belle think?"

"Likes him. We all like him. He's just right for Vanessa."

"She can't see him though," said Wendall .

"I know it. But she doesn't see any one."

It was lovely and cool and dark. Wendall lighted a cigarette and we walked slowly. "You know, it's that determination to be composed and gay that makes Fleta so tragic. Lord, I wonder if it will make any difference to her when her aunt marries Bope and gives her some peace."

I screamed with laughter. I was ashamed of myself because I consider understanding and kindness very important. But every time Bope is mentioned I still see him standing on his heels, his mouth in that round empty O, his bland eyes rolled toward the ceiling. I kept on laughing even though I knew I would be punished for it. I held my hand over my mouth but still I couldn't stop laughing, I was so glad to see him as ridiculous and idiotic and helpless. Wendall was out of patience with me for it. He stands up for the men.

"Grace, for heaven's sake!"

"I shall die." I gasped, and threw back my head and laughed again.

"Well, the poor guy," he said finally. "You're merciless. He didn't look as bad as that."

"And what about Edwin? How is Edwin going to look? I'll laugh at Bope all I please."

"Now, don't be silly. Bope's business principles are sound as rock and he's a good business man—Say, isn't that Vanessa across the street?"

She had on her soft white hat and she was hurrying toward Fleta's house. During the day you expected a bird to hop out their front door but now at night the heavy flower clusters tossed on the palmy foliage and the house looked luminous and remote, as if it were breathing in the darkness of the soft grass. I could almost see Vanessa's parted moist lips as she climbed the steps, her feet reverent and shy. Then she put out her hand to ring. I called from across the street, "Hello, Vanessa!" and Wendall said, "Hi!" but she did not turn. Her head was back so that her hair came out under her and curled over the edge like blonde feathers. She clasped both hands behind her back and when the door came open she stood like that until Fleta's fingers come out to her shoulder, drawing her in.

"Good heavens, Wendall," I said. "What if she urges Vanessa to live there after her aunt goes!"

"Did you say *urges?*" said Wendall.

"And she's making the most hideous pocketbook for her. She's trying to quilt it and it's made out of some high vibration color that Fleta told her about—orchid which represents love of humanity or something like that—and one end of it is so mussed and soiled that the poor child will have to have the whole thing cleaned before she can do anything with it. She made up the design and it's full of mystic stars and circles and whirls."

"Gosh," said Wendall.

"Oh, I'm going right over there now. I don't care. I am. Perhaps I can find out what Fleta is going to do when her aunt leaves. I'll just set my foot down in case she is planning anything—"

"Don't you mix in, Grace. Listen, Grace," he said, "I don't want you to go mixing in—"

"Good-by, darling." I simply ran across under the trees and up to the black screen door. I could see them inside by the big window. I called, "Hello, may I come in?" and burst into the hall. Wendall was waiting under the firs as if he expected me to come flying out to him again, but I waved the end of my cape and while I was doing it and making rather foolish love

faces that he couldn't possibly see, Fleta came and took my hand
vaguely. I couldn't help flushing and I felt ridiculous, standing
there like a child. She didn't invite me into the living-room or
do anything but stand holding my hand, her tiny pointed face
back on her white shoulders, her ears showing beneath the
waves of netted hair, and her large sad eyes and mute mouth
close to my face.

"I was waving to Wendall," I explained. I felt like a child
who has her handkerchief pinned on her dress in front.

She glanced out into the darkness. "Won't he come in? Is
he outside?"

"No, he went home. I saw Vanessa run in and I just
impulsively came too. Do you mind?"

"Not at all. Not at all. But will you amuse yourself with a
book or something?"

"Oh, of course. But are you sure I'm not intruding?"

"Come," she said. "Oh, you have such a handsome husband.
He is one of the best-looking men in town. I always notice him
when he walks to the bridge sometimes with your little children."

I knew that my clothes were all right, that my hair was as
nice as it can be made to look, and that I was completely all
right from the outside. But as I watched her face, with the mute
pity shining out on me, I knew that something inside me was
wrong. I knew then that I was pathetic in a way I didn't even
glimpse, that Wendall was handsome and pathetic and that the
children were, too. There was something pitiful about us but I
couldn't imagine what it was. I felt ragged and torn, like an
angel who has been dragged like a muddy branch through wet
gutters.

"I'll sit down here," I said, "If you don't mind. I want to
see this book. I've been looking forward to it." I sank down
without glancing at Vanessa and I wondered what sad fate there
was in life for us all, not in material things or circumstance, but
inside us, something tragic that I couldn't name or fully believe
in with my Christian optimism.

Suddenly I felt cold. I could see empty corridors and bleak

entry ways and street-cars filled with people waiting to get off but never, never getting off. I could see trains with huge engines plunging through the country with no destination, the smoke pouring over green fields and blackening white houses and transitory cattle staring, their hoofs fastened deep in futile mud. I opened the book and bent over it as if I were deeply interested, but I saw only frightening machines and people standing in the rain without umbrellas waiting for something. I resented it because I don't believe in futility, questioning, but I had no mind of my own then. And my own eager face was gone and in my breast was that tormented mute pitying mouth with the large eyes above, the ears gleaming, and the crests of hair rising under the loose net.

"Father won't go to him," murmured Vanessa. "He says it won't do any good. He says nothing will do any good."

"I wonder."

"But Daddy says he's just as helpless as the other men in the company. He says they're all going to get done in, robbed—"

Fleta got up and went to the couch. She stood with one hand on the tufted arm and the other out vaguely in the air, the polished nails held together like the shining beak of a bird. "I know, I know, I know."

Vanessa raised her shoulders, her tranced head back, her high white forehead gleaming with little fine dangles of hair from her half-grown fringe. "Please show Aunt Grace your new picture, Fleta. I want her to see the little boy with the pail."

Fleta laughed. "No one really wants or cares to see my pictures." She smiled at me graciously and settled her lace in a cold, composed way, one grayed tooth caught in her lower lip. "They always ask what they are of."

"Oh," cried Vanessa, rising, her hands twisted together, "but you would be the one to understand that, Fleta. You would be the only one on earth to see how pitiful they are, not knowing what it all means, and not having an interpretation of life and a goal. Why, Fleta, how can you laugh? Why, you are the only one who understands about those things. I've never, never been the same since that time when the man who was selling coffee came in and looked at your abstraction and said, "What's it mean?" and then just perspired and fairly groaned. Don't you remember? And you said that we all feed on the trampled empty husks instead of the golden ears."

"Good heavens, Vanessa, is it possible I said that? Grace, forgive me if I did. Vanessa, you forgive me too."

"But it's beautiful! It's noble!"

"Yes," she said tenderly, "and rather like a large gray goose."

"But you've never been this way before," said Vanessa slowly, in horror. "Oh, I want to go, I can't bear to be here, I want to go home."

Fleta caught her arm, laughing again, throwing back her head, her eyes half closed. "No, no, don't go. We're going to have some lemonade. Grace, you are an authority on cooking. Will you supervise this mixture? We want it to be good." She giggled then, looking me in the eye, and fastening up a strand of hair. "I am sure my lemonade needs supervision."

We went into the tiny kitchen and Fleta handed me the lemons. "I really ought to go home," I said. "I've been to a party."

"I thought you had been somewhere. You look extremely nice." She laughed suddenly. "I didn't mean it that way, Grace. Here's the ice but we mustn't make any noise on account of my aunt. She is sleeping just above." Then she and Vanessa stood looking out the kitchen door into the dark.

"Could a person if she tried real hard bring a great gift to all?" asked Vanessa in a desperate voice. "Could a person work and work and be worthy in time to serve humanity?"

"Yes, darling, I think so. You could. You can. No, you are doing it already."

Vanessa shook her head impatiently. "No, not yet, not yet. But the thing to do is to keep our eyes on the vision. We must work toward that end and toward seeing the hidden

struggling part in every one. We must not see what we feel but
what things really are and mean."

"Right, darling."

Vanessa gave a tremendous sign, as if dimly she felt some
restriction on herself after such a statement. She laid one hand
over her burning cheek and slowly rubbed her tongue up and
down on her large front tooth.

"How many lemons shall I use?"

"Oh, nine or ten. Four probably. As many as it takes. I
really have no idea. Oh, have you seen how heavenly it is to-
night, Grace? Why don't we all love one another until—"

I dropped the knife. "Until we start singing together all
over the earth, with our arms out and our heads up, shouting
exactly like angels until God actually hears us."

"Well, I wouldn't care to have my arms out," said Fleta,
"or my head rolled back. I think I could stand quite still and
feel I was doing it just as well. No?"

"That would mean almost nothing to me."

"But what has the body to do with it?" she murmured, and
when I started to speak she turned her back and pressed down
the edge of the run. "The sugar is in this little tub. I don't like
mine very sweet. How about you, Vanessa?"

"What? Oh, I don't care for any. I'm not thinking about
food."

"But you will take a glass if Grace goes to all the trouble
of making it, won't you?"

"But you put in the sugar, Fleta, and it will be worth
drinking."

"I like that," I said. "Thanks a lot. I just adore your pretty
sayings, Vanessa."

"Don't mention it, Aunt Grace. You're all right."

They stood facing the darkness and Fleta suddenly said, "I
wish your father would have a serious talk with Mr. Bope. There
is something very exquisite there."

"Somehow he doesn't seem like the type that wants to
work for humanity, though," said Vanessa.

"Perhaps none of us has ever seen him," she said gently. "Had you thought of that? You know we don't understand the slightest thing about each other."

"But *we* do, Fleta."

"Yes, we do."

"As soon as the ice melts and it's cold we can have it," I said. I put the pitcher on a tray and walked lightly for fear of waking that old witch up-stairs. But I had a feeling she would appear some time before our departure. We all sat down and suddenly Fleta pointed to a face on the magazine cover. She gave a horrid little laugh and said, "My, I'm glad I'm not married to *that*."

"Or this," said Vanessa, turning it over eagerly.

"Or this thing that looks like a gorilla."

"Or this perfect bull."

"Or this rather sly gentleman in the hairline stripe. Ugh, see those soft white hands and that mustache. Pretty awful, isn't it?"

"Or this—or this—or this—or any one," said Vanessa, closing the magazine with a bang and crowding her fist down on it.

There was something puzzled and willful about Fleta's expression then. She half smiled, then her lips moved as if she were about to speak.

I handed each of them a glass of lemonade. "How nice," they said at once. Then they sat down on the couch together and asked me about the party. "Who was there?"

"Mr. Bope," I said.

"Isn't it strange," said Fleta quickly, bending over her folded hands, the cold glass beside her on a small table, "isn't it strange that no matter what you paint it isn't ever the thing you meant to paint? It's never the great thing you think you are painting? *Never.*"

"Oh, yours, Fleta," cried Vanessa, "Oh, every one of yours is. I want to be a great painter like you when I see them. Oh, I feel as if I am a great painter just when I see that little boy with the pail. That meant everything to me. It means there's hope for something more than this materialism and viciousness and greed and dishonesty." She looked straight ahead of her, the light shining on her young face, her nose tilted, and those crazy fine hairs dancing on her grave forehead. "I am changed into something magnificent when I look at your pictures. But it hurts me," she said suddenly. "I hurt. I don't know why. I hurt. Now she turned her whole body to the woman. "Did you like Robert?" She snatched a book and began turning the leaves.

"Robert? Robert? Do I know a Robert?"

"Why, Fleta, you said he was nice."

"Not that little man with the brown eyes."

"Oh, *no.*"

"Yes, I think I do remember—I think I almost—"

Vanessa walked over to the window in silence. I drank slowly. Finally she turned. "Do you think a person would be making—do you think a young girl, for example, a young girl would be making a big mistake in life, for example—" She rubbed her hand over her forehead as if she felt dazed at her own words. "Would a person be able to help toward a new world and marry too?"

"Some think they can," said Fleta. "People claim it can be done."

"What would your opinion of Robert be if some one asked you what you thought of him?"

"I think he's exactly what he appears to be—a nice lad. There's something rather exquisite there and fine, of course, but that's not enough." She sighed impatiently. "I'm so eager for you to get through wasting your time with young fellows like that who are merely nice, agreeable, and a few other things. He's not good enough for you," she said shortly.

"Robert is a darling," I put in quickly. "He's about the finest boy in the world."

"Yes, I know, Mrs. De Vries. But I suppose I'd think no man was good enough for Vanessa." She gazed at me for a second as if I had no place in their world. "You see I have always felt like her mother."

"You mean that I am better than Robert?" asked Vanessa slowly.

"My dear, don't let's talk about Robert. I'm not saying anything against the little chap. It's just that some day you will look back at the whole thing and laugh."

"Then you'd say I'm not in love?" she questioned. She stood there horrified and silent, her arms straight at her sides, her face toward Fleta.

"I would most assuredly say you weren't. Love comes like an eagle."

"An eagle," she murmured. She moistened her lips. "And do you feel sure night and day and all the time?"

"Utterly. And no one can influence you or change you. You are certain."

"If I could do it quickly without thinking—I guess if I marry I'll have to do it that way," she said wretchedly.

"Not if you're marrying the right person. Why, darling, you've years and years before you. Some day some one magnificent and remarkable will come and help you do all the things you're living for and must live for."

"I feel as if I want to be a wife when I'm with him—"

"Well, look around at a few wives. Look at the wives here in this town."

"A wife is like a bird," she cried. "They are beautiful— they are so—so—"

"Does Mrs. McGeehee look like a bird? Or Mrs. Bulgren? Have they done anything for the world by being just wives? It's all absurd because you don't know what you're likely to get into. You know nature does strange things with us if we aren't watching all the time."

I burst out laughing but they didn't look at me. I even said, "But that's our trouble. We're too watchful. We're either that or being watched." Fleta heard but she didn't look up.

Finally she said, "The lemonade is very good, Grace. And

don't feel that I'm being personal. My talk sounds very rude indeed but you understand."

"I really don't," I replied but she took no notice of it.

"Would a young girl like me, or, I mean, any young girl," Vanessa began and raised her chest for a second, holding it until her frightened eyes fairly stood out of her head, "would a young girl who had my ideas and who married be likely to take to dope or drink if she married the wrong man and had her idealism destroyed in a single night, on her marriage night, for example," she added, flushing, holding her hand over her cheek again. "For example, if a man couldn't see the fine idealism in a young girl, would she be utterly destroyed from a single contact with him? What I mean is—do we become like the thing we love? Do we become base if what we love is base? Well, Leonardo said that in his note-book."

"My darling, it's just that I—" She burst out laughing. "You must excuse me, Vanessa, but I can't help laughing at the thought of you and that little fellow. Somehow, the thought of you with your fineness coupled with that little man—"

"There is something wonderful about Robert," she said as if it were an act of will.

Fleta sighed. "I don't doubt that. That is true of every one on earth. I'm not saying that he isn't a splendid little fellow for any girl in town. But for you—well, you know what I believe you are—"

Vanessa twisted herself to the side of the couch, dragging her fist across her eye, and then pounding it softly on her lap. Suddenly she drew up her breath with a great jerk of her chest and clenched her jaws, the tears starting out of her eyes.

"But we've had the crisis," said Fleta icily.

Vanessa did not move. Then she bent over her lap and stared at her thumbs, her lips closed tightly as if she were holding her breath. Sweat sparkled out under the little bunches of hair on her forehead and she bent lower, her arms gripped over her waist as if her stomach hurt.

"We're divided now. The way you acted about the cake.

The way you told your aunt what I had said to you in confidence. But the pupil always rebels and then transcends the master. Why does the master always resent it so much and suffer over it? It's something to be radiant and grateful about, happier than you have ever been." Fleta's grayed tooth showed on the edge of her lip. She held her head firm, her fingers, with their long polished nails, feeling of one another forlornly. "You must transcend me, Vanessa. You must make me see how worthless I am and how—Oh, you must really be what my pictures will never be. You must be what I thought they were going to be. All my life I've seen something and believed in it and tried to paint it but it never, never came out that way and what I did—was always nothing at all. But, Vanessa, darling, you are the real thing and you are going to be happy—if you will do what I say."

The girl rose unsteadily. She put her hand up in one of those vague, helpless gestures, as if she were wiping webs off her face or felt amazed that her fingers could touch real flesh. She swallowed so that it jerked her whole body. Even her flowered dress looked mute with all the tiny blossoms on it and the broad velvet under her breast. She tried to smile and then she glanced away, clenching one hand. Suddenly she knelt down on the carpet, gazing across at Fleta, her hands up, her face toward the woman. "Please tell me I'm not as good as Robert!"

"My darling child, don't be absurd."

"Tell me, tell me I'm beneath him—and every one—or I can't love—I can't—love—"

Fleta looked down at her fingers. "Perhaps you are beneath him," she said coldly. "Perhaps I haven't understood you. Perhaps you are just a girl like any other girl in this town or any other town and I'm just putting my own wishes on you. But I did see something. I *do* see it. There is *something*, Vanessa, I am sure of that."

"Really, Vanessa, it's time to go," I said. I got up feeling too angry and wracked to do or say anything important.

"I thought you had come to the place where you had

escaped karma and where you could choose and live and be perfect without all these mistakes and sufferings and pointless tragedies and violences. But it may be you aren't ready and that in your inner self you feel that and are warning me not to harm you with my high conception. It probably means you aren't ready." She turned her face away, her cheeks grayed, her hands folded.

"Come on," I said. *"Vanessa!"* I plunged toward the door, my cape gripped around me. "I'm going." I muttered, and tripped over the edge of a rug. Fleta turned and looked at me as if she didn't remember who I was. She stared for an instant, as strange as a bird with her small pointed face and her polished beaked hands. "Just a moment," she said. "I want to say something to Vanessa, if you will excuse me."

I went into the hall and stood by the big door. I was pounding my toe without knowing it and smoothing my hair in back and looking straight into a dark tiny glass above a table without seeing myself or knowing I was looking in at my blurred dark cheeks and eyes. Then I looked at the ceiling, calming my mind, staring at the empty flat space. Bending over the stairway was that figure I had expected to see. She wore an enormous gray flannel nightgown that had deep cuffs trimmed with pink tatting and a big quaker collar that met the full gathered top of the sleeves. Her bloodless ears showed below the strands of thin hair turned over rags and she held her lower jaw out, the lip drawn down so that the teeth shone grimly. I caught her eye. I knew then that she saw me, that she had been looking straight at me, and a shudder went down me through every notch in my spine. I bowed and muttered, "How do you do?" like a formula for the aged. I saw her clenched hands, bony and purple under the full cuffs, and then she shoved away in her long gray felt slippers with pointed ratlike toes. I sprang into the sitting-room, catching hold of the curtain, my lips drawn down and no breath in me.

Vanessa stood with her head forward, her arms at her sides, her eyes on Fleta. The woman was speaking while her mouth twitched and red lines came in little patches around it and under the eyes. Her hands were tightly clasped in her lap. She sat rigid, chin up, those little ears shining beneath the waves.

"If I have disappointed you, Vanessa. . . . Oh, of course I have disappointed you time and again. I'm not going to pretend that I haven't. But if I could only give you something in payment for all this. . . . Oh, could anything make up for my not being all you think I am?" She rose. "You don't even know that I've failed you." She was still rigid, looking straight into the girl's confused, frightened face. "But your love makes me feel very, very quiet, like sitting somewhere all alone and not thinking of anything, just closing my eyes."

Vanessa reached for a piece of paper. She moistened her lips and sat down on the floor before Fleta, a black thick pencil in her hand. She laid the paper on the bare floor and she drew quickly, her tranced face determined, her large eyes suddenly cold and strange. Now her jaws were clenched and she looked up quickly and then down at her paper, glancing impersonally, her arm moving as if all her will were in it. Once she seemed to shift her sight, as if there was a possibility of sudden confusion and defeat clutching her and making that hand tear it apart. Then she bent lower over her paper, her teeth pressing her lip, the wild little hairs on her brow swept together in damp tails.

I was standing in an uncomfortable position but I did not move, even though I was more and more aware of my leg aching and all the hornets of heaven and hell seemed suddenly to sting my heel. In my discomfort I saw for the first time that Fleta's chin wasn't firm, that soon the flesh would hang gray and soft like moss, and that it would shake as she spoke. I saw that her hair was thin and that she certainly tinted it. But all of this made her ravaged lovely face more beautiful than it had ever been, and the shine of her eyes, like something inside her looking out in fright and dismay, too strange to describe or try to understand. Then Vanessa jumped up and thrust her picture into Fleta's hand. She waited, her lips tight again as if she could not breathe until she heard the answer. Suddenly she clasped her hands before her as Fleta does, lifted her face, and with indescribable earnestness and pain said distinctly, "Am I a great artist?"

A strand of hair had fallen over Fleta's face. She did not hesitate. "Yes," she said with determination.

I went toward them. I looked over Fleta's shoulder at the drawing. It was made with many short blurred lines, some of them redrawn and not erased. It was sharp and almost piercing. But somehow it was Fleta even though Vanessa thought she had drawn an angel, a beautiful bare face shorn of experience, shining mildly from the eyes and the too delicate, lovely lips. It was really Fleta and in one corner was a great smudged print of Vanessa's thumb, like the definite earthly seal of her will. Or perhaps I put this into it. Did I see from the eyes that were drawn rather crookedly under the brows, Fleta's look of fear, as if sin were all about her and the way of life would change her from a pearl to an empty trampled husk if she reached out with her body toward the real sun, the real flesh of man that brings us whether we care for it or not, to what we are, to our real selves?

Fleta looked at me. I remembered suddenly that she hadn't asked me for my opinion of the sketch. She looked into me. She did not move. Then she said, loving the universe with her eyes as if we were all clasped together, "Help me take care of her!" And I cried out in a different voice, with different eyes, holding my body firm and restrained, feeling my blood and bones vanish, standing like a wraith, an empty cherub, "I will. I will."

VII

Belle and Edwin couldn't see anything in the picture that even dimly resembled Fleta. When Vanessa had left the room Edwin said it was a shame not to be able to nourish the budding genius in one's own child but that he, for one, had the spirit of truth in him and a social spirit as well that would prevent him from ever urging her to paint or draw. Belle was hurt and worried over it. She insisted that it wasn't as bad as Edwin made out and that she did see something in it but not very much. They both looked so worried that they made me feel slightly deranged. But I liked that sketch. Perhaps it was because I knew how Vanessa felt when she doubled her fists over her chest and bent over her paper with a torrent in her that held all her parts together in agony and awe as she drew.

Edwin held the drawing off and took out his pencil, pointing to the bird hair, the serene brown cheeks and mouth. "God," he said, "I'm afraid Vannie's painted a picture of what she's going to become. That's why it worries me such a lot."

"Robert telephoned three times last night long distance," said Belle. "I didn't like to connect him with Fleta's but I suppose I should have done it."

"Yes, you really should," I said, "but it wouldn't have done any good."

"Now if Vannie is going to start in painting those damned bowls of flowers, and those pots of daisies and sad pansies for women's magazines, I swear I'm going to do something desperate." He walked up and down in front of the fireplace. "You know a man can't stand everything. But I've had every kind of bitterness and failure a man could have. Lord, I know every hour of the day just what kind of failure I am."

"Don't be selfish," said Belle. "Please, Edwin. Now *don't!*" She went over to him and took the sketch out of his hand. "I'm going to put this away."

"I wouldn't do that," I said. "Vanessa will be insane if you do. Don't say anything about it except that it is interesting."

"Interesting!" said Edwin. "Good Lord, woman, won't it be interesting if she starts in copying Fleta's pictures and turns out to be a childless, manless, lost—God," he repeated, and held his head.

"But Fleta does draw out of every one a perfectly radiant power of expression," I said. "Really, I have felt it too."

Edwin shook his head like a great bear and simply plunged

out of the room. Belle said, "He's almost wild. I've had such a time with him. You know he had a talk with Mr. Bope and everything is going to be horrible. Imagine it. Our Neighbor. I went to grade school with Pliny. Our pews were right together in church. He's our most dignified elder. You know that, Grace. But—"

"It isn't really dishonest," I said. "Wendall said it wasn't."

"But is it neighborly? He knows he could save Edwin and all the others but he wants to run the thing himself. He's putting in a lot of money and instead of buying us out he's just taking whatever we have."

"But the company is bankrupt, Belle," I said.

"What if it is! He's rich. Edwin said he was just as hard and hypocritical as he could be and Edwin outlined a plan to be used so that every one would be saved but he just laughed at it. Oh, when I think of getting up in school with Pliny and reciting together and then being so near him in church—I can't think—I don't know *what* to think."

"I know," I said, "I know just how you feel."

Vanessa came down with her hands full of papers. Apparently she had been drawing every second of the time since she left Fleta the night before. She shook them in my face and I saw a series of older angels, their cheeks filled in with sooty smudges and their large eyes staring out of the blank paper. But even in that glance I could feel something alive in them, as if in Vanessa there was something so extremely alive that it flooded the lines she drew, even the uncertain ones, with a kind of immediate livingness. They were almost as good as Byron's and Myrna's, and when I say that I am paying Vanessa a compliment, because everything my children make on paper, and I don't care what any one says, everything they make is alive, and if they make a tiger it does roar out of its crayon cage, or if it is a princess stepping along on frozen glass toes you can actually hear the little gusts of sighs coming from the blue velvet bosom.

"Darling," said Belle, "I thought you promised to clean your room this morning."

"Can't, Mother. Sorry. But I'm going to take these to Fleta. Look how many I did!" she cried.

"Oh, please stay at home for this once and help me with the cleaning. Please, Vannie."

Vanessa opened her lips. She looked outraged and pale, her eyes seared around the lashes as if she hadn't slept in weeks. "Mother," she said sternly, "you may not know it or care but I am a great artist. I am greater than you even imagine and — Oh, I can't help it if you don't understand—I can't help what you and Daddy think of me or the low things you have in mind for me to do. I am *determined!*" she cried.

"Come on, I'll take you around," I said. "I have the car this morning. Come on."

"Are Byron and Myrna out there?"

"Of course," I said. "Come on. She'll be right back, Belle," I promised.

"I wish Daddy and Mother *could* understand."

"They're horribly worried."

"Well, Aunt Grace, I think I'd forget material things if I had a child who was going to be great. I know I would. I'd simply worship that great talent and give my life toward furthering it, because think what a great artist can do for humanity."

She didn't speak again until we got to Fleta's and then she ordered us to wait and not to move. "And don't bring Myrna and Byron in even if she invites you," she insisted. I had to giggle and she laughed a little herself, rubbing one smudged hand over her eye.

But Fleta was at her bedroom window and she called out to us to come in, and when she saw Byron and Myrna she leaned out and made noises to them like a bird. They flapped their arms and hopped up the walk before I could pretend we had to go to the market.

"Now, it's going to be just hideous," said Vanessa. "Those children always spoil everything. You don't mind my saying this, Aunt Grace," she said, and took hold of my arm warmly. "I love them of course when I don't give them a thought. You know how it is."

"Sometime," I said, "I shall be really angry without being able to help it when I suddenly remember all these insults to my darling children."

"Oh, no you won't," she said carelessly, "you're sensible. You know too much to do that."

"Hello!" cried Fleta.

I am sure she was fresh from her meditation and Yogi breathing because she looked all loosened and moist around the face, dewed about the eyes and mouth. She kissed the children on the hair and Myrna put up her hand instantly and felt of the spot. We stood together in the doorway and Vanessa, waiting for more privacy, held the papers behind her.

"And do you want another picnic soon?" asked Fleta, kneeling to them.

"No," said Byron, "I hurted my toe."

"I'll make you another princess," said Myrna. "I'll make you one with longer hair and flowers and a castle. I can."

"Oh, Auntie, dear," called Fleta, "have you seen that little book of mine called 'A Light on the Pathway'? I want to loan it to Mrs. De Vries."

"I can't keep track of all your crazy books." she snapped. As she swept past us I got the odor of crackling singed flesh, like a fowl, and I saw instantly Vanessa's horrified description of those bony arms held out over the gas.

"I shouldn't have left it around," said Fleta. She gave her sad little laugh. "I'm so sorry, darling."

"Say, all I want is for you to quit puttin' me in the wrong with your nice talk."

Fleta gasped. Then she smiled, turning to us. "Isn't it strange that with all our discipline and effort we are likely to grow more selfish? I mean this. It's never right to even be kind if it makes some one else appear to be in the wrong. Isn't that true?"

"I've told you six times now, Fleta Bain, that Oxford is calling you long distance."

"Oh, excuse me, please."

"May I wait, Fleta? Would you have time to see something?"

Fleta paused. Something strange flashed across her face. She caught her lip for a second. "I don't believe so to-day, darling. Some other time. I'm so busy. Good-by, every one."

Vanessa choked and then she rushed down the steps, her head lowered, and ran toward the car. I caught hold of Myrna, who was following Fleta to the phone, and I heard the beloved auntie say, "Might better be at her painting making money instead of dragging all the young 'uns in the town over to ramp on my rugs."

Fleta had the receiver to her ear but she turned. "Darling, I'll buy you some beautfiul new ones. Hello, hello, hello. I *must* have it this afternoon. I'm leaving town."

I opened the screen and pushed the children out on the porch. Fleta called again to her aunt. I heard—"some lovely new ones, darling," and then her aunt replied, in a tone calculated to reach the river bridge, "Well, they'll all turn on you in payment for your sympathy. You see."

We simply huddled together and hopped down the walk as fast as we could, feeling rather guilty and strange. Even the children lowered their heads and got into the car without saying a word. Vanessa was in a corner, cold and lost, crowded against the plush. I got in without speaking and we drove away. That evening I went out on the porch for the paper. Jackie Gunsaulus usually rides his wheel up the bank and it's cutting a deep rut in the lawn. I thought I had caught him this time but the paper was folded in a packet and laid in the mail-box. I went inside with it and sat down by the table. I remember fixing some flowers that had come out of the water and were drooping down on the scarf. Then I leaned back. I read almost at once: "To-day, at the home of Miss Clavira Weir, 512 East Eleventh Street, was solemnized the marriage of Miss Fleta Bain and Mr. Pliny Bope, prominent citizen and owner of the local gas works."

I read it again. I walked into the kitchen and put on the kettle. I always do that mechanically when there has been an accident. I reread it. I glanced at other things in the paper and went back to it. Even yet it didn't seem like news and I couldn't connect it with Fleta. I read it for the fourth time but my mind wouldn't clamp over it and make meaning. It stayed apart, hanging like veils above the substance, refusing to mix and change. Very rapidly I caught up our old Persian with the long white eyebrows and whiskers, and washed his face with my handkerchief. Then I took him back to the kitchen and made him a big dish of corn bread, bits of cold bacon, and cream.

"Well, this is something like it," said Wendall when he came home. He carried the paper at arm's length, simply beaming at me. "It's about time. So that's what was happening and we didn't catch on."

"I don't know what is going to happen to Vanessa."

"The best thing in the world for Vanessa. Positively. You know that yourself."

"But she's going to suffer so much, Wendall," I said. "I— I—hate to even imagine what she will have to go through."

"Nonsense, she'll get over it. She'll come through it a lot better than to keep fastening and growing on to that starved woman. Fleta's better off too. But, Lord, I can't imagine it. It certainly does give a man a jolt to think of it." He opened the paper and read it aloud.

"I'm not feeling very well," I said.

I hurried into the bedroom. In some way I felt connected to Vanessa and it was as if at that instant she had seen the paper. Something inside me moved. I lay down on the bed and when Wendall came I said, "Really, darling, I feel as if I'm going to lose the baby."

My eyes felt strange and then it seemed as if everything inside me was pushing out. I felt so frightened that I caught hold of him, half moaning, and he said over and over, "Never mind, it's nothing, nothing. Just lie down, darling, lie back. That's right. That's right."

I let my head sink down and suddenly I started to cry and I can swear to you that it wasn't myself that was crying. It was nothing that I knew as myself. It was as if Vanessa lay inside me in all her youth, cold, pale, without breath, waiting, waiting for an unearthly torrent of grief to wrench her apart with scalding pain. Just for a second she lay inside me instead of the child and I felt somewhere a terrifying burning light that springs up from the bowels of the earth, through feet, body, and then in the last gasp of consciousness, pours like a silver stream out the mouth. "Oh, Christ," I cried aloud and vomited, strangling and crying, my head limp and pale, his face so close that I breathed in his breath through my acrid sour nostrils. "I'm better now," I said. "I feel all right now. I'm better. Please get me a drink—"

I went to Edwin's the next morning and they were all in the dining-room eating breakfast. Belle had on a blue morning dress and she looked thin and as if she hadn't slept. Edwin was scowling, his eyes set off on something far away. I tried not to look at Vanessa. I tried to ignore her and ask Belle how she was feeling, but suddenly I saw her. She glanced at her mother mutely, as if partially dumb, her eyes straining wide in her face. She had a round comb in the front of her hair and all the little funny fringe was held back in the teeth. Her blue sweater had a round neck and there was something so tender about her skin there under her throat. She looked at me for a second and then at her father, then she glanced at her plate, moving her eyes as she looked at the knife and fork, the spoons and goblet. She picked up her knife and then she laid it down, staring at it as if she was trying to remember something. She examined a place on the spoon and then laid it down, shoving it back and forth on the cloth, her forehead drawn so that her brows met. She moved her head to the side as if in that position she might remember something she had forgotten.

Edwin poured syrup on his cakes and finally said, cutting off a mouthful, "Well, Fleta's played her last card I see. Got married at fifty-one."

"Yes," murmured Belle. "Amazing, wasn't it."

"Well, one thing, she won't paint any more of those God-awful pansies," said Edwin. "We're going to have some compensation in that. No more pansies or verbenas or trailing arbutus for the delicate-minded."

Vanessa did not move. She selected a warm cake and buttered it, with stiff definite movements. Then she cut off a small piece and put it into her mouth, chewing slowly, her eyes ahead, all serene except for the way her eyebrows met above her nose, as if she were trying to remember.

"Bope's good for ten years more but his love of money has made an old man out of him. That barracks he lives in is no better than a hotel. Every damned room in it is like a furniture store."

"I'm feeling rather strange about it myself," I said.

He turned to Vanessa almost savagely. "Now you can see what is to own your own soul for a change. This is a lesson to you to always own yourself and be yourself and run yourself and not be afraid of anybody or God or the devil. I'd thank you for the sugar, Belle." He ran his fingers over his lips and swallowed.

"Don't let's get into an atmosphere now," said Belle.

"What about?" asked Vanessa.

"Please excuse me, Belle. Belle, I am asking you to please excuse me," said Edwin harshly.

"Dear, order that white paint as you pass Dowling's. Will you?"

"All right."

"Vanessa," I said, "won't you come for a little ride with me? I'm going out to the farm for eggs."

"Run along, dear," said Belle. "Please go with Aunt Grace."

Vanessa looked at me and then she glanced away. She looked at her mother and the table and the garden. "I don't believe I'll go this morning, Aunt Grace," she said.

"Oh, darling, come on," I urged.

"Yes, Vanessa, it will do you good."

"I think I won't go, Aunt Grace."

"Now you'll hurt my feelings if you don't. You really will this time."

She got up from the table and went out of the room. We heard her slowly climbing the stairs. I didn't see her again until the following day. I rushed over with a cake I had baked for Belle and I met Edwin in the garden. He was stone gray around the mouth and his clothes looked too big for him. He stooped as if already it was too hard for him to hold himself erect and when I asked him what was wrong he said, "Oh, nothing more than I had expected all along. Bope has done us all in. I can't go into the new company without mortgaging my home and I won't do that. I've worked all my damned life and here's what I get. Lord, I know now that there's a heaven because there must be some place where justice is. And it isn't on earth, so it must be in heaven." He looked at me coldly, as if he had forgotten I was his sister. He looked as if he hadn't a wife and a daughter and home and garden. He ground his teeth and then he turned his back. I ran away from him into the kitchen.

The dishes were standing on the table and there were some soft papers rolled together in a ball that they had used for cleaning off the food. The tea-kettle was steaming violently and the dish-pan was in the sink with the goblets soaking in the suds. There was a great soapy clot on the towel that looked as if some one had wiped her dripping bubbly hands hurriedly. I went on through the pantry and dining-room to the living-room. "Belle," I called, "it's me."

I opened the door into the sitting-room and I saw Belle leaning against the wall, her face bleached with shock, and her hands pounded against her blue work dress. The whole room was still and stark and cold. Vanessa stood near the piano, her arms at her sides, her face staring ahead. Just from the way she stood I knew that her mind could not hold for long the consciousness of her pain. She breathed quickly in a little sharp gasp when she saw me and lowered her face, as if now all the force and terror of her grief had passed into her bones, stretching them apart, filling her flesh; then suddenly her body was not large enough to hold it and she fell on the floor.

"Get some water, Belle. Vanessa! Vanessa! Quick! Oh, open your eyes! Water, water, please, quick, some water. Darling, oh, my little girl, please, please . . ."

VIII

Clackie Weir didn't come inside the church again that summer. She didn't ever wear her gay frightful hat with the Christmas-tree cherries and the tufts of cotton and lavender candy-box ribbons. Every one in town had a passion to call on her about two weeks after Fleta's wedding and at first she opened the door to them but later she never went down, no matter how hard or how long they rang. Mrs. Gunsaulus said, "Well, how'd she know I wasn't a telegram that her sister died." But nothing brought her to the door. She worked around her nasturtiums by the elm tree, her gingham bonnet with the starched cape hiding her face, and the only mention of Fleta that she made to any one was, "Living in the same house with that saint put a strain on every organ in my whole body."

One day I saw her in the drug-store giving Eddie Jevens a lecture because the gall-bladder medicine she took had been raised ten cents a bottle. "I don't mind paying, you understand," she said, "but it's being held up that I object to. I can't help myself. I have to take it or leave it. How do I know whether that's the real price or not?" She stopped buying her medicine. Mr. Jevens told us that she had been getting it for the last fifteen years and now she stopped. She dug up all the pansies. She didn't even go to the door when the minister came.

But as soon as Fleta came back from her honeymoon the Bope car was at Miss Weir's door every day. The Bope cook carried in pails of soup, baskets of cooked food, and Fleta brought even chairs and flowers. I saw Fleta one morning just stepping out of the big car, her arms filled with flowered curtain material for her aunt. She caught her breath when she recognized me and then she came straight toward me, dropping the material and holding out her hand. The skin under her chin had loosened and fallen and she was very pale with dark deep circles under her large eyes. But she came toward me with adorable swiftness and put her hand into mine. "*How* are your little children?" she asked. Now she came close to me, standing with that same composure, as if there were no time. Her eyes, above the ravaged cheeks and delicate strange lips, still held their pity and fear of sin. Then she smiled enchantingly. "Byron and—is it Myrna?" she said. "How are the tigers? Has she made a new princess for me? I do love those glass slippers she makes them wear and the castle in the background. Don't you love a castle? Except for the labor involved and the exploitation of workers. But I think they are *nice*," she ended and smiled a little sad smile. "I see you are hurrying along in the other direction, Mrs. De Vries, and I am keeping you. Are you well?"

"I am very well," I said, "very well indeed, thank you."

"Oh, that's splendid. But aren't we all well no matter what we think? Isn't wellness in the head, Mrs. De Vries? Isn't youth in the head, too? I'm *sure* of that now."

I nodded and she gathered up her materials and stepped up the walk on her high-heeled satin slippers with large steel buckles. She wore a pale green georgette gown with very short sleeves and a transparent slip that revealed her young-looking calves and hips. It was a strange costume for morning but when I remembered her bunched, tight-belted atrocities, her waists of commonplace material, I felt glad. She turned when she reached the porch and called back to me, "Your hair looks so lovely in the sun, Mrs. De Vries. I'm just standing here and loving it."

I was very much aware of her not mentioning Vanessa. I think she was aware of not speaking to her too. And around her mouth had been a new expression, not the worn compassionate delicacy of her lips but a hard, almost pert willfulness that matched her short skirt and transparent slip. She had run into the house with that light but determined air, practical and yet appearing to accomplish nothing and to have no purpose beyond leaning toward either the rising or the setting sun, one palm over her cheek, muttering, "Aren't we all brothers, aren't we all one?"

Vanessa was staying at my house because Edwin and Belle wanted to get her away from the rather bitter atmosphere at home. They felt too defeated and sad to keep up appearances and they didn't want to saturate her, and perhaps mark her, with their own hopelessness just then. So she spent her week-ends from college mostly with me. That evening some of our friends were in the living-room with us playing bridge and Vanessa was sitting near the window, her fingers on the curtain, staring out at the dark bushes. The men were laughing and the room was filled with cigar smoke. Suddenly the telephone rang. I went. It was Fleta. "I want to speak with Vanessa, please," she said.

"Of course, Fleta, I'll call her."

I went to the door. "Vanessa," I said, "Fleta wants to speak to you."

She did not move. Then she crowded herself down in the chair, gripped the arms, and shook her head.

"Why, Vanessa," I cried, "she's waiting."

She did not answer.

"Oh, come and just say hello," I begged.

She shook her head, her lips drawn together.

"But you must, Vanessa!"

She half raised herself in the chair with the effort to speak. "I can't."

I went back to the telephone and somehow Fleta's voice reminded me of that time when her aunt shut the door in our faces. I could see perfectly Fleta's eager pointed face at the front window, waving with pitifully forced composure at us.

"Oh, Fleta, are you there?" I said. "I'm so sorry but Vanessa will call you later. She's—she's—washing her hair and can't very well leave."

"Oh, don't bother her, Mrs. De Vries. Tell her it was nothing. I just thought of her and I wanted to say hello."

"I'm sorry, Fleta."

"Good-by," she said sharply and before I could put up the receiver she said, "How are the children? I'm so glad. And yourself? Spendid. And, Mrs. De Vries, tell Vanessa she needn't bother to call me. It was nothing at all important."

Vanessa was sitting forced down in her chair. When I came into the room she pressed her palms over her eyes. Then she said, "Oh, I loathe her, I hate her, I don't care if hating her keeps me from God, I don't care if it makes me go to hell, I'll keep on hating her and loathing her and knowing that I'm going to hell for it, too. I'll keep on forever, I'll never give up hating her."

"Well, I do think Fleta should have told Vanessa she was going to be married," said Evelyn in her casual voice that makes any strong emotion seem ridiculous. "I really do. What kind of hand have you, Art? Good. No, I really do. I think after Vanessa had been so intimate with Fleta, like a daughter and all that sort of thing, that she might have told her."

"I didn't want to be told," said Vanessa.

"Of course you did," said Evelyn. "If she'd let you stand up with her everything would have been all right. I was really quite surprised. Every one was. We all thought she was—I mean we all knew she must be devoted to you, Vanessa."

"Oh, yes?" drawled Vanessa.

"Sit down with me and help me play," I said.

She burst out laughing. "Did you know that she wears green georgette now in the morning and satin slippers? That's to attract her savior of humanity with."

There was a shocked silence.

"She tells lies," said Vanessa. Her handkerchief was rolled into a ball in her hands and she kept scraping her lower lip with her teeth so that the veins in her neck stood out. "She sent every one in town a card with Whittier's birthplace on it—but me." She laughed and opened a magazine on the table. She stared at me as if she had been mumbling in her sleep and then her expression changed and she clenched her hands in front of her and said, "I don't care if I rot in hell. I don't care if I never can love again or paint or draw. I would rather hate her than ever be happy again. If hating her means that I shall be separated always from—from—humanity"—she brought out with a choke— "All right, I don't care, I'll hate her until I die no matter what the price is. And she knew all the time what Mr. Bope was going to do to Daddy and she didn't make one move to stop him."

"Oh, I have a lovely joke," said Evelyn. "Perfectly lovely since we're being low. My cook heard that Fleta and Mr. Bope used to spoon under the lamp every evening and the people next door saw them—isn't it killing—and so now they sit in the dark for hours. Can you *imagine* it? Those two." She broke into laughter, covering her mouth with her hand. Then she took out her handkerchief and wiped her lips, breaking down again when she met Arthur's eye.

I looked at Vanessa. She was biting her lip and staring down at her fingers. She was feeling of them forlornly, holding them in the same tender way Fleta always held hers, knocking and smoothing the long nails. When she saw me looking at her she began to laugh.

"Make us something to drink," I whispered to her. "The oranges and lemons are on top of the ice-box."

"What?" she said.

"Come here."

"Sorry. Awfully sorry, Aunt Grace, but I'm going for a walk. Bye, every one." She stood still with one hand up in imitation of a gay little casual farewell and then that sound came from her lips. It raised me out of my chair. Evelyn turned. The men looked down at their cards. It came as if she didn't know it was her voice, like my own that time in the cemetery when my mother was being lowered into the ground. I sprang out of my chair and went to her. For a second it seemed as if she could not move. Then she ran swiftly out of the house.

"Excuse me a moment," I said.

She stood near the banked bridal-wreath that hung in those

soft white ropes, curved down to the dark grass. She had her hands in the cool faces and leaves and her head was lowered so that her hair swept down over her cheeks. Far in her throat, deep, as if it came from that same place where all those startling cries of labor come from, she was murmuring, "O my God, O my God, O my God, O my God, O my God," all in the same tone, eyes closed, hands out mutely.

"Darling," I said, "oh, please don't ever talk in front of Evelyn. Just Wendall and me. Please. They don't understand. Please."

It was very still. She moistened her lips and opened her eyes, lifting them to me, still with that angelic adoring look she unconsciously had when she gazed up at any one. "I don't believe what I say about her but I can't stop."

"But you must!"

"I can't. I want to go out and tell the whole world. I want to tell every one on earth. I want to spend my whole life telling them that she is a loathsome, damnable, despicable—liar." Then she clasped her hands in front of her and looked quickly all around, drawing up her breath. "Oh, Aunt Grace, but what if she isn't—what is she really *isn't*—"

I heard a great peal of laughter from the house and Evelyn's high scream. Arthur was simply howling and then there was the sound of cards being shuffled, like little sharp gun-shots.

"We're waiting for you, Gracie," called Marshall.

"Coming," I said.

"I think I'll go around and see Daddy," she said. Again she lifted her arm stiffly, her face turned away from me, and said, "Bye."

IX

One morning I found Vanessa in the garden picking flowers. She had a great pile of phlox that she had brought over from her house and she was cutting my white daisies and some delphiniums. "You don't mind, do you?" she said. She sat down on the grass and dropped the garden shears into her lap.

"Why didn't I go to the telephone?" she said. "Oh, I couldn't."

"Put in some of the baby's-breath, it looks charming with the phlox."

"I couldn't move, I *couldn't* have spoken." She bent her head and then she pulled on my arm, "Aunt Grace, when I woke up this morning I could feel her breathing and I was breathing and every one else in the world was. I'm going to take her some flowers."

"Well, that's nice."

"I kind of hate to go alone," she whispered, "I'm so afraid I'll meet those hateful girls. I just loathe them."

"I'll take you over," I said. "I promised Fleta some of those large lily-of-the-valley bulbs. I hate having them mowed down every time the grass is cut and there are a lot spreading out from the bed."

"And do you think it looks all right to take these?" She gathered them together and looked at me over them, her eyes very earnest and sad.

"It will be lovely. Come on. I'll take you right over."

We went around to find the spade so that I could get the bulbs but Wendall had set it away somewhere. So I told Mrs. Weston to take the children for a walk and we started.

"Suppose some one wronged some one she loved very much and would die under a car to save but she couldn't be sure what the person really was and so she changed all the time and said horrible things—could a person make it all up in time to the person she had wronged?" She looked into my face eagerly. "Could she? Do other people?"

"You know what they say about time," I said. "Time heals all wounds and all that sort of thing. We forget after a while."

"But do *they* forget? No, Aunt Grace, I can't take these flowers to her. I'm not worthy to give her anything. Really." She put them in the back seat and sat rigid. "I have no right

when I spurned her gracious advance toward me. Oh, why when
I knew how she loves humanity, why did I have to hurt her like
that, just like her horrible aunt was always doing. Oh, when we
went on picnics she always looked up at the hospital and
wondered if the people inside were feeling sicker because we
were having a good time."

"And then what," I said, "what did you do then?"

"But she always decided that they would enjoy it more and
be grateful that we were out there having a good time even if
they couldn't be."

"Well, that was optimistic of her," I said.

"Oh, Aunt Grace," she said and put her hand over her
mouth.

We got out and went up the steps to the porch. I rang. A
very severe-looking maid with a boil opened the door. "Mrs.
Bope will be right in. Won't you sit down?"

The room looked as if the furniture had been pushed into
every conceivable position to make the place seem more livable
and intimate. A little stiff table had been pulled against a large
remote armchair and over the fireplace hung one of Fleta's flower
pieces. Vanessa went straight up to it and gazed. She turned to
me, her eyes filled with tears, and shook her head, as if she
could not speak. "You see everything she does," she brought
out, "everything is a gift to people and how many of us can see
what she means or the beauty in them?"

I couldn't look at the picture because I kept forgetting I
was looking at it. I saw the lamps. She was filling it up with
lamps. They stood there, lonely and ornate, sending out their
futile light on the imitation mosaic, the early American desks,
Tudor walls, and Florentine leather. But I kept seeing Fleta
directing the rearranging. I kept seeing her with that measureless
love of harmony and quiet, that passion to be happy and
exclusive, ordering the imitation tapestry to be hung on the east
wall and then for a few hours feeling complete and at rest, as if
it was all more wholesome and intimate now. Then another
morning I could see her supervising the moving of the chairs,

warding off the cold and empty spaces in that room by bringing
in more lamps. I saw Fleta for the first time as uneasy in her
heart, not sure of herself, incomplete.

"Can't you see how she *loved* these petals when she made
them?" asked Vanessa. "You can tell. They are so warm and
real."

Fleta came toward us. She looked at Vanessa and then she
came straight toward me, holding out her hand. "How do you
do, Mrs. De Vries?" she said. "Hello, Vanessa. Do sit down.
I'm so sorry to have made you wait. Isn't it a perfectly heavenly
day?"

"I am about to bring you some of those giant lily-of-the-
valley bulbs you said you wanted."

"Well, how sweet of you, Mrs. De Vries. I shall put them
in my garden."

Vanessa sat down. Beside her was a table with a huge
leather Florentine box on it. There were two lamps behind her
head. She moved uncomfortably and then folded her hands in
her lap, gazing at the toe of her slipper.

"Have you been well, Vanessa?" asked Fleta, glancing at
her.

I caught my breath. It grew still. Vanessa lowered her
head, picking at her fingers, her feet rigid. She did not answer
or move.

"How are your little children, Mrs. De Vries, little Byron
and Myrna?"

"Oh, they're always well, you know."

"How fortunate you are."

I didn't know what to say next. I didn't know what Vanessa
would say or do and so I looked around and smiled and said,
"This is a lovely home."

"Yes, isn't it," said Fleta. "There's something so—Oh, as
if one had dreamed it or imagined it when one was a little girl
and full of anticipation."

Vanessa jumped up. "Fleta, why do I hate it?" she cried.
"Why do I hope in my heart, all the time, so that it's eating

me up, that this house will burn down or the roof will leak and spoil the ceilings?" She steadied herself now with her hand on the back of the couch. "Why do I feel glad you can't raise any flowers?"

"Oh, my darling, but look at them!" she cried and threw open the French window. "I *can* raise flowers."

They stood in straight rows, in full bloom, newly transplanted from a greenhouse. Vanessa glanced at them and then she went over to Fleta. She stood in front of her looking up. "Would a person be able to make it up to some one she had wronged? Would she be able to give up her life to the person to make up for the violence and the betrayal? Oh, can it be done? Or doesn't the other person want it any more?" She opened her mouth and caught her lip with her teeth. "I thought I would always be with you and we would work to make humanity—better," she said.

"Sssssh," said Fleta with a delicious listening look coming over her face. "Listen. It's a whippoorwill," she whispered. "I heard him last night, too. Delicious." She drew Vanessa toward her. "Listen. Did you get it? Simply delicious."

"I don't think so," said Vanessa. "And it's a wren anyway."

Fleta laughed. "Well, let's talk about you then. We'll talk about Vanessa, Mrs. De Vries, shall we? I was coming to you anyway, darling, because I have a thrilling plan. You know, Mrs. De Vries, you always emphasized cooking and housework so much for Vanessa and I was wondering— Oh, would you do this, Vanessa? I wonder if I dare ask it or even suggest it? It would be so wonderful for me. And we'd have time to read together. I'm reading a history of oriental philosophy that is one of the greatest things since Plato, one of the most charged things I have ever touched. Exquisite. Well, would you consider coming here and helping me, darling? I told Ella that she deserved a month's vacation and I sent her away yesterday morning."

"Oh, now really, Fleta," I said, "that's not going to be possible."

She lifted her hand. "As an experiment? Just for the

experience? Just to know? Well, why isn't it possible?"

"Would a person be able that way to pay back the evil he had done to some one he loved—loves—loved—thought he—really loves—would it be possible to show through devoted service—"

I was furious. "Fleta, I know Edwin and Belle would never let her come. I know that."

"But if it is going to develop her? I thought you were so enthusiastic about domesticity, Mrs. De Vries?"

"But I don't dare even think of telling Edwin and Belle. No after what has happened," I said and looked into the fireplace. I couldn't meet her eyes. I felt horribly gnarled to even bring it into the conversation and I felt sure, at that moment, that Edwin had made up the story about Bope's hypocrisy and treachery to the others.

"I wanted to speak to you about that," she said. "You know Mr. Bope did one of the most generous things I have ever heard of. He didn't ask the members of the company to share his failure, he let them out, and he took the burden of reorganization and loss on himself. The night he made up his mind to do it Mr. Lewis got down on his knees in the meeting and prayed. He thanked God that some one was left in the modern world who would sacrifice himself for the people and who would be generous and brotherly." Her eyes filled and she pressed her handkerchief to her lips. Then she turned to Vanessa. "I know how ugly it looks from the outside but I know the inside of it and I see that Mr. Bope has done one of the most highly spiritualized things I have ever witnessed."

"I'll see that you get the bulbs," I said and got up.

"Vanessa, dear," she said, taking her hand, "think it over. Let's both be maids and wear caps and aprons and find out what we are making our sisters do. Let's! She pressed her hands together as if she wanted to feel airy and gay and smiled enchantingly. "Let's."

"If a person could wipe away the guilt—"

"Nonsense," she said. "We don't know anything about guilt."

"I do. I have it. If a person could make right the awful wound—"

"But I have no wounds," she said, laughing, lifting her tortured, ravaged face. "I can't be hurt. Really. It's something I've worked on for a long time. No one can hurt me. I won't permit it. I'm so proud of it that I shall probably be punished for feeling satisfied."

Vanessa stared at her in the most infinite love and confusion, all the violence and resentment washed away, her eyes fixed on Fleta's face, her whole body leaning toward the woman's. Pliny Bope stood in the doorway.

"Ready, dear?" he said. "Oh, excuse me, I didn't notice you had guests." He came toward me, adjusting his glasses, his polished slender shoes sinking into the rug. He was safe and happy with a white piping in his dead-black vest. He put out his hand generously. "Well, how are you, Mrs. De Vries? It's mighty fine to see you again. How's Wendall? Well, well, isn't that fine. And here's Vanessa. How do you do, Vanessa? Don't you know me any more?" He went close to her, smiling graciously, and took her hand. "I'm so glad to see you here. You know I'm mighty nervous for fear Fleta's friends won't like me. And I want to measure up. Don't I, darling?" he said and laughed. "Of course I do. I'm mighty glad you came, Vanessa. Come often."

I moved toward the door, my feet plowing over the rug, and Vanessa followed looking cold and strange. We came face to face with the Bope twins at the door, Jane and Julia. They were in blue with white hats and gloves. Vanessa deliberately pushed against Jane.

"My word!"

"Good heavens, you needn't shove us off our own porch, Vanessa Bodley."

"Oh, come in, daughters," said Fleta gently. She kissed them and took their hats off.

"My word, Mother, she acts as if this porch was hers."

"Ssssssssh."

"Come, girlies, let's forget it."

"Well, Daddy, I want twenty-five dollars."

"What for?"

"Well, I need it," she cried and flopped in a hall chair.

"Vanessa," cried Fleta, "Vanessa, darling, are we going to do it? Together?"

"I don't know."

"Say yes. We'll read and talk and find out more about life."

Vanessa whitened. Then she said slowly, "I want to come."

"Spendid. And shall I telephone your parents about it?"

"Please don't."

Fleta flushed and followed us out on the porch. "Oh, I hope there isn't any misunderstanding. I asked Pliny to speak to your father but he wouldn't. Naturally after doing what he has done he wouldn't want to. You know I've always felt that there was deep good in people that they simply couldn't show to the world and now I've seen it." She looked at us sadly and triumphantly, her large eyes suddenly earnest and grateful. "It makes me feel so silent."

"But, Daddy!" cried Jane.

"No, we're spending too much money. Our electric bill alone . . . Laundry . . . Telephone. I'm not made of money, you know, even if all I do is write checks. I tell you I've go to call a halt somewhere. I'm under terrific expense just now." He came out into the arched doorway. "Well, I'm glad to have seen you," he said. "I suppose I sound like an old miser moaning over my bills." He laughed. "This wedding trip wasn't done on any small scale, either, was it darling? But it was worth it," he said boyishly.

She leaned toward him slightly, her eyes closing a little, and said, "Oh, *yes!*"

Jane and Julia came up behind him and jerked on his shoulders with their blunt fingers. "Well, Daddy, where do we come in?"

He swung round. "You spend a quiet day at home," he advised them.

"Then shall I send the car for your things, Vanessa?"

"Yes."

"Vanessa, Vanessa," I said under my breath.

"But if I can make it up to her," she whispered, "if I can wash away my guilt for the things I've felt and said. Oh, I feel like a Judas. I've betrayed her in front of those people and she has never changed toward me at all. Oh, when I think of what she longed for me to become and the way I repaid her. No, I'm going. I'm going to ask to scrub even."

"Well," I said, "if she is really in need of help I doubt if you will stay very long."

"This isn't practical, Aunt Grace. This is an experiment. This is my big chance to wipe away my sin and if I fail—"

"And look at all those lovely flowers," I said. "I can't see why after you'd picked them you couldn't have handed them to her."

She pressed back the hair from her eyes and laid one hand over her ear, looking off into the distance. "A person has to be worthy to give gifts. A person has to—" And then she threw her arms around me and cried, "Oh, when I'm purified, when I'm free from this remorse, oh, would a person then be ready to help humanity to a higher road?"

We got out at Belle's and I went in with Vanessa. Belle was ironing, Vanessa went up to her and kissed her ear. "I'll do the tablecloths," she said, "then I have to pack."

"Good heavens, now what!"

"Mamma, you created me, of course, but she did too and I must be forgiven. Oh, when I die," she said, rolling back her eyes and laying her fingers under her chin, "when I'm dying I want to know that my soul is inside her and I am safe."

"Oh, for heaven's sake," said Belle. She heaved a deep hurt sigh. "All she wants to do is keep you on the rack. Let her alone."

"She wants to free me from this remorse and she took this

way of doing it. There is a purpose behind it all."

"But what have *you* done to her?"

"Oh, why didn't I force myself to the telephone that night? Why have I told those dreadful things about her? Why? Oh, when a person possesses you one ought to feel it all and suffer and be happy and polite—polite—I'm not—Oh, I haven't politeness."

"What is this great guilt of yours?" I said.

"Everything in me. Every word from any one brings up my guilt. I think all the time of how she must have suffered when I didn't understand and stand by the way a real friend does. I've just learned that. But I don't know her yet and I want to know her—all of what she is—"

"And she doesn't intend you to know her," said Belle. "She doesn't want you to because she's cruel at heart. She intends to keep every one on the rack who ever doubted her for an instant and if you can't idealize her she won't notice you. She wants to be thought unselfish and good and if you don't do it she will punish you eternally, or just as long as you will let her."

"If I believed that with my soul I would go insane. I know— I know— Oh, I won't accept her as a sinner like me."

"Then you're very selfish."

She ran up stairs.

"Oh, Belle," I said, "don't let her go. She's going to work for Fleta—housework. Please don't let her go. Oh, I'm going to find Edwin right away. Please, Belle, do something."

"What?" she asked.

"Something—anything—lock her up—anything—"

"I can't do a thing. Neither can Edwin."

"No, I suppose you can't," I said. "I suppose we have to let her go."

"Yes."

"She'd go anyway."

"Yes."

"Even Edwin couldn't do anything."

"No."

"Her own father."

"No."

X

"Darling, won't you arrange the flowers?" said Fleta the first day. And the second day she said, "Dear, there are some dishes to be wiped and poor Annie is so rushed." "Vanessa," she said on the third day, "Vanessa, would you put on a little cap and apron and answer the door?" And the fourth day she said, "Vanessa, would you make a cake? Why, dear, of course it will be good. You always made such delicious cakes. Of course it will be splendid. Come, I'm having guests and Annie has all the rest of the lunch to do. Come, brace up, and have faith in your powers. You can, of course you can, and I'll make one myself on Friday and we'll make it a contest."

"When—when are we going to talk about immortality?" asked Vanessa, pushing back the white organdy cap with the black bow on the side. "When are we going to be together and talk about time and space?"

"Well, on Friday I'm going to Chicago and Sunday I shall be home and on Monday we can surely have an hour together."

"I want two hours—I want more—Oh, I never see you—"

Fleta stiffened. Vanessa told me that she felt then as if she had been mercilessly greedy in asking for two hours. Then Fleta smiled and held out her hand. "Good-by, dear," she said vaguely, "I'm going to see old Gramma Hodges. I promised to take her some fresh spinach. Now *will* you take Auntie her soup this morning?"

Vanessa shook her head.

"Why not?"

"I don't want to go there now. I don't want—I don't like to—"

She said that Fleta sighed shortly and looked straight at her. "Good heavens, what difference does it make whether you want to or like to? If a thing is there to be done—Well, Vanessa," she said, biting her lip, "if you could ever see— Oh, if just for once you could forget yourself and see the immortal—yes, the immortal soul of that woman you would never be able to even remember such superficial, material things as liking and disliking. All you see anywhere is yourself. Yourself."

"Oh, I don't like it here," cried Vanessa and ran to the back of the house. "Annie," she cried to the cook, "when is Agnes coming back, for heaven's sake. I can't stand it much longer. When is she coming?" she asked and balanced herself against the gleaming sink. "Tell me it's soon because I can't stand—this—"

"Agnes?" said Annie, turning, a large spoon in her hand. "Why, Agnes isn't coming back."

"Oh, I can't remember her crazy name." Vanessa rubbed her hand over her head. "I can't remember anything." Suddenly she went toward the woman and stood stiffly, her head laid against her large shelflike breast. "Annie, why is the road to spiritual fulfillment so hard? Why, oh, why, do we forget what others are and only know ourselves and our love and what we want? Annie, am I the only one that feels that way and wants so much just like a selfish monstrous animal that begs and begs to be loved all the time? Oh, who was that girl, who was here— I can't even remember her name. The one before me."

"Her name was Agnes."

"Well, I thought it was."

"Agnes Feiss. She went home to Muirville."

"When is her vacation over? I can't hold out for more than two days longer. I wish I could go right now. Oh, I wish I could go to the tracks and lay myself down with my head on the rail and let the train come." She pressed her hand on her eyes and lowered her head.

"Agnes ain't coming back."

"I mean the Agnes who worked here as a maid. I didn't ever meet her but her name was Agnes."

"What did Mrs. tell you?"

"She said Agnes was so tired that she let her have a little vacation."

Annie shook her head, drawing the wind up through an empty tooth, and said, "Agnes went that day for good. She left her cold without an hour's notice."

Vanessa turned and ran out of the kitchen. She rushed up the stairs to her hot little attic room. She picked up a paper and wrote, "You *were* afraid of the cows that day. You try to make me think you are good but you tell lies all the time. You want me to work here because you don't really love me and you aren't doing it for my good. You are worse than the lowest on earth." She groaned aloud. "You are worse than an honest thief and an honest liar and an honest killer. You are a betrayer of ideals! Love from Vanessa." She erased it, sobbing in her throat, and then as she read over the note she rewrote it, "Love from Vanessa." She erased it again and put down, "Faithfully yours, faithfully always, I would die under a truck for you," and then she erased it and wrote merely "Vanessa." But in the corner she wrote in small letters, "If I have wronged you and if I am just seeing my own self, then I can't help it. I will suffer all my life for it. If I have misjudged you I think I will cut off my head." She folded it and crammed it into an envelope. Before she went to Fleta's room with it she wrote on the edge of the envelope, "You are gentle. I am rough. I can't help it." As she told it all to me later, she said that when she had written that on the envelope she stood still looking down at the table and she felt something in between her breasts crack. She pressed her hands over it and the pain pulled her down until her chin touched the bed and it drew her further, until her legs were drawn up and her face was on the bare varnished floor.

When she got up she said her mouth tasted like zinc and there was a kind of evil bubbling in her chest and her legs felt empty of blood and flesh. She stepped much higher than was necessary, as if the carpet was as thick as a stair step, and she laid the note on Fleta's desk. Then she went down and tried to make the cake with Swansdown cake flour and butter substitute. "Oh, Annie, could you help me cream this?" she said and ground the butter and sugar together, the bowl on the top of her knee. "Oh, it won't be good. I only made a few in my life and it won't be good." And when it was made she said, "I'll cover it with frosting and this soft torn part won't show." And when she had the icing on, it was so hard and sugary that she beat up some cream and simply threw it over the top and down the sides. "I wish I had some lovely flowers for a wreath," she said, and then she put it into the cupboard as quickly as possible and made sure that it was out of her sight.

Later Fleta came into the kitchen. She had on a white georgette gown with little capes on the shoulders that flung out behind her like wings and she had white slippers on her tiny warm feet and her hair was in a great mysterious net on top of her head with those fine ears gleaming beneath the waves. She simply ran to Vanessa who sat drooped on a kitchen stool and laid her cool hand on Vanessa's head.

"How warm you are!" she murmured.

Vanessa did not move.

"Come, let's sit on the porch for a minute and get you cooled off."

Vanessa bent over her knees, stiffened.

"Come. I have a new book by the author of 'A Light on the Pathway.' Come, dear. Oh, Annie, it's so warm, isn't it. I feel positively treacherous making you two stay out here in the heat. Why do we have to have parties and meals anyway?"

Vanessa looked at Fleta. Her lips parted and she gazed into the softened, benign face, the gracious partly opened hands. Then she suddenly lowered her face again. "Oh, you tell lies," she said stonily.

Fleta bent over her. "Lies?" she asked gently. "Did I ever tell *you* a lie?"

"Oh, I believe you do tell them, I know you do."

"When did I ever tell you a lie?"

Vanessa raised her face to Fleta without speaking.

"Well, perhaps, I sometimes do tell one to save some one else. Is that so bad of me?"

"Why do you try to make yourself out so good?"

"Sometimes we can only make others good by doing wrong or seeming to do wrong. Isn't it worth it, Vanessa?"

"But we must never *lie*," said Vanessa. "You taught me that."

Fleta drew her onto the little porch at the back. She looked into her face, pushing the damp hair back from the white forehead. Then she ran her polished forefinger over the end of Vanessa's small upturned nose and suddenly turned away. "Why are you always—always—so adorable?" she said, gazing down at the rows of phlox with their dank sour leaves drooping to the sod. "I've always been you—*you*—from the beginning. I've been through all of it with you." She raised her handkerchief and put it to her lips. "When you said those dreadful things about me I suffered because I knew how *you* would suffer over it later. . . ."

"I wrote you a note—" she cried, pushing her hand over her forehead. "You didn't read it—you mustn't—I want it back!"

"I did see a note on my desk but I haven't had time to read it, darling."

"Oh, thank God. Oh, Christ, thank you," she murmured and ran.

She snatched it off the table and flew to her room. She fell on the bed saying desperately, "What am I? What am I to have thought such things about her? Oh, when I'm so vile—so low—oh, I didn't deserve to have her understand and forgive me." Then she quieted herself and it seemed for an instant as she remembered that strange deep look of love on Fleta's face that all her guilt was gone. She chided herself then for the frosting and the torn places. She closed her eyes, letting her body relax on the hard hot mattress. "Forgive me for hating Jane and Julia. They too have immortal souls," she mumbled. Suddenly she sprang up and reached for the note to rip it into a million pieces with her teeth. She glanced down at the flap as she tore it apart. She pressed her finger over it. Then she took it to the light. She saw that it had been opened and resealed. She saw the wrinkles at one end, the thumb mark, and a drop of foreign glue.

XI

The day Vanessa went to Chicago to make her fortune she came to say good-by to us. It made me remember the day, the morning in September, when I had started off, my chest simply raised with the voice that I meant to send out into the world. I meant that voice to rush into every heart, every head, every body, and make them all new. I meant it to make singing, gorgeous deep notes and cries of pain and joy in all who heard. Then I imagined as I stood on the platform with my mother and Edwin, that all the plain little strapped trunks, some of them bound with ropes, held the souls of those very people who had packed them, and I imagined the ropes bursting off, the locks flying open, and those stern cold teachers stepping out into the light of day. I seemed to kiss the trunks as they passed, all loaded on a truck, a man with a bent back and black face pulling them and glowering ahead at the coal yards. I remember thinking, "You too. I shall sing for you. You will sing for me. And all over the world, all over the earth, we shall stop and sing together."

Vanessa had done up her hair. She wore a new suit that she had made and part of the bastings were still in the hem. I made her stand over near me and I pulled them out. She looked at me sternly.

"Now, Aunt Grace," she said, "I hope you aren't going to go on and on having these babies all the time. Really, I think this one is going to be enough."

I laughed. "I want to populate the earth with singers," I said.

"Well, it's too bad Byron and Myrna haven't contributed anything yet in the way of superb voices," she said. "Of course in time they may. Well, I hope they do and I'm going to send them each something nice from Chicago." She repeated Chicago with her head back and her eyes raised. She made a soft sweet sound in her throat, rather sad but full and deep, and then she clasped her hands over her breast and said, "If tragedy contributes to one's understanding and makes one better able to help humanity, then—then—I guess I don't mind what I've been through—"

"It does," I said, "of course it does. And you're going to—" but I couldn't finish. She turned to me with that quick earnest look. I couldn't go on and say—"you're going to do great things in Chicago, Vanessa"—I couldn't.

We stood there awkwardly and then she said, "I want to ask you a question, Aunt Grace."

"Yes, of course, dear, of course."

"No, this is a hard one. I want the truth." She bent for a second to look down at her shoe and she pressed her toe over the little block of deep red in the rug. "Oh, do you think it would turn out that another—another man will fall in love with me, Aunt Grace?" Now she looked into my face. "Could any one else be in love with me some time?"

"Of course, of course. Oh, yes, darling, yes, yes...."

"I hope I never see Robert again. Fleta spoiled Robert for me. He never looked the same after she said that—after she called him 'a nice little fellow' in that funny voice. I hope I don't ever see him."

"But perhaps you're different now—both of you."

"Yes, I'm different." She looked at me with that scared appealing face. Then she put her cheek toward my lips. "I guess I'd better go now," she said. "I just wanted you to see my suit. You've been in Chicago and you can tell if I'll look all right there."

"Oh, you do, darling. You look lovely—lovely—"

"Well, I mean by the highest standards, Aunt Grace. I

mean do I look all right to be with those—Oh, I guess I'll go. But you know sometimes I wonder if Orestes was ever cleansed from the guilt of killing his mother." She put her hands over her face suddenly. "I've killed my mother." Then she jerked her head up and said, "I'll see you at the station," smiling a little sad smile.

"Yes, dear, I'll be there."

Now she cleared her throat elaborately, blinking, her white fingers on her neck, and then she tried to speak in her bright laughing voice. "Before I go I want you to promise me not to be quite so productive. I think that one new baby a year is enough and remember—no more twins!"

"All right, darling," I said. "I'll do anything you say."

She laughed. "And if I should take to dope or drink, you can use me as a bad example to your growing children."

Then she ran out the door, her miserably fitting coat bunched out over the shoulders, the seam on top standing up like a tiny growth. She went straight to Fleta's, straight up the stiff walk and rang. A young girl admitted her.

"Is Mrs. Bope busy? Could I see her? Will you ask her if Vanessa Bodley can see her for a minute?"

The girl hesitated. "Mrs. Bope is very busy. Can't I have her telephone you?"

"Please ask her if she will see me for just a minute, not more than a minute."

"Well . . ."

"Tell her I'm going away this afternoon—to Chicago—for a long, long time—"

"All right. Just be seated," said the girl more willingly.

Fleta came into the room after half an hour. Vanessa said that her face was like gray stone. She had on a short white dress that exposed her firm youthful legs to the knee. On her head was a white crepe sport hat, turned up in front, the kind of hat that a doting mother would find in the débutante room of a large department store. She put out her hand, not smiling, and turned her face away as she stood under a large lamp with a stiff parchment shade. Vanessa kept looking into her face.

"I'm going to Chicago to-day."

Fleta glanced up. "Really, Vanessa? How wonderful!"

"Yes," she answered faintly.

The woman moved to the table and opened a little book. "Here," she said, "is a book by the author of 'A Light on the Pathway.' It is one of the most highly spiritualized studies I have ever seen. It is simply charged with higher significance."

"Oh, perhaps you don't care, but I'm getting an understanding of you, Fleta. I can almost say now what you really are—"

Fleta drew up her shoulders and started rapidly out of the room. "I have something to show you."

Vanessa told me that when Fleta said that, just as if there were still things she saved to show and explain to her, she felt as if her whole self burst open inside her. She crossed the floor into the studio and when Fleta handed her a photograph of a young man she held the picture without looking at it and gazed into Fleta's gray face under her jaunty youthful hat.

"He painted those things you used to like so much. It's Jerome."

"Is this what he looks like? Oh, I thought he would be different. He looks so kind of faint and chinless."

Fleta drew the photograph away. She folded it and laid it in a drawer. "Even so there is something very exquisite there." She stood near the window and looked out. "He has that deep respect for life."

"What is that?"

Fleta raised her face and looked straight ahead. "He has that kindliness of appraisal. He couldn't ever hurt any one. He would never be violent and destroy life or destroy a fine sensitive relationship. He has too deep a respect for the spirit—he is like my husband—"

"I'm not like that," said Vanessa. "I'm violent. I haven't politeness or respect or casualness."

Fleta gave a little laugh. "I'd never noticed. He always sees

people as better and more noble than they really are. My husband
is that way, too. His only suffering is that he will belittle some
one, hurt some one, by not seeing what is noble and great and
lovely in her."

"You mean that I don't! You mean that I am just the
opposite and you're telling me in that roundabout way—"

"Why, Vanessa, such a thought had never entered my
head. You weren't in my thoughts at all. But you're always self-
centered—always. It's so terribly disconcerting to be with you.
I never know any more *what* you are imagining and attributing
to me. No, really, I never know from day to day what vision
you have conjured up and called me—me—"

"Oh, but when you love you want to know the person,
you have to know what she is, what she is made of. Oh, you
have to know all—all—"

"Of course. But when you can walk with a lovely radiant
creature, why be aware only of the flaws and the small parts and
the evil? Why not see the angel instead of the other, even
though the other is there? Why do you waste your time denying
the beauty to accept the ugliness? And you deny the celestial
and radiant to brood over the animal part, the ugly part."

"No, that isn't the ugly part, it isn't!"

Fleta shrugged. "When I was a girl those theories about
the body were just in vogue. It's time we had a change. It's too
bad you can't be standing with those who are working for the
next thing instead of waiting with the mass that— Oh, people
are mad, they're mad."

"But does maturity mean telling lies? Does it mean you are
able to? Oh, do you have to tell lies to adapt yourself to a larger,
better world?"

"A lie is never an adjustment," Fleta said firmly.

"But what are you supposed to do? Do you have to pretend
things?"

"I don't know what you're talking about, Vanessa. Pretense
is always a vice. It's a waste of time."

"But—but—" she said miserably. "Oh, I hadn't planned it

this way. I thought it would be different. I thought you would be and I would be and I would always—always remember—my last— Oh, Fleta!"

"Aren't there more important things in the world than ourselves?" said Fleta sternly. "Why must we talk about ourselves all the time?"

"So I can understand. Oh, so I can *know* for sure what you are. I do try to understand and accept it. I really do." Vanessa turned her face away and then she said suddenly, turning to the woman again, "If you would only tell me one thing I did that hurt you so that I could make it up and know that you cared."

"Why should you want to know that?"

Vanessa's lips came open, she backed away. "Oh, when you look so cold and hard I feel as if you may be on a plane with me and I can't"—she bent over swallowing, pressing her lips tightly—"I can't—I won't accept—that."

It was still. They heard the lawn-mower from outside. A bird sang. Fleta glanced out the window and then she turned. She clasped her hands in front of her and now that earnest strange look burned out of her cold face and she swept back a strand of hair into the coy white hat with the diamond pin in front.

"Twice you hurt me," she said very low. "That morning you wouldn't take Aunt Clackie the soup." She laid her fingers over her lips for a second. "You refused to see her reality. You accepted what was obvious and you didn't look for the other, the real part of her. I counted on you to give her something." She choked in her throat. "I counted on you to bring her that other message. She is hungry for the real things and the important things and it seemed as if you failed me then."

"Oh, but she didn't like me," murmured Vanessa. "She..."

Fleta looked at her sadly. "Liking doesn't matter, you know. It's what we can give." She glanced around the room and that boundless love came into her face as she looked at her possessions, the imitation mahogany, the manufactured antiques, the hideous lamps that stood forlorn and lonely like gaunt people in a wooden inarticulate universe. "And I wanted—to share— all this beauty with you. I wanted you to love it with me and tell me"—she paused and tears came into her eyes—"tell me that it is lovely."

Vanessa said that suddenly she felt uplifted, exalted, as if she understood everything in the world. She moved into the center of the room and stared at the furniture until her eyes seemed washed of her personal vision. She stared until she felt blinded. Then she put out her arms and said to herself, "Oh, Vanessa, take this furniture into your mind, these walls, the flowers, the curtains. Take this day into your body, the trees bending over the opened windows, the soft day-air puffing and blowing, the great tufted foliage of bushes and plants below all smooth and deep. Take the breathing of the world into your breathing, relax and let this air of God puff slowly over your bones. Sink then, sink away, until only the bright spark of you is left, the burning star of you that travels the universe and can enter any house, any body, any heart—"

She turned quickly and now like a great tearing pain she saw Fleta's sharp little hat, her composed features, the complacent fall of her hands against the short skirt. It seemed to her in that moment of torment that her whole soul was breaking open and that she must ease it in the old way with stinging words that brought down burning tears and the momentary relief of weakness. She felt the dark giddiness coming over her and she knew that in another instant there would be no choice. But it seemed to her that she would die if she did not hurl out her revenge, her gigantic wound, and her lips slowly opened. Then in a second she bent her head, forcing her mouth shut, her hands clenched at her sides. And now the little hat, the skirt, and the ravaged, beautiful face—the hands, the body, the eternal spirit— were woven together in great pain. She bent lower, her eyes still closed, and she dropped to her knees as she had that day in the wood at the picnic, and touched her lips to the toe of Fleta's shoe. Then she stood up. She put out her hand, her eyes fully opened on Fleta.

"So you're going to Chicago!"

"Oh, Fleta—good-by—good-by—"

GISELA

To Jessie Gruner

S HE liked to sit there and think of the things she wanted. She wanted glasses because Isabel Van Buskirk, her best friend, wore them. She wanted an accordion-pleated dress, a red one, with an ivory lace collar and a big velvet bow in back with the lace draping over it. She wanted cloth top shoes with patent leather bottoms and black pearl buttons fastening them up to the white—pure white—ribbed stockings. But her mother said only little girls with younger sisters could have accordian-pleated dresses. Virginia Coleman had one and first she wore it on a tiny yoke with the pleats up under her arms and next it was lowered to her waist and the part between the yoke and the belt was filled with gathered silk—red. And now Virginia's little sister had the dress and there was a new collar on it that fell softly over the red stuff and in the back was a large bow of velvet, making a flower under the lace. She began moving her hands in and out from her hips as if she were jerking the beautiful skirt as far as it would go and then letting it collapse again into the tiny pleats.

Her mother always said, "Yes, and you'd have them kicked out in two weeks!" but the Coleman girls wore their cloth top shoes every day and they didn't. You could wear cloth top shoes even when they were ragged and had some of the buttons off and they would be almost as good as new. Even when the patent leather cracked so that the white showed and big holes came in the cloth over the ankle bones—even then they would be better than ordinary shoes with lacings and gunmetal tops that did nothing but squeak and pinch your stockings. Even if they did cost four dollars and a quarter a person could get a lot more wear out of cloth top patent leathers than any other kind. A person could wear them for Sunday the first year and the second year just for school and the third year for Saturdays and the fourth year a person could wear them in the winter when her toes itched.

She turned quickly and saw her little brother Evan standing on one leg in the woodshed door. He always filled his bedroom with pine boughs in the winter and he kept odd-looking acorns, like old men's faces, in his pockets. When company came he hid behind the stove but she liked him best when he pounded himself and came to show her the place. Now he just stood there smiling and she could see through to their picnic baskets hanging from the woodshed rafter. She ran to him and led him to the kitchen sink.

She wet her comb and ran it through his pale-gold hair that was so soft, slicking it to his head until he looked up at her with his jaws parted and jerked one hand up for the comb. She caught his hands and rubbed the cake of soap over his palms. Then she wiped them on the towel. "Now!" she cried, standing back.

His legs looked very thin in the black-ribbed stockings and his blouse was unfastened in front. He had crammed his hands into his pockets and he was shyly smiling, his cheeks shining with the quick rub she had given them and his eyes looking very strange and clear under the slicked hair. He wriggled inside his blouse and drew up his chin as he jerked his neck free of the starched collar.

"Can I have a doughnut?"

She shook her head.

"Please, Gisela. . . ."

She always loved the way he said "Gisela" and she ran instantly to the bread box. There was only a coffee cake squashed down in the bottom with a big dent in the corner of it where the sugar had melted. "Want some nice coffee cake, Evan?"

He looked in. "Sure."

She cut two large pieces and while she stuffed hers into her mouth she ran to the parlor and took her lily plant from the east window and put it in the north one that faced the street. Then she pinned back the curtain and turned the lily face toward the people who might pass.

"Mamma coming to-day?"

"No," she said, cramming down the last hard end of her cake. "Maybe to-morrow."

"I'm going to Henry's."

"I'll walk a piece with you."

They went out together and she stopped in front of the house, lifting her thin arm in the gingham stiffly and just letting her hands make a little sign to the lily plant that looked out at her. Evan turned his back and hunched, as if he felt she was shaming him. She gave a little laugh then, her hungry beautiful mouth twitching at the corners and she pressed her hands over her tight-fitting dress, smoothing down the stuff until she reached her knees. She caught up with him and walked sedately, switching a little behind, the fine curling hair blowing against her white temples with the blue veins standing out.

"Evan . . ." she said very low. She looked at the sky, that hungry eagerness twitching her lips again, her eyes moving rapidly as she seemed to see the whole sky at once. "How about you and me having a picnic now?" she said, clasping her hands and giving an awkward jump to the side.

"No, sir!" He shook his head. "I'm going to Henry's. I haf to go."

Before she could describe the lunch he howled something and flew down the street. "You be back for supper, Evan!" she called. "Evan!"

He stopped and jumped up and down nervously. Then he shot round the corner. She hurried on the Van Buskirks' house. Perhaps Isabel would let her polish her glasses with the little gray flannel rag or Mrs. Van Buskirk might let them spread the horse blanket on the lawn and have a sewing bee. She loved the way Mr. Van Buskirk teased Isabel and pretended to be Isabel crying and then it was wonderful to see Mrs. Van Buskirk in her best clothes. She wore gloves and a feathered hat with a veil and she took small steps on the sidewalk with her chin held out.

Floyd Werner was coming and she bent down, pretending that she had a thorn or something in her thumb. She even stopped to examine the nail, her brows drawn together until he had gone past. No one in the fifth grade spoke to Floyd. In reading class he always read with expression. You were supposed to read right along without changing your voice at all until the end. So when Floyd read everybody got embarrassed. And when company came into the room Floyd always stepped up and handed the guest his book. That made everybody embarrassed, too. And he always kept his big rubbers under his desk. She began to run down the sidewalk to Isabel's house. Then she stood by the kitchen latticework, her head among the morning glories, and called, "Is-a-bel!"

Everything was still. She wandered in the garden, looking at the rows of vegetables, her hands behind her. Then she picked up a tomato can and began knocking potato bugs off the green leaves with a piece of shingle. She worked rapidly, bending over the plants, her long thin tail of hair swinging against her cheek. Once she paused and looked at the silent house. Then she went on working.

"Hi!"

"My God, look who's here!"

Isabel and her mother stood at the edge of the garden in their best clothes. Isabel was wearing her glasses and Mrs. Van Buskirk had her gloves crunched in one hand. With the fingers of the other hand she was lifting her elegant skirt from the fringe of grass that grew too close to the vegetables to be cut. Gisela ran into to them, holding out the can.

"Look, isn't that a lot?"

"You're sure a nice girl to come and help."

"Say, I've got a surprise in the house," said Isabel. She looked very solemn and fat in her sash and short dress. She joggled her glasses over the bridge of her nose and pulled up her lip so that her big front teeth showed. "Gee, Gisela, it's something *you* never saw before!"

"Honest?"

They began to move over the grass. Gisela walked close to Mrs. Van Buskirk's elegant skirt and smelled. She moved her nose pleasantly as if she were smelling the woman's being, and then she took a piece of the material between her fingers and followed them into the house.

"Change your dress first, Isabel."

"All right, I'm going to, Mamma," she said pettishly. She twitched up the stairs importantly, her new slippers gleaming. Then she stopped and looked back at them, gnawing her fingernail. Her hair was cut in a fringe across her brows and her face was thick and pink like her mother's with blonde hairs around the lips and a little furry fuzz of gold on top of her ears. "You be guessing, Gisela."

"All right."

Mrs. Van Buskirk laid off her hat and ran her fingers into her blonde stiff hair that was matted and crimped like a doll's wig. She loosened her skirt band. "Aaaaaaaaa . . ." Then she loosened the straps of her slippers. "I'm so fagged out to-day."

"I have a cough," said Gisela.

"Is your Mamma back?"

"No."

"Is Mrs. Hurst better?"

"Yes. They took out four stones from her."

"I had that once, too," said Mrs. Van Buskirk. Then she let out a little scream and leaned back, closing her eyes. "It seems as if there's nothing but trouble on this earth."

"I guess you're right," she answered politely, trying to look worried.

"Trouble all the time. My head is simply splitting."

Isabel ran through the kitchen. "Gisela!" she shrieked.

"Do be quiet now!" said Mrs. Van Buskirk.

"I went to Mr. Regan's funeral," whispered Isabel as they went through to the porch. "He looked so funny. . . ."

"Was you scared to look?" whispered Gisela.

"No. Mamma looked and then I looked. But he looked so—funny—"

"Did anybody cry?"

"I think Mrs. did and Jimmie."

"Is it nice going to funerals?" asked Gisela. She sank down on the couch and looked eagerly at Isabel, her lips parted and moist, her eyes very serious.

"Oh, sure, if you get a ride out to the cemetery."

"Gee, I imagine."

"It lasts quite long, too."

"How long about?"

"Oh, I don't know. You don't get tired though."

As Isabel spoke Gisela formed the words she was saying after her, silently. Then she asked, "Was the flowers pretty?"

"Just beautiful."

They were still now and Isabel began winding her handkerchief around her hand as tightly as she could. Some people passed but they didn't look up. Then Isabel began picking the scab on her knee. "Say, I just love to put on winter underwear, don't you?" she said.

"I'd rather put on mittens."

"I heard Miss Grunky's got a diamond. They say her grade's awful hard—"

"Sure seventh is hard."

"I wonder if Miss Grunky feels awful smart knowing such a lot."

"I bet she does. I bet she's good and happy to know so much."

"I don't want to know that much. Say, when do you suppose a person's real happy?"

Gisela spoke softly, as embarrassed and ill at ease as if God had been mentioned. "When we get big and know everything we'll all be happy."

"Yah, grown up people all are. Wouldn't you like to make teacher scared of you?"

"Not Miss Mittenbhuler."

"No, Mr. Harney, though."

"Sure."

"He's got rubber rulers in his office and he hits the kids. Johnnie Ashley told me. He got sent in."

"Sure, I know that," said Gisela. "He's got a rope in there, too." She jumped up and down and began slapping herself with both hands. "Like this—good and hard, too—"

"He can't do that to me. My Daddy'll come up."

"What'll we do now," said Gisela.

"Say, I forgot the surprise. I'll be in the nutty house next," she cried, screaming with laughter. "Wait!"

Gisela went on tiptoe through to the sitting room. Mrs. Van Buskirk lay on the couch, one hand trailing the floor, the other over her eyes. She had taken off her slippers and they stood together with the heels far apart and the toes touching. There were pieces on the piano—Rainbow, Pony Boy, and some waltzes with colored ribbons and roses painted on the covers.

"Come on," whispered Isabel. "Now *guess!*"

"A pencil box."

"I should say not."

"Accordion-pleated dress," she said shyly, her eyes still closed, her hands clasped behind her.

"No," said Isabel sharply, "but I'm going to get one."

"A shell that sings a song."

"Got one."

"A—pony—" she whispered.

"No, but I can have one if I want it. Oh, you're no good guessing. Give up?"

"Uhha."

"All right, put up your hands. Now take them away."

Isabel was squatting on the floor, her red lips in a long

smile, and slowly she took a tin duck from behind her back. It was painted gold and there were bright red streaks on its wings. The long foolish neck jabbed the rug in deep pecks and it walked straight ahead, its flat tin feet clanking. Finally Isabel clapped her hands over her mouth and screamed through them, *"Look!"* Then she turned her face toward the screen door, bending down to laugh, while the goose gravely laid three brown eggs in a straight row.

Gisela opened her lips in joy and the goose stopped, its neck flung up, the tin feet together on the carpet. She put her hands over the eggs, warming them, her eyes very still. Then she heard Isabel's sharp giggle and she looked at her quickly. The little girl lay on her side, her fat legs drawn up, and she was shaking with laughter. She peaked out of the cover she had made for her eyes and then she went off again, the tops of her ears burning red under the gold fuzz.

"I don't think you'd ought to laugh," said Gisela.

Again Isabel gave her evil giggle. "Oooooo." She pressed her hands tightly over her face and rolled over on the bare floor.

"I don't think you'd ought to laugh," said Gisela again.

There was silence. Isabel did not move. Gisela glanced at her nervously and then she made a screen for the goose with her handkerchief. "It couldn't help doing it," she said.

Isabel jerked up. "Well, that's what it's for—so's you can laugh. I guess my Mamma laughed," she said angrily, "and so did my Daddy and my Uncle Will."

Gisela opened her lips, her eyes large on Isabel. *"Did* they?"

"Sure they did. And my Daddy said you didn't live in a nice house, either, and that your *father,"* she brought out harshly without looking at Gisela, "got drunk and chased you with a knife under the beds."

Gisela did not move. She turned her eyes away from Isabel and began picking at the rag she had braided into her hair. "He don't either," she said suddenly. "He don't, he never did."

Isabel kept looking at the floor, nodding her head back and forth, her mouth clenched firmly. "Yes, sir, and that pickle

pin you got didn't cost a penny even. Your Mamma got it for
working in the canning factory and my daddy said your father
can't keep a job and your mother has to go out to nurse and
you haven't got a piano so's you can practice and take lessons."

Now Gisela looked at Isabel, rubbing her thumb nail over
her front teeth, and then she put her fingers between her lips,
stretching them into a big smile as her eyes filled. "I guess I'll
do something," she said and got up. She walked into the kitchen
and went behind the door for the broom. The cat's dish was full
of ants and there were dust tracks on the linoleum. She began
sweeping as hard as she could.

Isabel stood in the door. "Well, you needn't do that!" she
cried angrily. "The last time you swep' my mother said there
were more crumbs than before. She said you must have made
the dirt, there was so much, and she don't want you to ever
touch our broom again. Here!" she shouted passionately, and
rushed for it. "You let go or I'll call my mother. That's my
mother's broom. You let go now!"

"Say, what's the matter with you kids?" called Mrs. Van
Buskirk.

"Mamma, Gisela's got the broom. She won't let go."

"You run home now, Gisela," called Mrs. Van Buskirk.

Instantly the little girl let go of the broom. She sprang to
the door and ran out of the house, flying up the sidewalk with
the long shy movements she always made at Sunday school
picnics when she darted from rock to rock or finally crouched
behind the bath house to look at the shining water, wishing for
some one to invite her to eat supper. She ran on wildly and
then from the corner she saw two ladies were sitting in the
parlor rockers out on the side lawn. They were erect with their
hands in their laps and high net collars coming up to their ears
at the sides. They wore hats too and they had seen her. They
called. She wanted to go back, to hide behind a rock or a tree,
but she wiped her eyes and then clasped her hands behind her
as she walked toward them. It was Aunt Mildred and Aunt
Carrie. She let them kiss her. Their lips were hard and Aunt

Mildred squeaked as she leaned back in her chair. They both had rouge spread over their cheek bones in pink spots and Aunt Carrie had little flecks of powder on her dark mustache and sharp chin.

"How do you like your teacher?"

Then her father called her and she ran into the house. He was standing by the bread box, his lips parted in rage and his dark hair shaking as he jerked his empty hands in front of him.

"Where's the bread?"

"Isn't any."

"Why not?"

"We ate it."

"Oh, the devil anyway."

She stood by the door watching him, her nose all wet with tears. He slung the coffee cake back and groaned again, throwing open the cupboard door and jerking things off the shelves. She saw his black hat on the wood box, a great dent in the side of it where he had snatched it off his head. His coat was sagging at the pockets and there was a hard dark place on the end of his nose. She felt very still and small.

"Run up to the store and get some crackers," he said without looking at her. "Dash along now!"

"Where's the money?"

"In your bank."

"Mamma said . . ."

"You run along and bring home ten cents' worth of crackers."

He filled the tea kettle and put it on the range. Then he glanced around coldly. "Did you hear what I said? Say, will I have to take out papers to get you in a home for the feeble minded? Can't you talk? Can't you act like a human being instead of a dunce? Run along now! I'll give you five dollars to-morrow. Nobody's going to cheat you." He gave her a sudden slow look of scorn, as if he were better than anybody in the whole world and all the people, even the Van Buskirks, were beneath him. "Haven't you got a better dress than that rag?"

"Mamma said . . ." she cried and then jammed her hand into her mouth.

Aunt Mildred stood in the door. "Don't bother about tea, Horace. Come out and talk." She sniffed as she glanced at the wood box, the kitchen sink and the clean oil cloth on the table. "Come," she said and leaned to him with a long squeak of her corsets, "come and tell us what you've been reading. Carrie and I don't know what to read. You always kept us informed."

He flushed and let his hand fall awkwardly on Gisela's shoulder as his sister led him out the door. Then the screen slammed and she saw him sit down at their feet, his face thrown back as if he were a king, his eyes all calmed and loving. Aunt Mildred reached out her freckled hand with the rings and picked something off his shoulder and then Aunt Carrie pressed back his hair in front. He began swinging back and forth, his arms around his knees so that his stockings showed. One was gray and the other red and black mixed. "Don't read him. Modern writers are no good. People are just insects to them. No nobility or vision. The best books had the right dope on it—"

Gisela felt a pang of pride go through her and she watched that loving look come on his face as he closed his mouth and looked toward the black roof. She glanced at the room but now nothing in the kitchen looked nice any more after Aunt Mildred had looked at it that way. Even the new clean oil cloth looked poor and so did the sink and there wasn't any carpet in front of the stove. Suddenly she thought of her green pickle brooch in the drawer upstairs. She couldn't ever show that again or pretend she had something nicer than any one on earth but she wouldn't tell Mamma.

"I've been thinking of having mother's fur coat done over for me. What do you think about it, Horace? I mean, would mother have want me to?" Aunt Carrie leaned toward him, her gold watch swinging out from the pin.

"Edith was to have it," snapped Aunt Mildred. "Mother expressed that wish."

"Well, where is Edith then?" said Aunt Carrie, her nose and chin looking sharp and blue.

"That unpleasantness I married?" He turned toward the house. "Fortunately she's out of town for a few weeks. *Gisela!*" he shouted.

She ran to her money and counted out ten cents. Then she tied the pennies together in the center of her handkerchief and dodged out the front door, fast, so they wouldn't ask about school.

II

Mittenbhuler's gave you the most crackers for ten cents but they were the farthest away, and when she finally came up the street with them no one was on the lawn. Evan was sitting on the little front stoop, his hands on his cheeks and his face staring ahead. He sat there alone, the dark house behind him, the little uncovered porch that was only a door step, beneath him. The whole street was quiet. Sun was shining through the leaves and soon it would be darkening, the sun would be turning a deep flame red and burning in a wild ball, then falling behind the darkened trees. Soon they would take hold of hands and climb the stairs to bed. "Did you wash your feet on the bottoms, Evan?"

Suddenly she ran as fast as she could, her loose dress blowing against her spare body, one hand on the end of her pigtail and the other holding the sack of crackers high so that he could see it. He sat there, looking toward her, his smile getting larger and larger until he couldn't smile any more and he bent his head, staring down between his legs at the worn step.

"Papa home?" she whispered.

He shook his head.

"Did you see Aunt Mildred and Aunt Carrie?"

"Uhuh."

Suddenly she wanted to hold him on her lap and press her hands over his hair. She wanted to comfort him. She took his hand and they walked around to the side door. Then she began smoothing his face and looking at him, giving little shakes to her head as if she were a real mother. She jerked him close to her suddenly while he squirmed to get loose. "Are you very sad, Evan? Did somebody hurt you?"

"No!" he cried indignantly and backed off, smoothing down his hair so that no curls would come.

"Yes, they did," she insisted, "and we're going to have a party."

"Gee, will Papa come?"

"No, he's gone with Aunt Mildred and Aunt Carrie."

"Gee, I'm glad."

"Let's talk about when we're big, Evan. What'll we do then?" she cried, and gave him the nutmeg balls and a rusty grater. "Don't start telling yet!" She ran to put the kettle on and then she laid some crackers in a neat milk white pile on a large plate with "Compliments of Mittenbhuler's Grocery" on it in gold. She moved close to him smiling. "I'll get Mamma something nice. I'll get her a feathered hat like Mrs. Van Buskirk's and gloves and a fan and I'll work hard and she won't ever have to leave us and go nursing. Will she?" she whispered, bending to look into his face.

He shook his head. "Oh, boy, I should say not, and we won't let Papa come around, neither."

"I should say not!" she cried. "Shall we have our birthday cups, Evan?"

He stood against the kitchen table working, scraping the hard surfaces of the nutmeg against the grater and letting the dust fly into a tea cup. "Sure," he said and waved one arm to rest it, heaving a great sigh. "You know, one of them boas for her neck," he explained. "A brown one with long hairs and we'd make her tell stories every single night, wouldn't we, Gisela," he said warmly. "Gee . . ."

She laid the cups together on oil cloth. One had cats and

dogs on it and the other was all pink with gold flutings at the edge and three gold feet.

"Is this here enough?"

"That's enough."

She poured hot water into each cup and sprinkled some of the gratings on top. Then she sat down and Evan took his place opposite. They bent over their steaming cups, gazing into each other's eyes as they blew on the water, and then they began to stuff crackers into their mouths.

"Nobody hurt you this after, Evan?" she began again, her lips raising over her white teeth.

"Course not."

"We'd better let Papa come," she said suddenly, half imploring him with her silent opened lips and quiet eyes, "because when we're big maybe he'll like us better. Maybe we'd buy him something as good as Mr. Van Buskirk's got and then he'd like us. Sure he would," she insisted.

"No, sir. When we're big we're going to have just Mamma. Not him. No, sir."

"Maybe he'll get different, Evan. Maybe, you can't tell."

"Uhuh, he won't," he said, leaning his head on his arm.

She began to laugh suddenly. "Here's the way Mrs. Van Buskirk eats," she said. "Look!" She broke off a piece of cracker with two fingers stretched out from the others. Then she took one of the tiny bits and chewed with her nostrils parted haughtily and a vague indifferent look on her face, the other hand held out, her chin stretched over the table. Suddenly Evan began to laugh. He looked at her and laughed with his head held stiffly and his eyes glancing at her in pride. "Look!" she cried again and chewed slowly, her jaws grinding and her eyes fixed sadly on the sink strainer. Then they leaned back in their chairs, gazing soberly at the crumbs.

"As black as a bear, a three-cornered square?" she asked him.

"Say, I knew that last year a'ready."

"Around and around the house it goes and only one track it leaves. . . ."

The screen door opened and slammed. Gisela sprang out of her chair, one hand pressed against her mouth. Her father threw his hat at the wood box and then he sat down with his back to them, his big shoulders bent and his head looking tender and young.

"Any mail?"

"No, Papa."

"Paper come?"

"Evan, run and look!" she cried and gave him a shove.

She stood still for a second, watching the back of the man's head, and then he bent over his raised hand and laid his face on it. The room got still and everything looked poor again the way it did when Aunt Mildred looked. She went to the doorway on tiptoe. The sun was falling. It had gathered into a solid burning world in the pale cold blue and it had darkened the furthest trees into a deep black. She put her cheek on the screen and leaned against the door with one sandy shoe over the other.

Evan came up on tiptoe, the paper in his hand. He looked scared and white, very small, as if he had just come out of a press. He drew his brows together in a little frown as he looked up at her. She went softly to her father and laid the paper beside him on the sewing machine. He did not move and she went back to Evan and they began talking with their fingers and whispering over the big black stove. Finally she pointed to his box of playthings and gave a push in that direction. "Bring it over here," she said very low.

He went silently to the place behind the machine, his body half turned so that he could see his father as he went so softly on his toes. Then he bent over and lifted the wooden box. It was too heavy. He had to put it down. Then, before she could speak, he got on his knees and began pushing it before him with the scrape of sand on wood. "The little saw ain't here," he said in a loud whisper, as the box gave a long eerie shriek on the bare floor.

The man was out of his chair. His black arm shot down and jerked the little boy to his toes so that he hung limp and white from the shoulders, his scared face deathly pale, his mouth gaping. A little whine of fright came out of him and his father struck with a quick savage blow, half moaning as he shook him back and forth. Gisela sprang at them. She pulled on the huge hands but she could not loosen them. She hung with all her weight on his big arm but his wild movements shook her too. Then she darted behind him and set her toe with all her might into the back of his leg. The shock went down her and her eyes went red and whirling with fear. She grabbed Evan's arm and they ran. Then they huddled in the parlor near her plant and she knelt down and tried to wrap her skirt around him.

"Does it hurt now, brother?"

He kept his hand over his cheek, his head bent, half leaning against her.

"I'll make him scared. . . ." Her lovely eyes were still and she kept one hand on her brother's head, her frightened face motionless. Her voice sounded squeaky and far off to her ears and all through her pounded the great hollow boom of guilt and fright. "I'll slap *him*," she said louder, with a groan.

Evan sniffled and she let him out to the front step. They sat there close together, their faces turned toward the big sun as it fell behind the forest of dark trees behind the swamp. The little boy put his face in her lap and she smoothed his head and jerked the twisted seams in his stockings straight. Finally she whispered that he must go to bed and they went into the dark still house, hand in hand. They went softly up the stairs, touching the walls on each side as they climbed, their eyes lifted, looking ahead.

"I feel so—funny—" she said weakly.

"When's Mamma coming?"

"In the morning."

"To-morrow morning, Gisela?"

"Maybe in the evening to-morrow."

"Let's write her to come, Gisela."

"You know they took four stones out of Mrs. Hurst," she reminded him. "Mamma has to nurse her so's she'll get well. Oh, if you could have a present, Evan, what'd you want?" She looked at him anxiously but he lay down in bed and pressed his face into the pillow so that she couldn't see where he had cried. "Go on," she said, "what'd you want if you could have a present?" She held his hand but he did not speak and as it grew dark she glanced in the corners nervously, rubbing the end of her nose with her finger. Now he was breathing quietly and she turned him over so that his face would dry, the way mothers always did.

She stumbled slowly down the dark stairs and felt her way into the kitchen to the wood box. She put her hand in but her father's hat was gone. Now she went over to the chair where he had sat near the sewing machine and stood there a while, bent over it. Then she went slowly out the kitchen door, closing the screen so that it wouldn't bang. The white chickens had all gone into their house to plump up their feathers, close their eyes, and roost on the long pole above the bits of hay and droppings on the floor. Their yard was bare and silent, no kernals of corn or grain showing on the darkened sand. The big trees looked as if they were sleeping, bending down with trailing soft leaves over the barns and houses to breathe and rest in peace. Everything was cool and still, so silent that she felt she must run fast somewhere.

In the street the houses were all lighted and she looked hard into each bright window even though she felt lost and scared. Minnie Puffer was practicing her recital piece at the piano and the Brandon twins were leaning over a big book on the davenport. Their tricycles stood on the front porch, the empty saddles looking desolate and bleak in the darkness. There was one roller skate on the walk and at the next house a little wagon was drawn up as if it were waiting for some one. "When I'm big, when I'm big . . ." she whispered to herself and began running fast, her tail of hair beating against her back. But when she stopped suddenly that funny feeling about her father was still inside her. She sank down by the group of elms at the corner and pressed her face against the trunk. Then she looked up into the dark branches for a moment but suddenly her face jerked down to her knee and she put both arms over her ears.

She sprang up. Some one was coming. She crawled to where she could see. It was Floyd Werner hurrying home, a neat parcel under his girlish arm. Now her heart beat hard. "Hello, Floyd," she said for the first time.

He jumped to the side, drawing up his breath sharply, and then he said, "Hello," without looking and hurried faster, his black legs twinkling in and out. Vonberg's black Persian cat came prowling over the dark grass, his long tail sweeping behind him, his short legs rushing his soft body ominously along. "Kitty . . ." she cried and jerked her handkerchief to tempt him, but he sprang wildly up a tree. A dog came smelling the walk and then old Mr. Eulberg pounded past on his cane, breathing in hisses through his teeth. Suddenly she flattened herself into the dark by the tree, not breathing at all. And then she changed her mind and crawled into the light, pulling grass on each side of her.

"Hi Gizzie!" said Mr. Van Buskirk heartily. She could see his big stomach and watch chain and one hand was in his pocket as if he had lots of money, five dollars, maybe. Mrs. Van Buskirk was taking her small elegant steps and Isabel was jumping high between them.

"Hello, Gisela, see you to-morrow, maybe."

"Your house, Isabel?"

"All right. I don't care. I'm going to the show now. King Baggott," she added, giving another leap between her parents.

"Your mother back, Gisela?" asked Mrs. Van Buskirk.

"No, she isn't yet."

"Maybe she'll be up there all summer. You can't tell. If Mrs. Hurst's as bad off as I was that time. . . ."

"Too bad about you," said her husband. "How about coming to the show with us, Gizzie?"

She clasped her hands over her neck in delight. Then she

patted her dress in front. "I can't," she said, "I'm—"

"Then you'd better run home," said Mrs. Van Buskirk. "You shouldn't be out so late."

"Aw, let the poor kiddie alone," said Mr. Van Buskirk.

"Well, you know perfectly well that Hazel Murphey was murdered just three years ago yesterday and she was only thirteen."

"Goody-by!" shouted Isabel.

Now it was silent again and she began making pleats in her skirt to keep that funny feeling away from inside her. Then she knew her father was coming. She knew he was kicking the bricks as he walked, his head lowered, and his sad face very white and hurt. Now that funny feeling was so strong that she couldn't breathe very well and she had to move her whole body in a big jerk so that she could swallow. He was coming fast and he was big and dark like a moving cliff. "Papa," she said over and over to herself, half crying. Then she crawled down the bank and followed quietly in his big dark shadow. Once he turned and she saw his large soft eye look at her. He waited but he did not speak and she walked beside him in little jerks and runs to keep up with his nervous gait.

"Cold?"

She reached out then and caught his coat that hung down limp and moist. She felt his arm brush her cheek and she shrank closer, smiling her eager twitching smile.

"What if I went away and you never saw me again?" he said suddenly.

"Papa!" she said as if she were screaming for help.

"No, seriously, what if you never saw me again?"

She put her arm up toward him awkwardly, wishing that he would suddenly hold her in his arms and kiss her so that she could fling her arms around his neck and kiss him again and again the way she did Evan when he was hurt. Then that funny feeling, like a frightened spinning inside her, went away and she felt all shaky and empty down to her toes.

"Maybe some fine day I'll be gone. Not that any of you'd

care. Your mother'd be glad to be rid of me and I wager you'd be glad too from the way you treat me."

Now she was sure he meant her kicking him and she mumbled in shame and fright, "Papa, if you could have a present. . . ."

"What's that? If I could *what*? Now don't act sullen the way you did with Aunt Mildred and Aunt Carrie. I was ashamed of you. I've been ashamed of you a hundred times but it's no use. You're just like your mother. Doesn't do any good to correct you. Some day you'll take another view. But then it'll be too late most likely."

"If you could have a present," she cried wildly, "what'd you want?"

"What would I want?" He gave a cold little laugh. "Well, I'd want to be happy for one thing. And I'd . . ."

"Cloth top shoes," she offered, "with black pearl buttons. They'd look so pretty on you, Papa. Maybe a nice hat like Mr. Van Buskirk's with a feather in the bow. Maybe . . ."

"I'd want to forget everything that's happened for the last thirteen years. I'd want it all wiped away as if it had never been. That's the one thing that could make me supremely happy."

"Maybe a diamond tie pin like Mr. Van Buskirk's . . ."

"Say, for Lord's sake, what kind of trashy people do you associate with anyway. But it's no use saying anything. Listen! Have you got wits enough to understand me. I'm through. I'm going to get some happiness as soon as possible before I die. I'm through. You can tell your mother that I'm—"

"Maybe when I'm big," she cried in a terrible voice that scared her, turning her body toward him, "maybe . . ." Then she broke away from him, gulping down great mouthfuls of heavy night air, her eyes ahead on their dark silent home.

MARRIAGE EVE

S HE wondered why, now on the eve of her marriage, she was walking toward her father's house. Five years before, when he had told her that her writings were curses on him and on her, she had lifted her hands to beat against him and then let them fall. She had rushed toward the door murmuring, "I'm going—I'm going away—I'm going—" and as she turned she saw him standing fixed in a strange rock-like position, his head thrust forward like a bull's, the jaws spread wide apart, the eyes slowly closing, and his broad tough shoulders spread solid and dark and impregnable.

"Some day your father will be dead!"

She had felt deaf and insensitive to all he could say, to any words he might now speak, and yet from inside her came a scream, as if she could endure no more, and then she had rushed outside into the street and down the sidewalk.

During those five years from her little room over the bakery she had always left her table at a certain hour, stricken with something vague and confused, and sometimes as she stood there she would see him stride into the post office for his mail, his feet coming down with the same rock-like tread, his huge hands bare in summer grasping his cane, and in winter in stiff huge gloves—oh, father!

She would go back to her desk as if nothing had happened and perhaps strike out a few sentences she had written and then she would go on with her story which always contained an ideal father, a strong, noble man who played games with his daughter and always let her win, who enjoyed little suppers served on creaky tables in front of the fire, and who said to the townspeople, "Yes, my daughter is a marvel. She cured me of asthma and she selects my clothes and what a woman she is for keeping me cheerful. And as for her writing—well, the world will soon hear of her!"

As she recalled the massive solidness of his legs, his frightening man's voice, the energy in him that had terrified her and made her flee, she suddenly wanted to turn back. But her body kept moving forward, up the street toward the house. She closed her eyes and she could see the way it used to look. A brick house set back in a tiny park of trees and bushes with a two-seated swing in the side yard and a barn at the end of the drive with doors that always used to stand open. Sometimes they kept a few hens in the shed and let them pick what they could find from the alley and the patch of green near the back door where Winnie threw the dish water. And Honey, the big brown and white collie dog, always used to meet front door callers at the white picket gate and escort them up to the tiny porch with open shuttered windows on each side and fresh white curtains blowing in the breeze that came through the dark screens. Soon she would be on the first step, the porch, ringing, waiting. Everything in her was silent and fixed, determined, and she could not turn back. She was going quickly up the steps as if all were well. She was opening the screen door and one arm was stretched out in the darkness. She rang, her lips parted, her face mute. And when she lifted her finger off the bell she kept her hand stretched out in front of her stiffy, her fearful eyes watching the pine door.

The key creaked in the lock. Then there was a tremendous shaking of the door knob, a curse, the same baffled shaking again as if a force inside there, behind the door, were rising to shake mightily not only the door but the entire house, and all houses, and all people. "I must be pretending, I must be exaggerating—" she thought. And she tried to think of some real, positive desire in her, something she could say when the door suddenly opened, and then in fright as the door began to give, she tried to think of why she had come. But still her body would not move, still it would not turn back. It faced the door stubbornly as if it knew what it was about and would not suffer defeat. "I'll stay—I'll face him—I'll stay—" Tears started to her eyes as she seemed to know in a dim, unworded way why she was there seeking her father, why, on this night before her marriage she was there waiting. "Only one father—only one father—"

The door swung open. He stood with his head lowered, his eyes peering out to see through the darkness, his dry lips parted. But he stood with the same massive dominant stature, as if he wanted to feel rooted to whatever his feet fell upon, as if he wanted to own whatever he saw, as if his hands wanted to possess, in their huge palms, anything he touched. She had forgotten the strange jangled throbbing that had made her scream before, even though she could not understand why she was screaming, and now as she determined, willed not to scream, she closed her mouth so tightly that her jaws felt locked and stony.

"Why, Clara!" he said with an odd squeak. "Come in!" He threw back the door so that she could see the hall table with his panama on it and his silver topped cane and the evening paper that he had thrown down when he heard the bell. "How are you?" he said, bending to look at her as if she were small and weak. "Have you had supper?" He turned his head. "Winnie! Winnie!" he shouted. "Put something on the table!" He went into the dining room for a moment and then came back closing the door, his huge arms flung out by his heavy movements. He led her to a chair and sat down, facing her. "How've you been?" he said weakly, now that they were exposed to each other under the electric light.

She nodded, swallowing and biting her lip.

He sank back in his chair, his feet apart, and his forefinger pressed against his large reddened nose, the palm on his mouth. His eyes, very blue and intense and bright, gazed at the fireplace and the light gleamed down on the thin white hair, loosened and blown on his flushed forehead. Then he began to rock solidly, his chair giving out a long eerie shriek. The sound was so intolerable that she sprang up and faced the bookcase, bending down to look for a book. She remembered, in shock after shock, how like a father he had seemed with all the space of the courtyard park, the road, the post office walk between them. How like a father he had been when she peered out at him as he strode into the door of the post office for his mail, his head, his eyes, all set as if he missed his daughter, his body human as if a daughter could run up to him and give him a kiss and throw her arms around him, warmly, humanly. And then at dusk sometimes how like a father he had seemed with all those walls of houses between them, those walls that rose between the bakery room and his house here on the hill near the river. With all the distances of town between them, in her room alone, then he had been real, then he had been a father, then, then—

"If you want a worthwhile book I've got one for you. Wilson's speeches all collected in one volume." He jumped up, his eagerness driving out of his face, the amazing force of his body plunging him across to her so that his arm swept her chin as he reached up for the book, placing his hand on it in the dark with a sigh of pleasure. He opened it and stood reading. Then he closed it gravely, examining the binding, and with a handsome bow, he handed it to her. "Real American stuff. A-number one."

He gazed off over her head, breathing heavily through his parted lips, while she took the book out of his hands and looked down at her worn oxfords that had just been whitened. Even with her ample body, her sturdy solid build that seemed almost as absolute as his, even with her firm mouth, her ardent eyes, even with all her attributes of strength she seemed shrunken now, powerless, bent. And she kept turning and turning the pages of the book while her eyes filled and the cords of her neck thickened and got taut. But still she grasped the volume hard as if she would not let herself hurl it against the wall.

He began rocking first on his heels and then on his toes, his eyes still held far off, intense and ardent. "Wilson is a fine writer. And any one who can write about what will be in the hereafter and what will help us to get there, can make a lot of money and in addition help humanity. Now take your poor mother, for example," he said, fixing his eyes upon her bent head and yet seeming not to see her. "As long as she lived she tried in every way she could think of to displease me. I'm a lonely man now because of her. And she would be living to-day if she'd listened to me instead of grieving herself to death over nothings." Now his eyes blinked shut unexpectedly and he gulped, pressing his lips hard together. "But there's an after-life even though we can't conceive of it," he repeated huskily. His eyes lifted as if he visioned a meeting place far removed from human life, far far away, where all that had not happened on earth would happen.

She laid the book down and turned to the window where the street light sent a glow on the rich dark leaves of the vines. Now the agony of her parents' relationship came over her again, her father thundering, her mother cowering, and she, the little child, between the two. She remembered her mother, suffering with an incurable and dolorous affliction of the bladder, and her father raging against the unwholesome atmosphere of illness, roaring when she mentioned her pains, and swearing that he would protect her from all doctors. She remembered with a quake that made her wince the way her mother gave up mentioning her seizures, her burning skin, and would simply excuse herself from table or cards and go away to lie down, weak and stricken, one hand clamped over her yellow brow. The day she died her father walked up and down the floor with awesome tread, up and down, up and down, his cheeks sucked in between his teeth and his startled eyes ahead. "We don't know where we're going—where we are—but there's an after-life even though we can't conceive of it—"

"How's Winnie?" she asked suddenly.

"What?" he said, as if he had answered her.

But the thought of going into the kitchen to speak to her made her draw back. After the funeral services Winnie had let her come into her room while she changed into her third best dress. Over this gown she always wore her crocheted grape arbor. It was white with wads of cotton for grapes and formidable-looking leaves, veined and substantial. Her two best dresses had buttons the size of butter dishes down the front and they were always cool and stiff as they hung, gleaming with starch, from the hangers. And that evening in the kitchen Winnie's indignation against death and the sorrows of humanity were dramatized by sticking out one bony arm with a gray damp rag wadded in the palm, and to keep from crying she had rushed to the table and gathered all the plates in a tottering pile that reached her goiterous chin, and then, breathing heavily, she had run for the sink and reached it just in time. "Whew! And it don't do a bit of good to make any complaints. No, *sir!*" And before bed, that night of the funeral, with the house smelling of flowers and wafting strange air over them, her father had stood under the cage of love birds in the bay window and stared out into the darkness, trying to see the furthest stretch of sky, and then he tried to convince them that it was all for the best because all that could not be carried out on earth could be achieved in heaven. He had fallen asleep while they watched him in a kind of trance and he had frozen their blood when he jumped up suddenly and called, "Is that you, Mamma?" But the next morning he was more formidable than ever before, guilty and embarrassed and snorting, and his morning kiss was once more wanting and more bleak.

She glanced up at him and that frightened vibrating and thrumming came on her again, more terrible now because she could not control it or even dimly understand. Suddenly she was aware of his raw heaviness for the first time, his eyes that could not regard any one, his being that was as dead and weighty and solid as coal, and from the pit of herself, as if now her most essential voice were speaking, she affirmed that he was not her father, that he hadn't made her or helped to conceive her, that none of his blood or bones corresponded to hers and nothing in him had given birth to anything in her. She kept gazing at her shoe, her head dropping. And then she felt her whole being rise against this thought, as if her happiness in marriage depended in some way she could not understand on her finding her father, on being enclosed in him in mutual understanding at last so that she might be given by him in marriage to the man and to the world, the great man and the great world that she wished not to hide from, that she wished to circulate freely with without obstruction, to breathe with and understand as she could not understand or circulate with or breathe with her father. Now the huge obstruction, like looming rock, that she had faced before when she rushed out of the house, rose again until she dropped down in a chair, her hands pressed stubbornly over her eyes, her body sagging until her covered face rested on her strong knees. "Oh, *why?*" she cried suddenly in a terrible voice.

He glanced at her in amazement. "Uh?" he gasped, as if a blow had knocked the wind out of him. He ran his hand over his forehead, as if he were hunting the spot a physical thrust had made, leaving him a bit stunned. He began breathing heavily, his eyes distending in resentment and confusion. But he did not speak. His lips rounded as if he were about to say— "You"—but he seemed to be without the power or will to do anything but swallow and swallow, his dry tongue struggling to wet his parted lips.

As she pressed her head against her knees she thought of her inheritance from him, the distrust of the world, the cowardly knowledge that all joy would have to pay its price and that after all struggle, after the ultimate reconciliation even, no desirable contact could be gained except the rock of one self facing the desperate rock of another self, intact, enclosed, incapable of understanding. "Oh, I will pretend he is my father and none of this has happened, only love, only joy—" and she imagined herself going to him as if she loved him, affirming as she had never affirmed that he was her father, that she was his child, that between them there had never been the dark years and the strife and the vast bleak space, but instead that she was warmed and acknowledged by him. But it was too hard to imagine and the sense of her desolation spread over her like the memory of those infinite meals at home with her mother senselessly rubbing her hand over her yellow cheek that seemed turned to stone and Mrs. Wheatley, Winnie, striking out with her gray damp wad of rag, her lips curling in resentment against his commands that she was always quick to obey. The whole flat plain of dark suffering unconscious life spread over her and no desire for happiness rose in her now like some powerful bird, lifting and wrapping itself with the best part of her being, rising free and glorious into a new kind of life. And now she remembered the man she had wanted to marry and their love-making, her ardent reaching out to meet him, her sudden flashes of light and life in a kiss, as if her being had turned to vines, opening now in the light of his being, the sun of his essential love and faith in her so strong that they turned endless when their hands touched and their flesh alone denied all her former life.

But now that love was a dream and she remembered it as a dream or a play that she had acted in. Now the real part of her seemed her orphaned suffering state, her desolation, and she believed that greater than all was her desperate separation from and her loathing of her father. It was impossible to tell him that she was going to be married because now she could not imagine herself marrying any one, now she was doomed to hide from any more torment like this, doomed to shrink down so that she might never again be pitted against that dark obstruction, forget in the darkness of herself that she had ever known another kind of life, that she had ever sprung up as fresh seeds spring through dark hard soil into light. Of what help was struggle and of what use was all the seeming deep knowledge that impelled her so mysteriously forward to discover and understand him? "No!" she mumbled, her body jerking straight in her chair, and her hands clasped tightly together and pointing upward, as if with their physical force she could raise her spirit from its blankness.

"No—*what?*" he half shouted. "Young lady, I've seen enough of your moods. You're on the same track your mother was on and you're working yourself up into the same kind of temper she used to get into over nothing. Calm down now!" he ordered, his eyes still held distended and wild, his lips gaping open now that he could say no more.

Such a wild thrumming and hatred of his mass started in her that suddenly she felt impelled to strike at him with all her force, strike until she fell exhausted and dying, having protected her spirit against his brutal heaviness and non-sight, and striking, too, because he had never been her father, never once read anything she had written, letting her always struggle on alone with only herself to urge her on and believe in herself and her power and her ultimate victory in despairing days, all with no help from him, only resistance and denying. And again she felt his fight against her that seemed always to be going on, his stern indifferent attitude of one who is always unselfish, always right, always a dictator. "Oh, if only you *were* right!" she thought, and yet something in her fought his being right, fought his being strong and knowing more than herself.

"What have you got against me?" he began testily, pacing up and down with his hands in his pockets. "What is it now? What have I done? What's wrong with me? What have I done?" One of his gold cuff buttons was caught in his dark sleeve and the ring of white looked like a bandage around his hand. She thought of him desperately wounded, stretched out dead, and she felt no terror, no sadness, no regret that he was dying without a daughter as she would die without a father. "Why haven't you been a father to me?" she cried, jumping up and facing him. She stood staring at him, a slow smile like that of a demented person coming on her face, idiotic in its simplicity, ironic and jeering when one saw her tormented eyes and bleached face. As she closed her lips there was only the sound of her breathing as it rose and fell in a weird threatening murmur.

"Huh?" he said.

"Why?" she cried again, her face still distorted.

Instantly the force of his body and his rage hurled him toward her and she felt his huge hands tear at hers and twist them together until she was too frightened to scream and the great strength of him made her jerk to get free, until she began to cry piteously, dragging away from his hands with all her strength, blinded and enraged and ready to lay waste to him so that he could no longer wound and destroy. She sank to the floor, her arms pinned against him, and then she raised her head and her eyes to his terrible face as he stood looking down, the blood vessels in his eyes distended so that his startled pupils were veined in blood. She saw tears in the deep crevices of his cheeks but his white mouth was stubbornly, impotently closed, as if he would hang on until death.

"You!" she cried with her last strength as her head struck out toward his hands and her teeth bared to sink into his flesh. But before she could grasp it her arm was jerked back. She felt his huge hand placed over her hand, forcing her palm toward her face. She pushed against it with all her force and then she saw the flat of his hand rising nearer and nearer and suddenly she closed her eyes as he brought it in a stinging crash against her face. When he let go of her she dropped down weakly, stretching out on the floor. She lay there crying and struggling to breathe, empty, confused and blank.

Suddenly she saw him, his nose twisting horribly, his lips, his cheeks, as if he could do nothing but that, and when she saw his eyes again, blinded and veined with blood, and his hands gripped over his chest, she cried, *"Father!"* She did not move toward him and he did not move. They stayed where they were, their eyes upon each other, their faces mute and terrible.

He cleared his throat, jerking his handkerchief to his mouth, and spit in it. "I heard," he said thickly.

"About to-morrow?"

"Yes," he said, the tears running down his face. Then he began to nod with his mouth gaping and his eyes shut and his huge hands hanging at his sides. But he kept clearing his throat and drawing the wind up through his nostrils until his nose looked red and swollen. "Asthma again," he muttered, reaching for his handkerchief.

"No—no—" she cried suddenly, "don't be sick—don't—nothing must hurt you again—"

"Umph," he grunted so that his body shook.

She went toward him as she sometimes did at dusk in her imagination, and she lifted one of his huge hands to her cheek, raising her eyes to his and smiling in a way she had never smiled so that all parts of herself were wholly free and open to him. And then she rested her head against him, as she did in dreams when she needed help and courage, and she said over and over, "Father—my father—father—"

He shifted his weight to his other side and sighed deeply as if her leaning against him must be endured no matter how long it continued and no matter how long he was forced to stand cramped and bent with devilish needles playing over one foot and a burning pain in his eyes that made him fear the light. "Well—" he said finally.

"Tell me to marry him!"

"Don't you ask me anything about it!" he shouted wildly. "You never asked your father's advice before about anything. All these years have passed and you and your mother never asked my advice or gave a damn what I thought about any of your doing. I washed my hands of you then. Both of you. You women will have to straighten out your own mistakes. I can't. I'm too old. And all you want of me now is to tell you to do something and then when it turns out badly then you can blame me and tell me I forced you into it and ruined your life. I tell you right now, I won't shoulder any of the responsibility of this so that you can come crying and say I told you to do it and that I'm to blame just like your mother—I tell you I won't—"

He turned his head quickly and closed his eyes, his head bent and his hands clutched together, as he sometimes stood in church when they sang hymns. But she still gazed at him smiling, her head resting against his arm as if after labor and violence and pain she dared keep close to him no matter what he said. Suddenly she saw him as a boy and a young man, frightened and unwarmed, forced to live as she had lived like the blighted, unproductive soil about them, the rocks and snow and bleakness of winter-driving cold working in deeper and deeper, thawing, then freezing again. She saw his parents suffering in the same way, enclosed, alone, driving their wintry bareness before them, sinking it deeper and deeper. On it went—back, back, oh, far back. And each generation could turn back and back and back so that there was no end and no beginning, no fixed body on which to place the crime, nothing but wintry death and sightless eyes trying to see and yet escape being wounded and melted, and the heart slowly crusting with the impenetrable substances of cold.

He eased himself away from her, snorting in embarrassment and then swinging back on his heels, his head lifted so that he need not meet her gaze and her far opened eyes and face. "It's a good thing to have a family—we live for that—we have to keep the world going—happiness doesn't count here in America—we have a bigger ideal than that—the next generation does count and nothing else matters—Have your family. I can't put up a kick against that—it's what we're here for—no one yet found a better reason—sure—go ahead—"

MONDAY MORNING

To Blanche Matthias

D EAR, it *is* a rose bug."
She turned the gas low under the coffee and ran in.
"Is it, dear?"
"Look! It is."
"Where? Oh, but it isn't, dear."
"But did you ever see a rose bug?" he asked. He straightened up and put his arm around her, laying his face against her hair. She turned to him quickly and pressed her lips on his ear. "Oh, God, I had a quake," she said, drawing back. "It seemed as if my cheeks flashed white. Just as if I'd turned the light on and off."

"I like the way you arrange flowers," he said. He began kissing the same place on her cheek as if he were absentmindedly eating something good.

"Oh, listen, it is a bee. That zzzzz comes right out of its stomach. Oh, the coffee!" She ran into the kitchen and poured a little cold water down the coffee spout. "Eggs, darling?" she called. "Both sides? A little cinnamon on your toast?"

He came running toward her, his rather firm short legs stiff, as if he were running on a track. He pushed back his cuffs and stood there by the stove, smiling and smoothing his ring. His body was so alive, she thought proudly, and his large mouth was generous, and sometimes when he tried to make her understand things all his eagerness and honesty seemed to push out of his pores. He would get close to her if she could not understand. He would bend over her, examining her eyelids, her face in its very center.

"I say, dear, can't I get the water?" He sprang for the pitcher before she could say, "Don't bother." He jerked the empty water pail then and went out the door whistling as she flopped the eggs. She heard him pushing the handle up and down, then the splash of water came as he emptied out the first bucketful. She shoved the hair up from her forehead.

Oh, that little room, that sodden bed. The broken chair in the corner. Oh, the body beside hers. The white restless hands. "You want courage, don't you? You want life, don't you?" Oh, the agony and glory of that face pressed on hers, the agony and glory of that giving. Oh, the light that came from their skin. All never ending. Life never ending. All around them the great world of tenements, sorrow, rage, bricks, joy, old brooms, cats, all—all never ending. The great world in whose body they lay, whose arms arched their heads, the roof of the house, whose hands put rain and snow and sun in their faces, brought money and took it away, ate them slowly, smiling, as they ate it—that world, never ending

She put the eggs on a platter. Parsley. She turned the bacon with a black spider fork. She laid it crisply, rolled like little blankets, round the side. She shook cinnamon over the pale toast and spread it, watching it mix brownly with the butter, and bubble under the heat. "Oh, I love my life." She took off her apron that was like a yellow Easter egg and laid her hand on her brooch. Then she glanced down, turning the pin up—a white dove in a basket of roses.

"Margot, the radishes are up, dear."

He set the pail down and filled the pitcher from a long dipper. He went in and filled their glasses. Then he dashed back for the food. "You take the coffee, dear. I'll take the platters. Go ahead."

She stood by her chair, gazing at the ceiling. She raised both hands quickly, her head pressed back against her shoulders.

"Dear God, thank you for our life." As she felt the cool chair, the hard cool wood under her hand, that other voice shot through her, "Margot, you're never polite to me." And her answer, "I know it. I love you. I can't be polite. I want the whole world from you."

She sank down, smiling at her husband. "Oh, I forgot the fruit. We were going to have casaba melon. It's in the ice box. Let me get it, dear."

He was serving the eggs. "Don't want it." The clean way he placed the eggs on the plate, just to the side of the gay French couple, made her open her mouth a little as if she were already putting the first precious taste on her tongue. He laid the bacon gently beside it. A bit of parsley.

She took it. "Thank you, darling." Now it came again, filling her head, her ears, now the room came again, the bare walls, the papers. Now the little windows opened behind her eyes, the lighted shops, the stars at night over city roofs, the sky at night above those cold white streets, those towers that went into the deep blue evening sky. "I won't let you lock me up. I won't. No. You can't. Cry then. Cry all you please. No, I'm not a monster." Girls holding their jackets together in front, a window of cloth roses. A card—Dinner .35.

"Oh, I forgot to pour the coffee."

"You're absent-minded, dear."

She lifted the proud silver pot. "Oh, I forgot the sugar, dear. I'll just put it in now. Three?"

"Why, no, dear," he said sharply, a wrinkle coming down his nose. "You know I don't take sugar."

"Of course, dear." She handed him the cup. "Shall I order fish for dinner? They're going to have trout to-day. Hollandaise? Of course I can. Why, I can too make it. I did last Wednesday and it was good." She closed her eyes for a moment, lifting her head the way she did when everything suddenly came to life, the chairs on their polished legs, the old table, the cloth, the silver, the big bowl of roses opened full. "Oh, husband, I love my life." She leaned over the table toward him, smiling, holding a piece of toast, a tiny buttered crumb on her red mouth. "I love you. I love my life."

He always sprang up, his very blue eyes almost closing too. He always choked her with his arms, bending over her face, pushing it back, back into his hands, kissing her then so gently, his hands, his body seeming to say, "Thank you, thank you, wife."

"You smell so good," he said. "You always smell that way." She felt his nostrils quivering over her cheek. She felt the melting joy of her arms as his swept hers. "Oh, I love my life," she cried, rising away from him, looking strangely into his face. "I love the world. I'm in the world with you." She pressed her hands against her womb, looking full at him now. "I love our baby. I wish there were three of them inside me." She laughed, her head far back.

"You'll have three," he promised immediately. "You'll have twelve. A dozen. A gross."

They ate, smiling at each other.

"I decided in bed last night that he will have to be named Wren."

"That's a silly name," he protested. "My poor mother couldn't think of anything else for me. . . ."

"Wren, I love your name."

He shrugged. "Have it your own way." He laid the top off the toast plate and took another brown piece. "Oh, say, Margot, I'm just joking. I'd be tickled pink to call him Wren. I just feel more manly not liking it. *You* know."

"Wren, Wren, Wren," she said rapidly.

"Dear, that is too a bee. Look, it's getting ready to sting you. See. It's sharpening its hind legs to sting you with."

Oh, save me now. Oh, master, save me now. Let him come. Let everything be the way it was at the beginning. Make him come, God. Make him come now. Make him, make him. "I'll always love you, Margot. I'll make one million babies for you." There is the train pulling out. There is his head in the window, his body, both arms waving. There are his eyes, sad, accepting all—every separation—every sundering—all, all. Oh, run, run by the train, run faster, faster, run by the train. Oh, run, run. Catch at the window, catch at the arms, hang, hang, be drawn up, lie forever near that face.

She ran into the kitchen. What is it? She thought. I don't really want to go back. I love this. I love him. I don't want to go back. It was like a clock striking in her stomach—"That was divine." She remembered the great wrenching she used to have to understand, to enter the world outside, the pain of life, of giving, the rockets that would break in her body when they sat together, then the soft gush of light through her pores.

"What *are* you doing, dear?"

"Heating the coffee."

"All right, I'll bring the pot," he called.

She bent over the stove, the lighted match in one hand, the other on the white knob. "Thanks, dear."

He took out his watch. "I ought not wait for it. I'll miss the bus again."

She stood with her back to him. "Why is anything—anything at all—always so good when you look back at it?"

"My dear, only the present is good," he mumbled. "What we do with our bodies in the present is good. What we say to each other and look. What we can express now, this minute—that's good."

"But, darling, the past becomes the present and the present seems the future and both are equally real. You know that."

"No, I don't."

"Well, it's ready."

They went in arm in arm, trying to squeeze themselves past the narrow cupboards with the rosebud china and the pewter. "Oh, my whole self is open to you, Wren," she said "I—I look back. I think of him. I can't help it."

"Of course not, dear," he said instantly. "It's all right. Why not?"

"Oh, those quakes. They come before I think of him. Just like turning on the light, Wren."

He forced her into her chair. "You drink the coffee, dear. Here goes the sugar. Here goes the cream. Here goes the spoon to stir it. Here it all goes into your red mouth. Isn't that silly, dear?"

"Thank you—thank you." She closed her eyes, pressing her lips against his hand, but there was space between. She laid her ear against his mouth but she heard that other mouth, that other voice, as if that rainy night were happening now, the cold wind blowing open the little window, the rain pelting their clothes, the clean cruel lightning crashing and blazing on the bare wall above them. In that little space between her ear and his mouth she heard those other words as if it were now. "Today I don't want a million babies, Margot, I'd kill them all quite cheerfully and without remorse. You bore me. I want to go one million miles away from you, angel. I'd as soon choke you and the kid as well if we had one. I'd murder you after six months. I'd be in the penitentiary and you'd be bringing me cigarettes and stale cookies. Don't talk. Every word you say you've said one million times. You bore me. Keep away. I haven't anything at all for you—ever. No, you've got me crazy. I swear any woman in the streets has more than you. They have bodies. They have senses. They don't hang on a guy for love all the time. Oh, shut up for a change."

She stood up, grasping the edge of the table, leaning over the fresh opened roses to him. He was standing there looking young and lonely. "What did I say to you, Wren, that day I told you all about it?"

"What? Which?"

"That day I told you how I lived with him. What did I tell you?"

"I can't remember."

"Think. Try."

He went to her. He laid his hand on their child, on her breast. His warm arms held her. He looked then into the center of her face, all of him pressed toward her, something inside him making all his particles seem loose and open, as if all his eagerness were spinning out to her from the tumult inside him.

"I said, 'What I am looking for is not in life. I can never have it.' I said—I said—'Now I want to give. I want to serve. I want to love. I want to understand.'"

Wack-ack-ack-ack-ack-ack-yeek!

"God, I can't miss it on Monday. Where's my case? To hell. Where did I put the damned thing anyway? Take a nap, dear, won't you. You're pale. I'll phone—"

"What about the trout? Shall I order . . ."

"Water the radishes, dear."

"Don't forget the receipt this time, dear."

Now he was climbing into the bus, reaching out to shake hands with his friends in gray hats and canes and crushed gloves. He was turning to smile back at some one as he straightened his tie, his big generous mouth very pleased and boyish.

Wack-ack-ack-ack-ack-yeek!

Now he waved at her as the bus was moving, making one of his hideous faces just for fun. Then he smiled quickly and lifted his hat. The long orange bus went.

"West End 2039-W." She fingered the telephone book. "No, operator, I said West End 2039-W. Yes."

Oh, to be nothing but a tree, to spread cool branches over grass and flowers, to let children climb my body and lie in my boughs, to shake off my leaves and fall asleep, making a soft zzzzz under the fallen snow. Oh, to be born again, to be new, to blossom.

"Hello, this is Mrs. Henshaw. I want you to send me a very nice lake trout. About one and a half pounds. I want half a dozen lemons. A dozen of the best eggs. A pound of the best butter and two casaba melons—no, not any melons. Cross that off. I have melons. Yes, that's all. No, I must have a bottle of prepared mustard. That's all this morning."

She went upstairs singing, shaking her bright hair. Then she stood before the opened windows, her hands on their child, her face light and beautiful as she looked down into the garden, then up to the branching trees that sprayed the house. She saw the bright perfect sky, the white clouds. But the clouds, the air, even, the great trees, all were still, gleaming in the sun.

The soft lavender quilt was half on the floor. The white mark of their heads had creased the pillows, denting them softly. There was her orange robe with the pale yellow flowers breathing softly out of it, shaking soft petals down it, vibrating on the cloth as if a little wind were underneath. She sat down on the hard cool chair near the desk. Instantly ice spread over the skin of her feet. It spread up and they turned hard and dead. They broke apart with lightning from that night and it ripped her open in long clean cracks.

"For God's sake, marry some one else, not me, not me, not me, for God's sake, where's my tobacco, marry some one else, please. I want you to be happy, you're the one I love best of all, Margot, marry some one else. I can't bear to see you unhappy, get that match over there for me, where the hell did I throw my pouch, I'll find some one for you, I love you, it will make me jealous, I want you to be happy, Margot, Christ, can't you see I'm cold, close the window, don't you ever see what I need, no, I won't regret it, don't fool yourself and that's the truth, don't reproach me for the truth, I won't regret it, I love you best, give me a dime, damn it, I want a dime, I do too love you."

She went downstairs and gathered up the cups and saucers. She threw the Easter egg apron over her head and turned water into the dish pan. Then she carried the plates into the kitchen, into the sunny window by the gleaming pan. She pushed the parsley aside so that she could look down on the gay French couple, hand in hand, laughing in their big shoes and funny peasant hats.

"I have a child inside me," she whispered to them softly. "I love my husband. I love the world. Thank you, God."

DEATH OF MRS. VANDERWOOD

S HE lay in bed before the open window, her gray hair
moistened and brushed, her cheeks a bright pink up under
the eyes on the high cheek bones, her hands folded on the
pansy quilt. "Mady," she said, and the girl in the rocking chair
came over to the bed. "That's a good girl, Mady. Sit down here.
Take hold of my hand."

The girl turned her face away for a moment and fitted the
starched frill of her white cap over her ear in a little puff. Mrs.
would want to talk about death again, ever since this last attack
she'd been going it strong, talking about death. And her hand
was like turkey flesh, purple and spare and cool, you could feel
those cool slim bones when she reached out with it.

"That's a good girl, Mady. Sit right here."

Mady got up and looped back the tan curtains from the
windows so that light poured in. They could hear the river
outside, flowing past, lapping the little stones on the narrow
beach. They could hear the sound of Sunday mixed with the
sounds of voices in the little churches across the river, voices
that sounded now as if they had sung forever on this bright
endless Sunday. Occasionally a car passed on the sandy road or
a bird flew by the window.

"Doctor said you could have milk. Don't you want me to
get you a nice cool glass? Come, Mrs., let Mady get you a glass
of nice milk."

"Just keep hold of my hand, Mady."

The girl stopped by the bed, as if she could not move, and her upper lip twitched so that her two large front teeth gleamed. She put the edge of her tongue over her teeth and her eyes rolled up in nausea and fright. She remembered her grandmother dying. She hadn't talked about it at all. She hadn't been a bother. She just lay still and then stuff came out of her mouth and she was dead. But her mother had made the little ones run away, she had made them go to Affeldt's back yard and look at the rabbits. She jerked in impatience. She never knew what Mrs. would say to her, what she would ask her, like as not it would be—"Was your mother really happy, Mady?" or "Tell me how you feel when you stand looking at the river?" or "Mady— Mady!" and this always frightened the soul clean out of her body—"Mady, it's a shock—a queer little jolt all over—when you *realize* you're going to die. It doesn't last, just a little shock, like electricity, but everything in you knows." And Mrs. expected a wise answer to everything. When she said something wasn't true or that life wasn't good or just she always looked into her as if *she* ought to prove the statement false. And what did she know anyway? Mrs. was unreasonable.

"Oh, come, and hold my hand, Mady."

"Doctor said milk was good for you. It's the natural food, Mrs. I'm going to get you some.'

"I've been thinking of Uncle Azra all morning."

"Oh, God help me!" thought Mady, "God save me now." She knew all about Uncle Azra. Her mother always brought him chickens during the winter, and she had heard about his death, too, but no one else made it sound like Mrs. when she went into it, no one else made it so frightening. Even when she mentioned Uncle Azra Mady always wanted to go off alone and get sick and she always liked him, too, when he was alive. "Don't let her tell it again," she prayed, as she saw the purple hand stretch out and the lids open.

"Now sit down and entertain me, Mady. Tell me something diverting. How do I look?" she asked very low.

The woman's face was still, her mouth closed in a line of firm acceptance of everything. Her hands were folded in dignity as if they were part of her, as if they were expressing as much as the mouth or the shoulders or the strong thin neck. Her eyes expressed the same but they were dulled over with a milky mucus like a blind dog's, and as she turned them to the light the brown eyes beneath looked serene and inquiring.

" 'Delia,' he said to me, 'Delia, good-by.' And I said, 'Oh, Uncle Azra!' And he put out his hand—here, Mady, take my hand—he put out his hand like this and shook mine. He said good-by to his wife and his children. 'George, James, Samuel, John—I see now you're all good boys.' I remember when he went to Chicago he said good-by to everybody just the same way."

Mady jerked impatiently. Her full cheeks were bright with hot color. She jumped up, her hand still in the woman's, the other on her cheek. "I heard the back door, Mrs. I better see."

She ran down, biting her fingernail and rolling her eyes. She stopped short in the kitchen and then she went into the front of the house and took up the telephone. "72R," she said shortly, and began gnawing her nail again. "Hello. Katie? Did you get the dress done? Swell. Is he? My Lord, that's swell. Sure. Sure I am. White. All white. Sure. Sure it's nicer. Sure. Oh, she gives me a big pain. Say, about everybody in our family's died with heart trouble but they never made over it, not one of them ever did. Why, she's going crazy. Honest, I think she is. You'd think she'd want her mind on something different than dying, wouldn't you? Say, she's got me wild. Talks about it all the time. My Aunt Minnie—you remember—never a moan out of her—just like that—then she was gone—not a bit of trouble—thinking of others—Oh, I don't know. No, I can't tell. Doctor said she was lots better. I guess as long as she's got wind to talk about death she's all right. But wouldn't you think she'd want to be talking something bright and cheery? Wouldn't you, though. Something happy and cheery. Sure, I know it. Sure. Ya, white. Ya. Sure. Four ninety at Graham's. Sure. Oh, you'll

look all right. Sure you will. That's a swell hat. Sure, I'll go if
I can. You know Doctor can't tell yet. She ain't as bad as she
makes out. Oh, sure she's a lovely character. Sure she is. Listen,
I think the world and all of Mrs. I sure do." She began smoothing
the goods of her skirt. "All right. If I can. Listen, you know I
don't mean a thing I say, don't you? All right. If I can, Katie.
'By."

She rushed upstairs and then before she could hunt for her
gum Mrs. had her hand and she couldn't get loose this time.

"Oh, what do you *do* when you run off like that? Now
you're to stay here. Sit down, Mady."

"If you was going to get a dance dress which'd you get—
black or white?"

"This place is going to my daughter," said Mrs. unexpectedly. "But I don't want her here for the funeral. It'll be bad
enough to be dead without having every one talking about how
I look. Oh, my God!" she cried suddenly. "Ooooooooo."

Mady cried out, too, with the pain because Mrs. pressed
her hand so hard. Her long cold bones gripped round it until
she burst into tears. "Oh, Mrs. Don't take it so hard. Listen, it
hurts my hand. Listen!"

"Lord, I'd rather walk out into that field and lie down and
be done with it where something is growing. That's the last
thing I'd feel—something alive under me. Here I am in a bed
that's already dead, in a dead house, closed in dead walls—
Bring me a glass of water!"

Mady scuttled to the door.

The woman turned over on her side. "I'd go down to the
river," she said very low. "I'd step into the living water and die
in life. I'd—*Delia!*" she cried sharply, as if she expected herself
to answer.

Then it came back to her. Once she had been sitting in
the sun on a Sunday morning like this. All Sundays were alike
through the whole world, all singing was alike, all voices lived
forever on a Sunday. The voices of the dead mixed with those
of the living and those about to live. She had been looking at

the river, listening to the voices from the little churches on the
other bank. She had let her book fall to the grass. Now it all
came back to her. But that day she had understood something
important, vital, and today she didn't. "Mady," she called,
"come back. I need you."

"Mady came in sheepishly with a glass on a tray. "Here,
Mrs. Now don't you want me to fix you up for a nice nap? You
look sleepy Doctor said you'd need sleep."

"Huh," grunted the woman. "Sleep. That reminds me of
Uncle Azra. 'Why, Azra,' said Aunt Liddy, 'Azra, your feet's
cold. I'll get the hot-water bag.' Uncle Azra said, "Course they're
cold. When a person's dying his feet's always cold."

"Oh, Mrs.!" cried Mady, the tears glittering on her lashes.

"Well, I can't help it. Women always want to keep things
warm forever. When my baby died I went down and bought
winter underwear and I put on her thickest dress and they all
thought I was crazy but I saw to it she had her hood and coat
on when they buried her. Oh, if a person could only die—
wonderfully—" she said, closing her eyes.

Mady's starched cap crackled as she bent her head. She
kept thinking to herself, over and over, "Trust Mrs. to act
special, as if she's the first to die." Then she thought of all her
family going with heart trouble, too, and the way they took it,
thinking of others and not talking crazy and scaring every one
out of their wits nearly.

"Sit up, Mady! I want to look into the face of one simple
honest natural person."

Mady slowly lifted her round freckled face and tried to
look into the eyes of her mistress without making up an ugly
face or drawing down her mouth until the cords of her neck
stood out. When those eyes were upon her she always wanted
to look homely, just make her ugliest face, because Mrs. made
her feel so queer, as if she was seeing something nobody else
saw and nobody knew about.

"Listen, Mady. I sat right out there near the river, near
those lilacs. I used to call it my lilac copse when Minda was a

baby. Get up," she said suddenly, "and look at it and don't forget what I'm telling you. Is the grass kind of thin to the right of the bushes, the side near the river bank—just a little spot there kind of poorly?"

Mady went heavily to the window and leaned out. "Yes, Mrs." she said.

"Does the river look all smooth and as if you couldn't ever stop it?"

"Sure it does."

"Do you see the cottonwood tree to the left? There were little cotton fluffs coming out that day and the wind was blowing them all over the lawn. Mr. Acres came in from the fields and he wanted to cut the tree down. Do you see the tree? Now what was I telling you about it, Mady? There's something vital connected with that tree. Do you see it? Did I tell you what's remarkable about it? Listen, go down and bring me up one of those little stones near the river, one of the white ones. They always remind me of baby's teeth. Hurry now!"

Suddenly the woman saw herself standing out on the river bank that Sunday. The calendar on the desk reminded her of it. Mr. Acres had brought the calendar to her on her birthday. It was from the Snyder Cement Company. "I ought to leave Mr. Acres a little something," she thought. "Minda'll run through hers quick enough." Then she recalled that Sunday morning again. She had dropped her book. She had known with utter clearness that her body—something about her body—"Mady," she called, "bring me my glasses!"

"All right, Mrs." called Mady.

"I know what it was, Mady," she said eagerly as the girl came into the room. "I was unhappy that Sunday. I guess it was the day I was so terribly unhappy only I can't remember. Anyway, I suddenly realized that I was in pieces. Just as if I'd been knocked apart and never got together again." She turned her eyes to the windows. "Oh, when I knew," she thought quietly, "when I knew that why didn't I do something, why didn't I try to get all fitted close together again." The curtains blew into the room softly, rippling out with the slight wind, and there was the noise in the cottonwood below of leaves moving. "I don't know, Mady, I think I'd get white. A pretty white with lace and then white slippers. Do you want slippers?"

Mady came close to her now. "Can't I hold your hand, Mrs.?" she asked. "I saw some nice ones down at Graham's for four ninety. Just what I want." She couldn't help feeling indignant, though, even with the offer of the slippers. Imagine leaving the place to Minda. In books they always left their riches to the faithful servant. Anyway, Minda didn't need it. She had a home and a husband and a baby and she hadn't treated her mother or any one else right—no. "What do I slave here for?" she thought to herself. Then she pulled her hand away and pretended to examine it closely as if it hurt.

"I don't want to live. But I want what I have been to live. When I was very happy and when I was very sad. I want that to live. I want all the separate Delias to live and I want some one to remember one of me forever."

She looked confused again and then she closed her eyes and put her thin hand over them. It seemed to her as if she was swarming with lambs, as if all those memories of herself were lambs running about in her without a shepherd. She would die, these bones would die, and inside her all those lambs would lie down and die. . . . "Mady," she called, "I want you to telephone Mr. Clark and tell him I've decided to put in an oil burner."

"All right, Mrs." called Mady from the stairway. She rushed down. "2007" she told the operator. But before she could get Mr. Clark on the wire Mrs. was calling her again and she put up the receiver. "I never in my life," she said savagely as she went back to the bedroom.

"Mady, please come here. Now sit down near me again. Hold my hand. Mady, did you ever see any one die?"

"Well, *sure!*" she cried "Everybody's gotta."

"Oh, but it ought to be *different!*"

"Now listen, Mrs. You turn over—"

"How can I be remembered?"

"Well, I never forgot my grandmother because she left me her quilts for when I marry."

"All these *people* in myself. All different people. I don't know which—and I'm dying—"

"Mrs., I don't think you are," said Mady with a gulp. "I really don't. My Aunt Minnie didn't speak a word. She had the same as you've got."

"My grandmother had those pure white chickens with red crops. They were in a big chicken yard and I loved the smell of their feathers. When the sun shone—the white feathers, their clean legs, the bright grain, their shining bills— Oh, I've fallen apart. I'm dying."

"You look on the dark side too much."

"What do they call it? The river Charon? The dark boatman? That's it. Mythology. I need that. Uncle Azra had a mythology that's why he could die like a brave man. He thought he was taking a journey. He was stepping into a boat, crossing a river, and then entering the heavenly gardens, the heavenly skies and rivers and stars. He was more excited than when he went to Chicago." She turned to Mady, her eyes glazed over again with the gray film. "I've fallen apart. I haven't any shepherd to gather me together. Oh, my God," she said slowly, her eyes closing.

"Oh, don't you bother, Mrs. Don't you mind. Listen, listen," she cried, bending over the bed, a strange startled look on her face of grief and innocence.

"I felt something—I can't remember my life—I want it saved—all of it—please—"

"Mrs. Mrs. Oh, listen—"

The woman opened her eyes for a second and then she closed them. It seemed to her that she was reaching down into the infinite darkness of herself and lifting them out one by one— lambs; lifting them out and burying them; one near the lilac copse, one near the river, one under the cottonwood, another on the roof of the barn where it sloped toward the chicken yard, another in the south field, another in the mattress where she lay, and one, and one, and one; on, on, until she saw a dark figure bending and sagging, huge, black.

Mady went downstairs. "7086," she said. "Oh, Doctor, listen. She's gone into a comie."

AFTERWORD
The Life

*There's only one possession that's worth having and that is the
capacity to feel that life is a privilege and that each person in it is
unique and will never appear again.*
—Margery Latimer to Zona Gale, 1928[1]

Margery Bodine Latimer was born on February 6, 1899 in
Portage, Wisconsin, the second child and daughter of Clark
Watt and Laura Augusta Bodine Latimer. Her parents had met
and married in Mansfield, Ohio in 1890 and her father, a
traveling salesman, had chosen to settle in Portage because of
its good rail connections to his upper Mississippi territory. The
town of Portage in 1899 had not yet been put on the literary
map by Zona Gale's phenomenally popular Friendship Village
stories.

Laurie Latimer was a beautiful, gentle woman, low-key in
manner, who loved books, music, and comfortable surroundings.
Clark Latimer, a large, handsome, noisy man whose impeccable
dress verged on dandyism, held conventional views and his tastes
were uncultivated. He adored Laurie all his life and worked
extraordinarily hard to provide his family with the finer things,
but it seemed, when he returned from his long road trips, that
he was almost baffled by the three females living under his roof.

From the moment of Margery's arrival, she became the
center of her mother's emotional life; the six-year-old Rachel,

a robust and gregarious girl, fell into alliance with her father. Laurie Latimer sensed immediately that there was a special, other-worldly quality in her youngest child; Margery seemed to possess a sixth sense which enabled her, even when an infant, to "know" things inaccessible to others. She seems never to have grown a protective social crust; wise and vulnerable at once, Margery would face life with the directness and intensity of a Blake vision.

Margery's early resolve to be a writer was strengthened by the example of Portage-neighbor Zona Gale, though the two did not become acquainted until 1917. One of Margery's short stories, printed in the local newspaper, caught Zona's attention and she immediately summoned the young author to tea at her elegant columned home overlooking the river. At 42, Zona Gale had already achieved financial independence and fame through her writing and had returned to Portage several years earlier to live with her parents. Her finest work (and the Pulitzer Prize) was still ahead of her at the time of her meeting with Margery.

Zona was enchanted. "There is a wonderful child here," she wrote to a friend. "She is one of the most exquisite centres of intuitive experience imaginable."[2]

For her part, Margery was cast under a spell which would not be broken for fourteen years.

Margery entered Wooster College in Ohio in the fall of 1918 but seems to have been terribly unhappy there from the start (homesickness, mainly) and she withdrew at the end of the first semester. The following autumn she entered the University of Wisconsin, only forty miles from Portage, but was not much happier. The impersonality of the huge campus, the emphasis on football and the rah-rah spirit, the brassy social life revolving around fraternities and sororities—all repelled her. A fellow occupant of Barnard Hall recalls Margery at that time:

> My first impression of Margery was that on the whole she seemed
> somewhat remote, intentionally. It might have been a mask for

shyness. But when one got a little closer one found she set a lot
of store by being not different, exactly, but distinctive.[3]

Everyone agrees that Margery was a strikingly attractive
girl; the word most often used to describe her was "radiant."
Above average in height (about 5'8") and large-boned, she had
a mass of golden hair, variously described as honey blonde or
strawberry blonde, large, piercingly blue eyes, and perfect skin.
The poet, Carl Rakosi, recalls Margery vividly:

> She wore no make-up, no lipstick, no high heels, no frills of any
> kind and only the most plain dresses. Her walk was unselfconscious,
> very straight and direct, without being masculine. What struck
> one immediately was her radiant presence. Blake would have
> described her as a cloud of gold. . . . In a long life, I have not
> seen her like.[4]

Academically, Margery performed adequately but she could
not learn by rote; the canned lectures seemed only to skim over
the surface and left her bored and restless to find deeper
connections.

In May of 1921, while Margery was preparing to leave
Madison "for good," Zona was awarded the Pulitzer Prize in
drama for *Miss Lulu Bett*, the first woman so honored. The play
had opened in December and was still attracting standing-room-
only audiences; Zona was earning enormous sums of money and
was the most sought-after figure in New York.

Margery arrived in the city in June and signed up for a
summer playwriting course at·Columbia University. The class
was a disappointment but Margery found a friend there who
more than made up for it. Blanche (Mrs. Russell) Matthias, an
extraordinarily lovely, wealthy, sophisticated woman in her early
thirties, was intrigued by the "glorious looking young woman"
who was indolent and impertinent in the classroom and so
wonderfully alive outside it. Blanche soon became Margery's
closest friend, confidante, and supporter.

One of Zona's many letters of introduction finally paid off

for Margery in October when she got a job in the fashion department of the *Woman's Home Companion*. She promptly moved into a charming studio on West 23rd Street, bought a typewriter on the installment plan, and began her first novel. Zona wrote her from Portage that Mrs. Latimer marveled at the courage her youngest daughter was showing but Margery's brave new world didn't last long. She was fired from her job in the spring and, chastened, returned home to Portage. She wrote to Blanche: "If it weren't for Zona, I would feel like Nothing."[5]

Margery re-enrolled at Wisconsin in the fall but this time as a special student, taking only those courses which appealed to her. Money, as always, was a problem. Clark Latimer's earnings in the first nine months of 1922 amounted to only a little over a thousand dollars. Zona responded by initiating the Zona Gale Scholarship Fund which would grant to the winners the incredibly generous sum of seventy dollars a month. The scholarship terms were hand-crafted for Margery's benefit and Zona made certain that she was the first recipient.

Margery's third year at the university was a complete turn-about from the first two; she blossomed. She made friends with Kenneth Fearing, Carl Rakosi, Horace Gregory, Marya Zaturen-ska, and others in the literary group and her contributions (essays and reviews, mainly) began to appear in the literary magazine. And there was the excitement of Zona's visits to campus, which were frequent. Margery's feelings for Zona were intense, almost overwhelming. She wrote to Zona about this time:

> A new sense came to me as Miss Conklin sat there talking of you. I was filled with you . . . I thought I would like to serve you, serve you, belong to you. I feel as though now for the first time I am bound to beauty.[6]

At the same time, Margery's friendship with Kenneth Fearing had gradually deepened into a romance, to the astonished delight of their friends. Two more opposite people could hardly be imagined. Kenneth's looks were dark, frail, unprepossessing; he was appallingly grubby in his personal habits. Kenneth's gods were Edwin Arlington Robinson and H.L. Mencken and he deplored the romanticism of Margery's novel-in-progress which he blamed on Zona's influence. His upbringing had been very unstable (his mother was about to marry for the fourth time and would have seven husbands in all) and perhaps because of it, he played the role of *enfant terrible* to the hilt. His brilliance and talent were unquestioned, however, and though only twenty years old, his poems were already attracting notice in New York literary circles. The Latimers were vehemently opposed to Fearing as a suitor; Zona was not charmed by him either but had the good sense to base her objection to the match on the discrepancy in their ages.

Margery decided, in the summer of 1923, not to return to college but to live at home and concentrate on her writing. Her novel was now finished and Joseph Hergesheimer, at the height of his fame and influence at this time, had appointed himself Margery's unofficial agent and was trying to find a publisher for it. She and Kenneth visited back and forth between Portage and Madison but a shift of power in the relationship had occurred and Margery now found herself the pursuer, not the pursued.

Partly as a way of getting Margery's mind off Kenneth, the Latimers agreed to underwrite a combination holiday/writing trip for her the following summer. Zona recommended an artists' colony in upstate New York, near Rochester, where she had once stayed and where good friends of hers would be spending part of the summer. Margery boarded the train in July, expecting to be away only a month or two, but it would be almost a year before she returned home. She worked hard on revising her novel (the Knopfs, after showing strong interest, had finally turned it down) and exultantly wrote her mother in September that it was finished and that Blanche, who was visiting her, was lending her the money to go to New York to make the rounds of publishers.

The next ten months were among the happiest and most exciting of Margery's life. She and Mavis McIntosh, a friend from Madison, shared a room at the Old Chelsea on West 16th

Street and the "Wisconsin Gang" made it their home away from home. (Horace Gregory would celebrate these days in his first book of poems, *Chelsea Rooming House*, published in 1930.) She was dating the painter Walt Kuhn, among others, and there were dinner and party invitations from Anita Loos, the Carl Van Vechtens, the Hergesheimers, and Carl and Irita Van Doren. Georgia O'Keeffe (who was from the Portage area and who was, in addition, a good friend of Blanche's) was coming into prominence through Alfred Stieglitz's group shows at the Anderson Galleries.

Piqued, perhaps, by Margery's happy letters, Kenneth arrived in New York in December, eager to resume their relationship. They went to the movies (still silent), to the Provincetown Playhouse, and to concerts, when they could afford it, and simply walked the streets of New York when they couldn't.

No matter how hectic her schedule, Margery, at Zona's urging, tried not to miss A. R. Orage's Monday night lectures on the Gurdjieff philosophy. Like many other Americans in the post-war years, Zona Gale had become deeply interested in Eastern mysticism and this interest had intensified after the death of her mother the year before. Gurdjieff's movement had become famous (or infamous) in 1923 when writer Katherine Mansfield, a recent convert, had died at his Institute for the Harmonious Development of Man in Fontainebleau. Zona's credo was that "life is something more than that which we believe it to be" and she sensed that the mysterious Russian, Georgei Grudjieff, had a clue as to what the "something more" might be. Margery herself found Gurdjieff's teachings impenetrable but she was drawn to the charismatic Orage who soon became her friend and literary mentor.

Margery needed all of Orage's support and encouragement (he predicted that she would one day surpass Katherine Mansfield) as the new version of her novel had met with a cold reception. Originally entitled *Lilac Castle*, it had then made the rounds as *Pink Flamingoes;* Margery concluded that it wasn't publishable in any color and scrapped it. At the same time, she followed Kenneth's advice—or perhaps a nudge from Orage—and abandoned her highly romantic, almost inflated, style (although it would peep through later in *This Is My Body*) and employed sharp, minimal, effective prose for the short stories she was now writing.

Kenneth soon began pressing her to live with him and in the spring, restless to get out of the city, Margery agreed to share an apartment with him at Fort Place in St. George, Staten Island. They were, on the whole, happy together but neither was getting much work done and they agreed that they should part for the summer to concentrate on writing.

Margery arrived in Portage in June of 1925, intent on writing a novel with Zona as the protagonist. A month later she wrote to Blanche that she had finished seventy pages and "Zona . . . thinks it very good. There are parts that I shudder to read to her and when I have finished I feel that I can't go on but she sits there beyond emotion, poised, remote."[7] Margery was quite right to fear Zona's reaction. The central figure of Hester Linden in *We Are Incredible* comes off as a cold, sexless, domineering creature who ruins the lives of all those closest to her. Later, Margery would insist that she had not meant the book to be an indictment of Zona; rather, it had been a call for help. If so, Zona didn't answer it.

The novel was finished in December but before returning to New York, Margery accompanied her mother on a long visit to California. Kenneth complained, justifiably perhaps, that the Latimers were trying to keep them apart. However, when Margery rejoined him, it was Kenneth's idea that they share their apartment at 62 Barrow Street with a friend of his, Leslie Rivers, whom Margery disliked. It was not a happy ménage. Kenneth was notorious, among their friends, for his sloppiness and he was now drinking more heavily; the added burden of cooking and cleaning up after Leslie was the proverbial straw, as far as Margery was concerned. She felt that her own writing was being sacrificed in order to advance Kenneth's career, which was now in high gear. Even though, in 1926, two of her stories were sold and the following year Van Wyck Brooks chose two other stories for later publication in his prestigious American Caravan anthologies, Margery felt that her writing career was becalmed.

She had a sense of urgency also about getting on with her personal life; she wanted very much to get married and have children but Kenneth, after almost two years of living together, was still adamantly opposed to both. Looking back on this time, Margery would write to Blanche: "I tried to discover what he needed and I did but I can't live that way any more. I had to give everything—my peace of mind, my whole self, every kind of attention, and expect nothing."[8] In the spring of 1928, she made the final break with Kenneth and returned to Portage and to Zona.

Margery was unaware that Zona's life had taken an entirely new direction. She had, six months before, quietly assumed the guardianship of a homeless two-year-old girl, Leslyn, whom she hoped to adopt legally. The second turning point in Zona's life was a chance encounter in California with an old Portage acquaintance, William L. Breese. Breese was a wealthy manufacturer and banker, Portage's civic leader, and a widower just a few years older than Zona. The friendship deepened after each had returned home and Breese began a discreet but persistent courtship. It seemed, on the surface, an ideal match but there were deep differences between them. Zona was a feminist, a pacifist, a prominent supporter of La Follette's Progressive Party, and she had given up, long ago, on conventional Christianity. Breese was a conservative Republican and a Presbyterian elder, entirely traditional in his thinking. Will Breese was in love; Zona's reasons for accepting his proposal of marriage are not so clear. They were married in a quiet ceremony on June 12, 1928.

Neither Zona nor anyone else had the courage to break the news to Margery; she learned about the wedding only the night before it took place, reading the announcement in the newspaper. Convinced that it was a mistake or a joke, Margery ran in a frenzy to Edgewater Place to demand an explanation.

Zona kept her waiting for over an hour and then cooly told her that what she had read in the paper was true.

Margery saw Zona's marriage not only as a personal betrayal but also as a refutation of Zona's lifelong beliefs. In particular, her "failure" with Kenneth had finally convinced Margery that Zona had been right all along—that a woman must choose between the life of a creative artist and that of an ordinary married woman. One couldn't have both, Zona had always said. There was also the uncomfortable realization that if Zona was not uncommon, not a unique superior being, then what was Margery?

Her breakdown was so disabling that the Latimers considered hospitalizing her; even the publication of *We Are Incredible*, and the excellent notices that followed, did not lift Margery's depression. Surprisingly, Margery was writing her most accomplished stories during this tormented time and these, along with earlier stories, would be published in 1929 as *Nellie Bloom and Other Stories*. The volume was reviewed widely and the chorus of praise was overwhelming. Most critics commented that the promise of her first book had been more than fulfilled.

Returning again to the story of her own life, Margery worked throughout 1929 on a novel, *This Is My Body*. She intended the book to be both catharsis and communion; a way of reclaiming the girl that she had been and a plea, mainly directed toward her family, for understanding. In a state of exultation while writing it, Margery came back to earth with a thump when it was finished. "I have read half of the galleys and I am shocked and horrified. It isn't good the way I thought ti [sic] was."[9] When the book appeared in 1930, the reviewers agreed with her and though she had anticipated their reaction, Margery interpreted the reviews as a cutting personal rejection.

Still, in her words, "on the rack" about Zona two years after her marriage, Margery tried once more to exorcise Zona's ghost through her writing. The result was a long short story, "Guardian Angel," whose central character, Fleta Bain, is an even more damning portrayal of Zona than was Hester Linden.

Friends begged her not to publish it but when *Scribner's* chose
the story as a finalist in a $5,000 Short Story Contest, there
was no question of holding it back. By the time the story
appeared in the magazine's June issue, however, Margery had
already found her release.

The appearance in 1923 of *Cane*, a hauntingly beautiful
prose-poem about Southern Negro life, had established Jean
Toomer's reputation overnight. *Cane* would be cited later as the
harbinger and the highest achievement of the Harlem Renais-
sance but by that time, Toomer was no longer identifying himself
as Negro, which was only a small fraction of his ancestry. In
the 1920s, he had become an enthusiastic follower of the
Gurdjieff movement, traveling several times to Fontainebleau
to study under the master, and in 1931, at the age of thirty-six,
Toomer had succeeded A. R. Orage as the senior Gurdjieff
teacher in America. He had assembled a loyal group of about
forty pupils in Chicago and it was at one of their meetings that
he and Margery met.

If there is such a thing as love at first sight, Margery
experienced it.

> After dinner Lane played the piano and Toomer sat down beside
> me. Every one seemed to "observe" us, for some reason. He said,
> "Now, I'm going to hold Margery's hand if I may, Mr. Lane." I
> couldn't stand it for more than a second. His hand seemed moving
> inside and mine got perfectly static. I had to take it away and he
> said, "You're protecting yourself. You've heard things about me."
> Of course I hadn't at all, except from Georgia O'Keefe, who
> thinks he is simply great, much finer than Waldo Frank. But as
> I sat there not saying anything something quiet seemed to rush
> from my hand downward and I felt more quiet than before. I
> seemed to lose all memory, everything was washed away. I left
> early and suddenly as I said goodbye to those three—Lane, his
> wife, Toomer, I couldn't *bear* to go. . . . The next morning when
> I woke up I thought, "I was washed of my evil. I was washed
> clean. Now I can choose."[10]

What Margery might have heard about Jean Toomer was

that he had a formidable reputation with women; they adored him and continued to do so long after he had lost interest in them. He was tall, very handsome, charming, self-possessed, a superb athlete and dancer, a gifted musician, and had a "hypnotically beautiful" voice. Toomer had never married and he had openly cautioned the many women with whom he had been involved that he intended to remain single.

It had been Toomer's dream for years to establish a permanent community for his students, modeled after Gurdjieff's Institute, where they could live, learn, and work together. Margery immediately thought of Bonnie Oaks, a summer compound about ten miles from Portage owned by her friends Harrison and Mildred Green. The Greens sometimes rented the hired man's cottage to vacationers and though it wasn't suitable as a permanent base for the Institute, Margery thought it could be a starting point. The "Portage Experiment," as it came to be known, was wildly misconstrued at the time (outsiders thought it a haven for Communism, free love and nudism) and Toomer's explanations of his aims often were so layered in Gurdjieffian jargon that they only added to the mystery. Put in contemporary terms, the basic idea was to live simply and naturally, to get in touch with one's feelings, and to begin the long process of integrating one's personality. Margery loathed many things about the Experiment—communal living, manual labor, compulsory games—but the worst part, perhaps, was not having Jean to herself. One evening, as the group sat around the campfire, Margery lost her temper over a seemingly trivial incident and the next morning she was gone. Jean dashed into Portage to persuade her to come back (she did) and it was probably during this interview that Jean declared his love. She, usually so adept with words, could find only one phrase to describe her feelings. Over and over she wrote to her friends, "I am miraculously happy."[11]

The wedding on October 30, 1931 in the Episcopal Church was a large and lavish affair by Portage standards and the reception which followed was almost a community festival. The

Toomers honeymooned in Chicago and lingered there for a month before taking the train to New Mexico, still searching for a permanent home for Jean's Institute. His Gurdjieff lectures had been well received in Santa Fe five years before and Mabel Dodge Luhan had, in fact, offered her ranch in Taos as the site for a Gurdjieff community. Mabel was now bombarding the Toomers with telegrams, inviting them to stay with her. They arrived in Santa Fe in late November and rented a charming old adobe house in the foothills overlooking the town. New Mexico was colder (and more expensive) than they had anticipated but the month that they had together there would be the happiest of Margery's life.

Jean was working on a nonfiction account of the summer experiment (entitled *Portage Potential,* it remains unpublished) while Margery began a novel based on the same events. For some reason, the planned visit to Mabel Dodge Luhan's ranch did not take place, to Margery's great disappointment; she didn't mind missing the formidable Mabel but had looked forward to meeting Frieda Lawrence and Dorothy Brett because of their connection to Katherine Mansfield. Nor did Jean succeed in reviving an interest in Gurdjieff among his former students.

Zona had arranged for her daughter Leslyn and the child's governess, Evelyn Hood, to spend the winter in California while she and Will traveled. Evelyn now entreated the Toomers to join her in San Diego where they could live rent-free in the large house that Zona had leased. They were pondering the pros and cons of Evelyn's offer when Margery learned, to her great joy, that she was pregnant. Jean was ecstatic.

Jean and Margery arrived in San Diego just before Christmas and during the six weeks that they stayed there, Jean completed his Portage book and Margery made good progress on her novel, now called *The Ship.* The people of San Diego appeared oblivious of the Gurdjieff movement, however, and in February they accepted an invitation from Margery's aunt and uncle in Pasadena to stay with them. There were many Gurdjieff adherents in the Los Angeles area, especially in Hollywood, but none were able or willing, amidst a deepening economic depression, to pay for Jean's instruction. They were, however, buoyed by the news that Smith & Haas had accepted *Guardian Angel and Other Stories* for publication.

Jean was beginning to realize that the Chicago group, still loyally sending contributions every few weeks, was his best hope for the founding of an Institute. Both he and Margery wanted to visit San Francisco before heading back, however, and a Miss Bulkeley in Carmel (who had been valiantly holding together a group started there by Orage in 1928) promised them a warm welcome.

They thought they had fallen into paradise. Miss Bulkeley had found them a magnificent redwood contemporary overlooking the ocean; it had four bedrooms, two baths, and a view from every window. Also through Miss Bulkeley, the Toomers became acquainted with the Lincoln Steffens, the Robinson Jeffers, photographer Edward Weston, poet Orrick Johns, and others in the Carmel art colony.

To stir local interest in his lectures, Jean granted an interview to a reporter from the weekly Carmel *Pine Cone*. The risk of rekindling the scandal which had raged the year before seemed remote. (Two of the Portage Experiment participants, married but separated from their spouses, had fallen in love and run away together; the tumultuous publicity which followed had cited Jean and his "free love cult" as the instigator.) Jean opened up to the sympathetic reporter and talked idealistically (and naively) of the day when there would be no racial, class, or economic distinctions in this country—there would simply be Americans. A Hearst reporter in San Francisco spotted the interview, pieced it together with the scandal of a year before and added some lurid details of his own to produce an outrageously malevolent story which made headlines from coast to coast. The Portage Experiment was portrayed as the first step, with Margery as the first recruit, of a sinister conspiracy to "mongrelize" the white race. *Time* magazine professed to be shocked that the Toomer's marriage was actually legal. Reporters and photographers beseiged their house, cars filled with gawking sightseers caused a traffic jam on Ocean Drive, and the Toomer's mailbox was flooded with hate mail and threats. Portage was in an uproar and Margery's parents fled to Rachel's home in Montana.

Holding their heads high, Jean and Margery waited in Carmel for the storm to slacken before beginning the long drive back to Portage in June. It had been a shattering experience but Margery was more concerned about her family than she was about herself and the baby she was carrying. "I have brought suffering to you all—the one thing I have most feared."[12]

Jean rented a large airy apartment on Division Street in Chicago; there were separate bedrooms for the nurse-midwife and for Laurie Latimer, who would be with them for the baby's birth. Margery had, from time to time, expressed great fear about childbirth but as the date approached, she wrote to Zona:

> We expect the baby about August 12th and I look forward now, to the event, with such excitement and such eagerness that all thought of my inadequacy in pain and in life has entirely left me. It seems like my one supreme date with reality.[13]

Exactly what went wrong will never certainly be known. Margery probably contracted an infection for which, of course, there was no antibiotic. She remained conscious long enough to know that she had delivered a perfect baby girl. She died the night of August 16, 1932.

The day before Margery's funeral, Zona wrote to a friend that she had had an intense mystical experience sitting in her garden that afternoon.

> It was not until some time had passed that the meaning came to me suddenly (as in spring one will become abruptly aware that he has been hearing a grosbeak). It was Margery with whom I have been sitting—Margery, among her new flowers. Margery lies over at her house, by the fireplace, in a world of flowers—so beautiful, so incredibly adult. It is as if she had lived a life time

in one year—so beautifully, so surely entering, even here, upon her *more*.[14]

Nancy Loughridge

NOTES

WHS	The State Historical Society of Wisconsin
UW	Rare Book Department, Memorial Library, University of Wisconsin, Madison
P	Private collection
Fisk	Jean Toomer Collection, Fisk University Library

1. WHS
2. August Derleth, *Still Small Voice: The Biography of Zona Gale*. New York: Appleton-Century, 1940. p. 172.
3. Mrs. Frederick Knowles to author, Feb. 25, 1982.
4. Carl Rakosi, *Margery Latimer*, unpublished manuscript.
5. [August, 1922] UW
6. N.d. P
7. July 4, 1925 UW
8. [1928] UW
9. Letter to Blanche Matthias [Christmas, 1929] UW
10. Letter to Blanche Matthias [May, 1931] UW
11. Letter to Meridel Le Sueur [October, 1931] Fisk
12. Letter to her mother [April, 1932] Fisk
13. [July, 1932] WHS
14. Derleth, p. 225.

AFTERWORD
A Memoir

Deep in us, living its strange life, we are ripe together and complete and round with this perfect taste of living fruit. And in this moment of marriage, of perfect tasting and absorbing and fulfilling, I received and ate the best of you, the marvelous fruiting of your lives, the complete willing surrender of you all, lifted for a moment into full bodies and sweet blooded giving with eyes and bodies radiant, never to die but always to live.

—Margery Latimer

This appeared on the front page of the Portage paper the day of Margery's burial on the Fox River, on the old Indian portage from river to river—at thirty-three years, dead of hemorrhaging in childbirth, on Division Street, at the center of the Gurdjieff group under Jean Toomer, in Chicago.

Margery's stories, seized from women's prisons of the past, like messages left on a wilderness trail, warn us, guide us, and certainly give us a sharing in the pain of women between the centuries of struggle. The great span of years between 1880 and 1930 are anguished, mute years of women's struggle out of the torturous cocoon of dead structures. They went far to the edge of their blind exploitation and died there on the rim, leaving strange messages for us to decipher.

Strangely enough, Margery had four books published at that time. Then, there were hundreds of secret, masked writers, crying out their delicate, virginal assertions against the brutality of burying women alive, against seizing land and women, on the cusp of the twentieth century, the male barbecue, violent and destructive. The asylums were full of women, and the suicide rate was high. Before Pasteur, half the births ended in death, and you were lucky if your child survived its first summer.

The good woman could hardly walk on the street alone. She was covered from her chin to her ankles. She was cut off from immigrant women. She was isolated from sexual fulfillment. Every village had a brothel. The good woman covered the brutality with garden clubs, libraries, church doings, and sentimental poetry like Carrie Jacobs Bond—the "End of a Perfect Day." The good woman was imprisoned in the white, middle-class, Protestant cage. Zona Gale was the high priestess of the image of pure womanhood. Margery and I came under her terrible influence, a vengeful goddess against the male world, yet masked in sentimentality and goodness.

At our birth we were supposed to have been boys. We tried to appease our disappointed parents. Zona was an only child. Margery had one sister. Fortunately, two brothers followed me. Before the First World War and after it, a woman had four choices—to be a mother and wife, a nurse, a teacher, or a whore. You did not want the life of your mother, who had to give up her desires and career to have children. To be a writer you literally had to become a nun, to passionately devote your life to writing and success. The good woman also denied sex. Zona preached that sex was brutalizing, bestial, enslaving. And in her time it was.

Margery, born later than Zona, put up a magnificent fight against the caging of women, and against Zona, attacking her and her power often viciously as in "Guardian Angel." But Zona also was a nourishing woman, and with some of the destructiveness of "mothering." We flocked to her. Margery might not have written at all without her. I might have remained unpublished. She helped found the first experimental school in Madison to nourish the creative spirit. Here Margery was given a living for two years. You did not even have to appear at classes. You were "free." Zona nourished that special feeling of the "good," the purity, the delicacy, that special feeling of the nineteenth century, of the woman as a power against evil, of the secret guerilla strategy of "saving" us from reality, of the power of the pure, isolated woman saving the world from grossness and rape. Women died on this level of struggle, to illuminate the dangers for us, transforming through their own redoubtable spirits even the terrible loss and death of the frontier.

Zona made you feel important, a superior person. Member of a secret cult of purity and redemption. And we needed to feel important. Margery expresses often in her stories the ways she felt humiliated, at school and by her parents, because she was never winning or special or loved. The patriarchal world did not accept us. We tried to break from the maternal world, the biological fate. There were two paths, one of vengeful hatred and fierce attack on the male world, the other the spiritual, seductive power of the victim and saint. Either path led to a crippling of creative women.

We owe Margery a debt for the surgical precision and boldness with which she attempted to cut out the disease, to cure the dangerous and organic struggle, within the web of hunger and need. Zona masked her struggle in sentimental village stories, although *Miss Lula Bett*, for which she got the Pulitzer Prize in 1922, is a valid woman's struggle. The first woman to get the Pulitzer, Zona wrote a kind of *Doll's House* of the middle west, with two endings, one in which Lula Bett stays, and the other in which she goes out alone, shutting the door behind her.

Margery painfully tore the mask. She had to tear it from her own face, which reflected the old necromancies of woman's desire for the Knight, the rider on the white horse, the savior, who will at last recognize purity and beauty, at last elevate woman to the madonna. She took the risk of unmasking, even the risk of satire. In the agonies of *This Is My Body*, ending in the terrible abortion, she rings her own death knell. Her death followed these necromancies of the past, these stultifying images we still struggle with, the fear of our feminity, of our survival. Why did she want a dominating husband and a child? The fear of not being dominated, mistaking it as weakness, not the genius of containing. Her submission, the mark of the patriarchy upon us, the doubting of our own strength.

She also saw the comedy in her split desires, to be herself the redheaded glowing Guardian Angel, who threatened her lovers, remained an angel they could not bear, unable to participate in sex because she was so pure. She fled the loves of the body, and located her salvation outside her, in an unreal image. She thought he wanted to nourish her and went to his knife.

We still feel the fright without the old dominance, the father, the nourisher, outside ourselves. The prisoner can long for the prison. It was such a long domination. We still struggle with it. Submission, domination, invasion, colonization—is the power of the patriarchy. Patriarchy broods in us fear of our creative power, makes us court invasion, long for the old dominance, even for the disease of theft, abortion, colonization.

We must realize from these outcries, these hidden messages, how brave and bold women were in that time, to invade the altar of the good woman, to crack the distorted mirror they had looked into for so long. How bold it was to cry out. They wrote in a female language which in itself was subversive, they wrote on the walls with their blood. They were like the women in Poe buried in the walls of their prisons. Carefully we must decipher these messages. Our lives depend on it. They cared enough about us to warn us. Margery was willing to go through fire for illumination.

As we bonded together, escaping refugees along an unknown road, so they wrote for you not born yet. The three of us might not have survived without each other, without attacks on each other, even in the terrible web of our history. Zona never married until she was fifty, and then she married her father. Margery leapt over the edge of her desires and died at thirty-three. I survived, maybe by camouflage. Women of our generation

were murdered, or silenced, brutalized in their sex. Helpless,
trashed, they became non-beings, never spoke again.

All my writing is like hers, to make our pain and our death
articulate, illuminating. She wrote a clinical report. We operated
on ourselves at great danger. Like a great scientist, she exposed
the cancer. She is burning now. Her light reveals inside us what
she warned us of. Boldly she called her book *This Is My Body*,
a testament to the horrors and agonies of an adolescent woman.
She gave me my body in the agonizing image of her bleeding
death, birthing another woman. This is my body, she said. This
is what we have to glow in. This is what is born and dies. This
is what is murdered. They have killed my body. They kill the
body in many ways. They can make you kill your own body. "I
don't want any one to suffer as I did," she said.

But she left us these papers, this testament. She had to
record fast. She had so little time. She tried to kill the slave
girl image of love, as servant, the ideal of purity, of virginity as
a special granary in a barbaric society, the transformation of sex
out of the gross Christian body of defamed woman.

She turned her penetrating light on all our grandmothers
and mothers, moving out of a low pressure fog, history bound,
delivered to old again dying images, carrying with them into
this high and dangerous air their compressed food, their survival
kits, their sickened and enslaved bodies, full of old prejudices,
fevers, and deceits. They begin to climb out of centuries of
darkness, at first only a few, then joined by millions. They have
to carry their own oxygen, breathe in rare air, they have to
carry food and shelter and companions with them, they have to
find new ways to live where no humans have ever lived before.
They are attacked by their own sisters, humiliated, robbed.
Worst of all, they suffer the psychic fears and terrors of centuries
built within the subtle enslavement of patriarchy, on systems of
concealment, invisibility, dependence, those images held up by
the oppressor of weakness, by the exploiter of love, on those
ideal images of the female martyr (which means revealer) of

purity, wanting a guide, a savior, a defender of weakness, dependence, and purity.

Margery exposed the terrors of that journey and the death of succumbing to that deadly past. She died on the cold level of her climb.

These are her tablets preserved in the terrible cold of her hemorrhaging death. She was bleeding all her life.

She bled to death.

Read these sacred notes in the crevasses, decipher them in pain, trace each bloody letter. She tells you how to prepare for the journey, how to drop heavy equipage as you go, how to make bridges and prepare for survival, how to share the oxygen, build the bloody ladders to each other so that we may continue to live along the terribly journey.

Live in my body, O my town and my people! Do not perish! I partook of you and you partook of me, in this marriage, and it became two marriages—the marriage of myself to him, the marriage of myself to you and you to me, O town, O people. And inside you, Town, I had suffered, and from you, People, I had hidden and covered my face and walked alone. And now, through him and through you I have partaken of full life. Deep in us, living its strange life, we are ripe together and complete and round with this perfect taste of living fruit. And in this moment of marriage, of perfect tasting and absorbing and fulfilling, I received and ate the best of you, the marvelous fruiting of your lives, the complete willing surrender of you all, lifted for a moment into full bodied and sweet blooded giving with eyes and bodies radiant, never to die but always to live.

So live on in my body, O my town and my people, and when the evil river comes to sweep us down and away and along with its dark current, then, O then, do not die in me, do not be washed out of me, even though my body is swept along with yours and with all the wreckage and all the broken parts. O do not perish then, my perfect marriage! Live in my dark bones and burn behind my sightless eyes, if I, too, am swept away forever, forever.

—Margery Latimer

Meridel Le Sueur

AFTERWORD
The Work

Readers may be asking themselves whether they have
"enjoyed" these stories. It's probably the wrong question to ask.
Latimer's anatomy of small town life is always vivid, often funny,
but invariably grim. I found myself laughing while reading "Mr.
and Mrs. Arnold"; it was not a laughter born of good humor.
Latimer is not a local colorist trying to evoke the charm of small
town America. She can be that—witness the descriptions of
houses, gardens, furniture, clothes, local customs, and idiosyn-
cracies in "Guardian Angel." But there is always the sense that
the sharply etched surfaces, the well ordered exteriors, are about
to burst apart. Mr. and Mrs. Arnold's conversations are funny
because they are at the edge of lunacy: not the lunacy that
charms, but the sort that strikes fear into the soul. The laughter
comes out of disjunction; the incapacity to make one's words
mean anything to even the most familiar person. Here are Mr.
and Mrs. Arnold at lunch:

> "Will you have some tea?"
>
> "Certainly I won't! Have I ever been a man to indulge my
> stomach?"
>
> "I had on my yellow crepe when I bought this tea." She
> put her chin on her hand and looked out.
>
> "If I'd known thirty years ago what I know now, I'd have
> set the world on fire."
>
> The woman tasted her tea and heard him call from the
> porch, "Good-by!" She examined a dark spot on a silver spoon;

shuddered. "Don't forget your umbrella," she called.

He charged back to the doorway. "And make an ass of myself coming home in the snow, I suppose. Yes you want to make me ridiculous in every way, don't you?"

"It sometimes snows in October." Again she withdrew into unlimited space, he judged, from her look. "A rather nice little bowl."

"Who cares where we bought it? No wonder I'm a madman living in the same house with you. Not a day can pass that you don't make your remark about that bowl."

"You are looking for cake again?" she asked half sweetly. He rushed from the house.

My laughter chills me as I read this passage, for Mr. and Mrs. Arnold are involved in a balancing act which uses speech both as an escape and a deadly weapon. Their conversation is composed of the everyday banter one might hear in a situation comedy, yet it is just on the edge of lunatic babble. It is a literary mode familiar in our time through the works of Beckett, Ionesco, and Pinter. For Latimer it was both a literary method akin to surrealism and life itself; these stories reveal the sensibility of modernism rendering "local color" into a theater of the absurd. Life might go on as always; or it might not. Here, as in most of these stories, there is little promise of resolution, as the logic of association constantly threatens to veer out of control. It is just this threat which draws me deeply into these stories. But I can't say that I enjoy contemplating the possibility of one's ordinary intercourse being exposed as a cover for madness. No, one does not turn to Latimer's stories for simple pleasures, since even the most casual remark ("A rather nice little bowl") can draw one into lives questioning with unremitting cheerlessness the possibility of their own descent into meaninglessness. " 'Everything's different from what we think . . . ,' " Mrs. Beale advises her daughter ("The Family"), " 'Nothing is like what's in our heads. . . . Nobody's right, maybe, and it doesn't matter anyway.' "

Or does it? After the panic of a near breakdown, Mrs. Beale convinces herself that she knows what she believes; that peace and quiet are hers as long as "no one drips on the clean cloth." Her urgencies, however, cannot be wished away.

> But by the time she got back into bed all her emotion had slipped out of her, she felt vacant and strange but not unhappy. There was nothing in the world to be tragic about, she thought. People were as pleasant as they knew how to be, and yet she had a queer image in front of her eyes that would not go. It was a dog rooting in autumn leaves, smelling with his moist warm nose over dry, imperishable leaves, each different, each vivid and crisp, and it was so sharp in her mind that tears came in her eyes but she felt no sadness, only a little shudder in her arms because she understood so little and didn't begin to know the why of anything on earth.

The why of anything: of love, passion, loss, work, creativity, the root of things. Latimer's stories are elaborations of this desperate search. The narrator of "Nellie Bloom" recalls her return as a young woman to the town of her childhood. Wishing to understand the why of her own melancholy, she goes about reconstructing and elaborating the tale of Nellie's strange life and death. As with any myth, the town's memory provides the narrator with only a few bare bones. Nellie's unhappy passion must be imagined by the narrator, who takes on her subject's identity in the process: "this unhappiness of mine . . . made me want to be another person, made me Nellie Bloom the instant I heard she had suffered." She puts herself inside the town's myth so as to understand—both herself and the rituals of town life. In most of these stories, after all, the rituals of daily life— business, going to church, sitting down for dinner, tending one's garden, caring for children—are assumed to give living its meaning. Somehow it doesn't work that way. The narrator had left town in search for . . . something; she returned looking for elusive hints in the town's memories of Nellie Bloom, now dead forty years.

In "Guardian Angel" Vanessa, out of innocence or arrogance or both, rejects her family's ordinary decencies in her search for significance. She experiments with new modes of thought as if they were changes of costume. Near the end of the story, as Vanessa says good-by to Fleta before going off to be an artist in Chicago, she admonishes herself to "let this air of God puff slowly over your bones. Sink then, sink away, until only the bright spark of you is left, the burning star of you that travels the universe and can enter any house, any body, any heart—" Will such reduction to an essence—to me it has the sound of parody—give meaning to her art? To her life as an artist? We don't know, since the story comes to an end. But given the force of her passions, I have my doubts.

❋   ❋   ❋

Passion, sensuality: Whether expressed in sexual desire, the need for bodily comfort or love, through anger, cruelty, the will to exert power in Latimer's stories, they are the harbingers of disorder, the challenge to the meanings established by custom, civility, the church. Townspeople might recognize their existence, but they are to be hidden for the sake of decency. After hysterically asserting that she loves her husband, Mrs. Beale in "The Family" cries out " 'I'm nothing but a toad! . . . I'm a snake. Oh, I want to come out, I want to drop off my skin, Oh, you, too, your snake skin, Oh, God in heaven, don't forget me. . . .' " There is no wifely love, only something more threatening waiting to burst from beneath the skin. In self-defense, she tells herself "that it was better to have a man who was steady . . . than to be dragging around after someone you would love insanely for a year, say, and then cease to love."

Soon after Nellie Bloom is abandoned by her betrothed, Dorr, Grandma Sweeney tries to comfort her with this story:

> "There was a crowd of crazy men went into the desert and called themselves the self-tamers because they thought they should be something better than beasts. They called their instincts the wild beasts and they tried to tame them and make them useful to themselves. Think of those poor fellows leaving their own to go off and die like that!"

To me the moral of the story is not clear. Grandma Sweeney means to warn Nellie about the dangers of burying her passions while dwelling on her loss. Indeed, five years later, according to the narrator, Nellie comes to understand "the terror of her body's starvation." But isn't it passion—hers, Dorr's, Bird's—which has disturbed the orderly procession of events? Dorr and Bird could not help themselves: therefore the betrayal of a friend and lover; Nellie can not rid herself of the beast: therefore her slow death. Perhaps Grandma Sweeney's point, and that of the narrator, is that passions must be part of the fabric of one's ordinary life, lest they express themselves in self-consuming hatred. The narrator imagines Nellie wearing her Palm Sunday clothes, silently cursing Bird and Dorr:

> God, destory that last spark that cannot be destroyed so that they may know that from that instant their lives are out forever and that they may not even be earth that gives its life to plants and trees and can feel the soft bodies of lovers lying upon it and feel warm fruit falling in its grass and feel rain stir its substances. Put them out forever on that day when all should be rising from the dead.

The curse descended on her own head. Her passion is left to dry out in the desert; her death is final, since she has borne no fruit.

In "Guardian Angel" Fleta threatens to lead Vanessa down a similar path. Fleta's bloodless paintings are the expression of her escape from passion. At the children's party she tries to suppress what is playful, improvisatory, all that is vigorously alive in the children. Vanessa is ridiculed by Fleta for being in love, and wonders whether she will ever love again, or be loved. Vanessa knows herself: " 'I'm violent. I haven't politeness or respect or casualness.' " Fleta's response: " 'Why do you waste your time denying the beauty to accept the ugliness? And you deny the celestial and radiant to brood over the animal part, the ugly part.' " Vanessa's desires are powerful enough to break through the film of Fleta's vapid spirituality. In a frenzy she produces drawing upon drawing of Fleta. Her father fails to recognize Fleta in the sketches. Vanessa's Aunt Grace, however, sees that in giving play to her "animal part," by using expressive distortions, she has revealed the passionate fears kept hidden by Fleta's cool exterior. But the release of passion brings with it the loss of understanding. Vanessa feels guilty about her rejection of Fleta. Fleta's teaching had been the key to the mysteries of space and time. To Vanessa, they are mysteries still.

❈ ❈ ❈

Nearly all the people in Latimer's stories are convinced that it is their duty to be happy. "In all the dark houses all over the world . . . ," Mrs. Beale reflects, "are people who once were happy, who knew a day that was above all days, and now they can't remember how they felt or what it meant or what it was for." Happiness is elusive. It is there, not here; in the future, or in the past. " 'Say, when do you suppose a person's real happy?' " Gisela is asked by her rich friend Isabel. "Gisela spoke softly, as embarrassed and ill at ease as if God had been mentioned. 'When we get big and know everything we'll all be happy.' " But what do grownups know? What knowledge makes them happy? Mrs. Beale enumerates the components of her life: "Plate of meat. Dish of sauce. Dish of potatoes. Plate of bread. Tablecloth clean on Sunday. Napkins clean on Wednesday and Sunday. Bed of petunias. Jack Miller passing in a new car. Mrs. Peppen watering grass. Two sisters from the Sacred Heart passing in black robes." Where is the happiness in that list? Yet Mrs. Beale feels sinful for not being happy. Latimer's town is full of people who tell themselves that they ought to be happy with their miseries. But something inside them knows better, and gives their speech that edge of self-hating irony that distinguishes so much of Latimer's dialogue in these stories. When Gisela asks her impoverished father what he would want as a present, he responds " 'Well, I'd want to be happy for one thing. . . . I'd want to forget everything that's happened for the last thirteen years. I'd want it all wiped away as if it had never been. That's the one thing that could make me supremely happy.' " It is only a short step to the father's response in "Marriage Eve" to his daughter's desperate request that he bless her marriage:

> "It's a good thing to have a family—we live for that—we have to keep the world going—happiness doesn't count here in America—we have a bigger ideal than that—the next generation does count and nothing else matters—Have your family. I can't put up a kick against that—it's what we're here for—no one yet found a better reason—sure—go ahead—"

There is something terribly sour in that fatalism. It reduces humanity to its reproductive function. Is that what America is about? The father has made his daughter a present of a volume of president Wilson's speeches. Yet we know that he fiercely desires something more than that dour Protestant's sanctimonious devotion to duty. His physical violence toward his daughter is the twisted expression of a passion for happiness. That passion has to be stopped up, since it can have no meaning.

❋ ❋ ❋

Amongst Latimer's most solid citizens something has happened to the American Dream. Vanessa's father trusts his town's most respected businessman with his investments and finds himself bilked. It's all very legal, but is it "neighborly"? The townspeople barely understand that the America that rewarded neighborly folks—white, male, Protestant—for hard work and persistence is fast becoming the property of the financial and industrial operators who follow laws that are a mystery. Aunt Grace observes that she is about to lose her faith in the notion of God as a "fair bookkeeper."

Mr. Beale tries to do good; but no one listens to his crazed tirades. In no uncertain terms he tells his neighbor how to tend

her garden, and is cold-shouldered for his efforts. Filled with
disgust he recalls

> his mother who was friends with everyone in the town, who went
> where the sick were, who sent large loaves of bread to the poor
> and always gave largely when a family was burned out or had
> sickness.

His daughter he considers to be a coward; his wife is sick to her
soul with a disease he does not understand; God and the waters
might be vengeful and wipe everything away. Yet he thanks
God for the wife and child he claims to love and for the warmth
of his contentious home. He lectures Gizzie, the family's maid,
and the only person who will listen respectfully:

> ". . . with all our faults the United States is the greatest
> nation the world has ever seen. . . . We stand for democracy,
> right thinking, for right living, decent living, and we live for the
> next generation, that's our religion, that's our whole life, the
> next generation that is to make humanity better, leave it with
> higher ideals and hopes, a bigger conception of life than we have
> ever known. . . ."

The very frenzy of Mr. Beale's locutions belies his claims, both
for the present and the future. The next generation might "make
humanity better," but not for Mr. Beale. In Latimer's stories
the children reject the American Dream because they experience
nightmares in the privacy of their homes. Vanessa, though
treated with affectionate warmth by her family, feels that there
must be something more transcendent than the day-to-day
routine of her home. She finds a surrogate mother in Fleta, and
by dabbling in spiritualism tries to escape the realities her parents
must deal with—maintaining a home, making a living, protecting
oneself against a society that is little understood. But Fleta turns
out to be a liar. " 'I've killed my mother,' " Vanessa tells Aunt
Grace melodramatically after a confrontation with Fleta. Mr.
Beale's next generation may not entirely reject its parents, but
the relationship is deeply troubled, and always remains unre-

solved. I am struck by the depth and honesty with which Latimer explores the ties between daughters and parents. The daughter in "Marriage Eve," though terrified by her father's physical presence, wants his love and approval. The most touching scene in "The Family" shows Dorrit and her mother idylically splashing about in the water while Mr. Beale stalks about disapprovingly on the shore. Dorrit wants to take her mother away and rescue her from a death by emotional dryness. Gisela yearns to give her father a present. Passion spills over everywhere. The ties between parents and children can not be totally rent: Vanessa kisses the big toe of Fleta's shoe before leaving for Chicago. Latimer understands these passions profoundly. Therefore she can not portray the rebellion of daughters against parents as simple embodiments of the rejection of the American Dream. Latimer's young heroines do not really understand much about America. But they do understand the hollowness of Mr. Beale's harangues, since they are so little related to the passions lurking about in their homes.

The rejection of the American Dream in Latimer's stories is therefore never overtly political. The ideal of the United States as a spiritual leader has died not because Pliny Bope does in his neighbors ("Guardian Angel"), not because small towns are being destroyed by entrepreneurs, but because it seems to be unrelated to people's everyday culture. Where, Dorrit and Vanessa ask themselves, is the passion, the beauty? Why is everything hemmed in by unremitting guilt? Why is Fleta's furniture so ugly? Latimer's young women revolt in the realm of art. Dorrit fills her canvasses with scenes of nude sensuality; they are hung, of course, in Chicago, not at home. Vanessa is full of self-important blather about "what a great artist can do for humanity." She needs such arrogance to make her break and go off to Chicago. In their time, their place, their social situation, no other revolt seemed possible. For Dorrit and Vanessa art is both an escape from home and a means of engaging what appears to be emotionally real. There is a price to be paid. Such rebellions are lonely. Leaving home may give one air, but it also leaves one isolated and rootless. At the end of "The Family," Dorrit, now an expatriate in Paris, is observed drunk in an artist's cafe by someone from home. She is parodying her father's high-flown rhetoric about America. When the observer describes the drunken scene to people back home, her mother asks " 'How *can* such people be happy?' " She has a point.

❊ ❊ ❊

There is a matter I have left till the end. Surely it is something readers have understood while absorbing these stories. Underlying nearly everything that occurs in these pages is the condition of the lives of many women in the United States during the 1920s. These small-town, white, largely middle-class women play out their roles as wives, mothers, spinster aunts, whatever. Fulfillment and status is supposed to come through their husbands. Their duties are to be supportive and happy. Somehow it doesn't work out that way. Hardly anyone—woman or man—is happy. Even Grace, the narrator of "Guardian Angel," who revels in her role of mother, enjoys an affectionate relationship with her husband, and critically accepts the ways of her town, has a skeleton in her closet. In her youth she went off to Chicago to become a singer. The story does not detail the condition of her return, but here she is, apparently happy with her lot. And yet she stays involved with Vanessa because she identifies with her yearnings. Grace encourages her children's artistic talents, because, I assume, she wants them to escape her own fate. But she resolutely enmeshes herself in motherhood. At the end of the story she is pregnant, and admonished for it by Vanessa.

I am not sure what to make of "Monday Morning." It is surely one of the most thorny stories Latimer wrote. The young woman tells herself, obsessively, that she is happy in her role as wife and future mother. However, the language of her self-assurances sounds almost like a parody of popular romances. Breakfast with her husband, though affectionate, comes across to me as a ritualized dance performed on broken glass. Throughout the meal she is haunted by memories of rejection by a previous lover who resented her clinging dependency. Her husband goes off to work; she is left at home, and orders the groceries for supper by telephone. For the women Latimer writes about, there seem to be no alternatives. They are stuck in their social situation. If their husbands are decent, they can make a life for themselves by hooking into the rituals and networks women have elaborated for centuries. If their husbands are brutish, insanity may be their lot. There are no forms of rebellion which really free women from the ties of their towns, their families, and the emotional straightjacket of their upbringing. Latimer's understanding of this condition gives her stories a depth I do not find in the work of Anderson or Hemingway. Her characters' despair is grounded in the hard work of staying emotionally alive from day to day, not in the modish literary and metaphysical attitudes of the 1920s.

Latimer was not writing in the 1970s or 80s. She writes about her women (and men) with a bleak honesty some people might find dispiriting. The simplicity of her language, the calm of her syntax, are a mask for the passions that lie just below the surface. Her understanding of this hidden world is a revelation for me. There is so much wisdom, so much generosity and understanding in these stories, that I marvel at how someone so young could have written them. Such knowledge is surely beyond the "enjoyment" many readers conventionally expect of fiction.

In the "Death of Mrs. Vanderwood," as she is about to breathe her last, Mrs. Vanderwood tells her caretaker " 'I've fallen apart. I haven't any shepherd to gather me together.' " Latimer is the laureate of those without shepherds. She richly deserves a place of honor in the history of American modernism.

Louis Kampf
Massachusetts Institute of Technology

Nancy Loughridge earned her B.A. degree at Antioch College and her M.L.S. at the University of Michigan, where she was a Horace Rackham fellow. Formerly director of collections at the University of Cincinnati Libraries, she is now working on a biography of Margery Latimer.

Meridel Le Sueur and Margery Latimer were close friends and, together, protégées of the Pulitzer prize-winning dramatist Zona Gale. Now in her eighty-fifth year, Le Sueur continues her productive life as a writer, feminist, activist. A major collection of her prose and poetry, *Ripening: Selected Work, 1927–1980*, edited by Elaine R. Hedges, was published by The Feminist Press. A new edition is in preparation.

Louis Kampf was president of the Modern Language Association in 1971. His book, *On Modernism*, is a classic in cultural criticism. He is professor of comparative literature at the Massachusetts Institute of Technology.

The Feminist Press offers alternatives in education and in literature. Founded in 1970, this non-profit, tax-exempt educational and publishing organization works to eliminate sexual stereotypes in books and schools and to provide literature with a broad vision of human potential. The publishing program includes reprints of important works by women, feminist biographies of women, and nonsexist children's books. Curricular materials, bibliographies, directories, and a quarterly journal provide information and support for students and teachers of women's studies. In-service projects help to transform teaching methods and curricula. Through publications and projects, The Feminist Press contributes to the rediscovery of the history of women and the emergence of a more humane society.

FEMINIST CLASSICS FROM THE FEMINIST PRESS

Antoinette Brown Blackwell: A Biography, by Elizabeth Cazden. $16.95 cloth, $9.95 paper.

Between Mothers and Daughters: Stories Across a Generation. Edited by Susan Koppelman. $8.95 Paper.

Brown Girl, Brownstones, a novel by Paule Marshall. Afterword by Mary Helen Washington, $7.95 paper.

Call Home the Heart, a novel of the thirties, by Fielding Burke. Introduction by Alice Kessler-Harris and Paul Lauter and afterwords by Sylvia J. Cook and Anna W. Shannon. $8.95 paper.

Cassandra, by Florence Nightingale. Introduction by Myra Stark. Epilogue by Cynthia Macdonald. $3.50 paper.

The Convert, a novel by Elizabeth Robins. Introduction by Jane Marcus. $6.95 paper.

Daughter of Earth, a novel by Agnes Smedley. Afterword by Paul Lauter. $6.95 paper.

The Female Spectator, edited by Mary R. Mahl and Helen Koon. $8.95 paper.

Guardian Angel and Other Stories, by Margery Latimer. Afterwords by Louis Kampf, Meridel Le Sueur, and Nancy Loughridge. $8.95 paper.

I Love Myself When I Am Laughing . . . And Then Again When I Am Looking Mean and Impressive, by Zora Neal Hurston. Edited by Alice Walker with an introduction by Mary Helen Washington. $9.95 paper.

Käthe Kollwitz: Woman and Artist, by Martha Kearns. $7.95 paper.

Life in the Iron Mills, by Rebecca Harding Davis. Biographical interpretation by Tillie Olsen. $4.95 paper.

The Living Is Easy, a novel by Dorothy West. Afterword by Adelaide M. Cromwell. $7.95 paper.

The Maimie Papers. Edited by Ruth Rosen and Sue Davidson. Introduction by Ruth Rosen. $11.95 paper.

The Other Woman: Stories of Two Women and a Man. Edited by Susan Koppelman. $8.95 paper.

Portraits of Chinese Women in Revolution, by Agnes Smedley. Edited with an introduction by Jan MacKinnon and Steve MacKinnon and an afterword by Florence Howe. $5.95 paper.

Reena and Other Stories, selected short stories by Paule Marshall. $8.95 paper.

Ripening: Selected Work, 1927–1980, by Meridel Le Sueur. Edited with an introduction by Elaine Hedges. $8.95 paper.

The Silent Partner, a novel by Elizabeth Stuart Phelps. Afterword by Mari Jo Buhle and Florence Howe. $6.95 paper.

These Modern Women: Autobiographical Essays from the Twenties. Edited with an introduction by Elaine Showalter. $4.95 paper.

The Unpossessed, a novel of the thirties, by Tess Slesinger. Introduction by Alice Kessler-Harris and Paul Lauter and afterword by Janet Sharistanian. $8.95 paper.

Weeds, a novel by Edith Summers Kelley. Afterword by Charlotte Goodman. $7.95 paper.

The Woman and the Myth: Margaret Fuller's Life and Writings, by Bell Gale Chevigny. $8.95 paper.

The Yellow Wallpaper, by Charlotte Perkins Gilman. Afterword by Elaine Hedges. $2.95 paper.

For free catalog, write to: The Feminist Press, Box 334, Old Westbury, NY 11568. Send individual book orders to The Feminist Press, P.O. Box 1654, Hagerstown, MD 21741. Include $1.50 postage and handling for one book and 50¢ for each additional book. To order using MasterCard or Visa, call: (800) 638-3030.

OTHER TITLES FROM THE FEMINIST PRESS

Black Foremothers: Three Lives, by Dorothy Sterling. $6.95 paper.

But Some of Us Are Brave: Black Women's Studies. Edited by Gloria T. Hull, Patricia Bell Scott, and Barbara Smith. $16.95 cloth, $9.95 paper.

Complaints and Disorders: The Sexual Politics of Sickness, by Barbara Ehrenreich and Deirdre English. $3.95 paper.

The Cross-Cultural Study of Women. Edited by Mary I. Edwards and Margot Duley-Morrow. $8.95 paper.

Dialogue on Difference. Edited by Florence Howe. $8.95 paper.

Everywoman's Guide to Colleges and Universities. Edited by Florence Howe, Suzanne Howard, and Mary Jo Boehm Strauss. $12.95 paper.

Household and Kin: Families in Flux, by Amy Swerdlow et al. $14.95 cloth, $6.95 paper.

How to Get Money for Research, by Mary Rubin and the Business and Professional Women's Foundation. Foreword by Mariam Chamberlain. $5.95 paper.

In Her Own Image: Women Working in the Arts. Edited with an introduction by Elaine Hedges and Ingrid Wendt. $17.95 cloth, $8.95 paper.

Las Mujeres: Conversations from a Hispanic Community, by Nan Elsasser, Kyle MacKenzie, and Yvonne Tixier y Vigil. $14.95 cloth, $6.95 paper.

Lesbian Studies: Present and Future. Edited by Margaret Cruikshank. $14.95 cloth, $7.95 paper.

Moving the Mountain: Women Working for Social Change, by Ellen Cantarow with Susan Gushee O'Malley and Sharon Hartman Strom. $6.95 paper.

Out of the Bleachers: Writings on Women and Sport. Edited with an introduction by Stephanie L. Twin. $7.95 paper.

Reconstructing American Literature: Courses, Syllabi, Issues. Edited by Paul Lauter. $10.95 paper.

Salt of the Earth, screenplay by Michael Wilson with historical commentary by Deborah Silverton Rosenfelt. $5.95 paper.

The Sex-Role Cycle: Socialization from Infancy to Old Age, by Nancy Romer. $6.95 paper.

Witches, Midwives, and Nurses: A History of Women Healers, by Barbara Ehrenreich and Deirdre English. $3.95 paper.

With These Hands: Women Working on the Land. Edited with an introduction by Joan M. Jensen. $17.95 cloth, $8.95 paper.

Woman's "True" Profession: Voices from the History of Teaching. Edited with an introduction by Nancy Hoffman. $17.95 cloth, $8.95 paper.

Women Have Always Worked: A Historical Overview, by Alice Kessler-Harris. $14.95 cloth, $6.95 paper.

Women Working: An Anthology of Stories and Poems. Edited and with an introduction by Nancy Hoffman and Florence Howe. $7.95 paper.

Women's Studies in Italy, by Laura Balbo and Yasmine Ergas. A Women's Studies International Monograph. $5.95 paper.